Praise for *Lenswoman in Love*

"It's no surprise that Kim Gottlieb-Walker's wonderful *Lenswoman in Love* is as soulful and true as her much-lauded work in photography. Gorgeous with detail and gloriously filled with heart and adventure, this is the literary equivalent of a great song with the kind of magic that lingers for days."

CAMERON CROWE, FILM MAKER AND ROCK JOURNALIST

"Romance, sure thing! But more than that, *Lenswoman in Love* offers a rich evocation of another time—the Sixties and Seventies, from the West Coast to Swinging London—seen through the eyes of a passionate and talented young photographer. Her camera takes her inside recording studios and onto film sets, and her heart takes her on a journey of soulful self-discovery. Read on!"

STEVEN REA, AUTHOR OF *THE HOLLYWOOD BOOK CLUB*

"I was captivated immediately by Jake, just as Maddy was. And pulled right into the story not only by the romance, but by all the connections with a time and world in which I grew up as well. Author Kim Gottlieb-Walker has a way of keeping a reader wanting to know what happens to her characters next, and providing authentic backdrops at the same time. *Lenswoman in Love* is a wonderful read by a gifted storyteller."

INA HILLEBRANDT, SPEAKER, MEMOIR COACH, AUTHOR
BOARD MEMBER, INDEPENDENT WRITERS OF SOUTHERN CALIFORNIA
BOARD MEMBER, INDEPENDENT PUBLISHERS ASSOCIATION OF AMERICA

"Maddy experiences the excitement and adventure we all wish we could have had. Gottlieb-Walker lived it. The slow-burn romance with Jake—the boyfriend every girl dreams of having—it's there, too. A sweet, sweet read."

Robin Maxwell, bestselling author of *Secret Diary of Anne Boleyn* and *Jane: The Woman Who Loved Tarzan*

"Kim Gottlieb-Walker has written a novel that reads like a memoir, and in so doing, has created a work that captures the reality of the music business, the movie business, the business of living during the 1960s and '70s. In her honesty, and her passion for what she does as a photographer… she gives us everything—her mistakes, her loves, her body, her combination of luck and talent. Along the way, she gets educated—and so do we. As a former denizen of the music business, and as a professor of media studies, I found myself nodding my head in agreement. This is the way it really was."

Allen Levy
Director of Public Relations, United Artists Records
National Publicity Manager, A&M Records
West Coast Director of Public Relations, ASCAP
Assistant Professor, Media Studies, Chapman University

LENSWOMAN in LOVE

A novel of the 1960s and '70s

KIM GOTTLIEB-WALKER

Lenswoman in Love

Published by The Conrad Press Ltd. in the United Kingdom 2025

Tel: +44(0)1227 472 874

www.theconradpress.com

info@theconradpress.com

ISBN 978-1-916966-83-3

Copyright © Kim Gottlieb-Walker, 2025

All rights reserved.

Typesetting and Cover Design by: Charlotte Mouncey, www.bookstyle.co.uk

The Conrad Press logo was designed by Maria Priestley.

Printed and bound in the USA.

AUTHOR'S NOTE

Dear Reader,

Welcome to the 1960s and '70s, before the advent of cell phones, personal computers, and the Internet. This novel presents attitudes that were common during that era, and it is hoped that readers will understand if some may seem unacceptable by today's standards.

During that time, dozens of popular songs were written about "younger girls," and men in their twenties often dated teenagers without it seeming strange. Evolving cultural influences included the widening availability of birth control, the "women's liberation" movement, and the philosophy of "free love," which empowered women to make more choices in their sexual lives but sometimes created pressure to go farther than a young woman might have wished. We've come a long way between then and now, and we're not going back.

Readers familiar with my photography books (such as *Bob Marley and the Golden Age of Reggae* and *On Set with John Carpenter*) will recognize that I share a lot of experiences with Maddy. While I've traveled extensively and enjoyed a long and amazing career, *Lenswoman in Love* is a work of fiction.

I hope you will enjoy Maddy's adventures and be pleased with Jake as the hero of her tale. Please feel free to visit my websites and send comments via my guestbook!

One Love,
Kim

        www.Lenswoman.com
       www.TheRenaissanceWoman.net

For Jeffrey, my "Jake"
Our life has been an amazing adventure.
Here's to fifty more years together.

I've always remembered my father in the golden light of late afternoon.

The first time he handed me his camera changed the course of my life. He sat in a chair opposite a window when the sun was low in the sky, casting a warm glow, and he said, "Look at me through the viewfinder, Maddy. Look at the way light reflects off my eyes. Look at the highlights and shadows. Shoot when you're happy with what you see in that little rectangle."

My first portrait was of him, only a few months before he was gone.

With the thrill of capturing that moment, photography became my passion and the catalyst for my career. It was the main source of joy in my life…

…until Jake.

CHAPTER ONE

Police Riot

1967, Century City, California

The throng of peaceful marchers began to move forward together toward the front of the hotel, singing and chanting *"Hey, hey, LBJ! How many kids did you kill today?"*

With the shrill of a police whistle, row after row of cops suddenly charged into the mass of unsuspecting protestors. The chants turned to screams.

The crowd in front of me parted, and I saw a woman fall to the ground, blood gushing from her scalp. For a fleeting moment I saw my dad's face instead, covered in blood, and that feeling of utter terror came flooding back. I froze for a second. Then I took a deep breath, lifted the camera to my eye, and began to shoot.

A man to my right gripped his injured arm, calling out for help, but all those attempting to aid the wounded were plowed down by the relentless lines of cops moving forward and attacking everyone in their path.

Adrenaline pumping, I clutched the borrowed Bolex camera protectively against my chest and fought my way through the panic-stricken crowd to the sidewalk. Determined to capture the entire range of the bloodshed in the street, I lifted the camera and braced my legs in a broad stance to steady the shot.

Lines of police in full riot gear advanced into the screaming crowd and swung their billy-clubs again and again. Bloodied bodies fell in their wake, only to be beaten by a second line of police and then a third.

Dusk was swiftly turning into night, and I was no longer sure I'd have enough light to capture the horrors unfolding in front of me, but pure adrenaline and fury kept me shooting.

Our student film crew had scattered throughout the crowd of peace demonstrators when the police attack began, and I had no idea where they all were. I had last seen our sound man, Danny, trapped and helpless where he'd fallen into a hedge, hopelessly entangled in the mass of wires from his microphones and recorder, being battered by police.

I pushed through the throng and broke free to run up a small rise, where I had a perfect view of the no-man's-land between the back of the crowd and the steadily advancing police lines. The street lights glinted off endless rows of white helmets. Shouts and screams tore the air, along with the cries of hysterical children and the thudding sound of batons hitting flesh and bone. I gritted my teeth and braced my elbows against my sides to steady the camera as I panned across the advancing troops and the panicked crowd.

A sudden flash of black and white in my peripheral vision was my only warning, a split-second before a cop slammed me in the back and I careened, rolling and sliding, down the hill.

Clutching the camera to my chest to protect it as the world

blurred around me, I landed in a dazed heap in the street, my blue work shirt ripped and gravel burns on my arms and shoulder. I lifted my head and saw the uniformed line advancing toward me, nightsticks raised.

Suddenly, strong arms scooped me up, whisking me out of the line of fire, away from the advancing batons and deep into the frenzied crowd. I tried to struggle free.

"I'm okay. Put me down!" I was dizzy and shaken but knew I had to record what was happening or no one would believe it. "I've got to go back!" I insisted, shoving against my rescuer's chest and forcing him to put me back on my feet.

I looked up into the face of my astonished hero.

Blood was dripping from a deep cut above Jake's right eyebrow. He held me tight, trying to protect me while the crowd swirled around us.

"Don't be an idiot!" he shouted above the din. "You'll get killed back there!"

I was tempted to surrender to the protection of his arms, after three years of longing for them, but the imperative to record the history happening around us was stronger.

"Please! I've got to get this on film!"

I broke away and rushed to the danger zone at the back of the fleeing crowd, outrage making me heedless of the risks. Despite the darkness I continued to shoot, dodging swinging clubs as I documented every detail.

From somewhere in the night, the sound of a whistle halted the troops in their tracks and called them back to regroup. The police marched away in formation, leaving the dazed civilians to search for their missing family members and provide first aid to the injured.

The unprovoked violence against the peace marchers shocked and angered me to the core. I'd always assumed that the stories I'd heard about police brutality had been exaggerated, but now I had witnessed it firsthand. A veil of complacency had been lifted from my eyes, and I suddenly felt much older than my eighteen years.

Frantic parents ranged across the lawn, calling desperately for their children. The Bolex heavy in my hands, I searched for my fellow UCLA film students in the dim light among the bruised and hysterical survivors.

I finally spotted our teacher Wild Bill's broad, hulking form kneeling on the grass, his black cowboy hat miraculously still in place. As I got closer I saw that he was supporting Danny, who was clutching a badly injured arm, his face contorted in agony, his breathing quick and shallow.

My roommate, Darlene, stumbled toward them, sobbing, her long, red hair tangled with leaves and her elfin face streaked with dirt. She huddled next to Bill and Danny on the grass as our camera operator, Terry, dodging broken equipment and smashed picnic remnants scattered everywhere, rushed to the nearest apartment building to call an ambulance.

Billy glanced up as I approached.

"Fuckin' hell, Maddy. You're a crazy woman! Nothin' stopped you from shooting," he drawled, obvious admiration in his voice. "You must have gotten some goddamn amazing footage."

A familiar voice from behind me said, "Jesus, Billy! Are all your students that fearless?"

I turned and looked up to see Jake gazing at me.

Billy laughed. "Hell, no, compadre! This one's special. Maddy's got balls of steel!"

"Yeah," Jake said, grinning. "Even as a kid she was a ballsy little chick."

Blushing with pride and embarrassment under the scrutiny of the two men whose opinions of me I most valued, I suddenly became acutely aware of my tangled hair, free from the now-dangling clasp that had held it in place, and my badly torn shirt, which revealed more of me than I had realized.

Jake gallantly removed his bloodstained jacket and wrapped it around my shoulders. It was filled with his warmth… and it still had the peace button I'd given him pinned to it.

"I didn't have a chance to thank you for saving my ass back there," I stammered, finding it hard to return his steady gaze. I kept imagining myself surrounded by his arms again, my head against his chest, inhaling his strength. The intense attraction to him made my stomach ache.

A lopsided smile began to lift the corner of his mouth. "Anytime," he whispered.

Billy glanced back and forth between us grinning at what must have been obvious electricity in the air. "Hey, Jake, you gonna put this in your script?"

"I just might," he replied, his eyes never leaving my face.

Where are my "balls of steel" when I need them?

I forced myself to return his gaze. The cut above Jake's right eye had blazed a red trail down his cheek that was dripping onto the shoulder of his denim shirt.

"God! You're still bleeding!" I took him by the arm and sat him on the grass.

Terry returned from making the phone call and told us, "The ambulance should be here any minute."

I knelt on the grass, tore a strip from my badly mangled shirt, and pressed it against Jake's forehead to stop the flow of blood. He stretched out his long frame and rested his head in my lap. It gave me an opportunity to brush his disheveled hair back from his bloody face for an unobstructed look. The streetlight accentuated his elegant bone structure and patrician nose. He closed his eyes and sighed. I stroked his head, feeling for lumps.

"Do you have a concussion? Y'know, I learned all about phrenology in my psych class at Berkeley, and you have prominent amatory bumps."

He laughed. "I do? Does that make me a great lover?"

"I wouldn't know. You split before I could find out."

CHAPTER TWO

Meeting Jake

1964, Berkeley, California (Three Years Earlier)

"*Maddy, shoot us! Shoot us!*"

My schoolmates stood in clusters outside our high school gym in the warm afternoon light, laughing and hugging each other. They had crowded together to celebrate the last day of our junior year as I posed them in small groups, full of joy and radiating their friendship, all looking their best in that soft illumination. Since I was the photographer for our high school yearbook, everyone was used to me and my camera.

As always, nothing gave me more pleasure than capturing a moment that others would treasure forever, but halfway through my second film roll, I glanced at my watch and panicked. The legendary Pete Seeger was appearing at our family's folk music club for one night only, and I realized that I should have been back to help my mother half an hour earlier. Our lone employee had just flown back to Idaho for the summer, and my mother wouldn't be able to handle both the baking and the advance ticket sales for the show all by herself.

I shot the last few frames, rewound the film, and ran all the way down Telegraph Avenue to The Folk Scene, the two-story, wood-frame residence that my parents had long ago converted into a coffeehouse. In the fifties they'd opened up the bottom floor and added a small stage, and we lived upstairs.

The local community of folk-music lovers was already lined up around the block, and I rushed past the ticket line and in the front door.

My mother's voice echoed through the empty club from the kitchen in back. "Maddy! Thank goodness you're here. Go sell tickets!"

I yelled a quick apology, dropped my book bag and camera on one of the small, round tables near the stage, rushed back through the lobby again, hiked up my forever-sagging knee socks, and climbed up on the stool behind the ticket window.

After everyone in line had bought their tickets, I started to close up the till when I heard a firm knock on the front door. I called for whomever it was to come to the window, and a tall, lanky guy strode into view. The sun was setting behind him, casting his face in shadow.

"Can I help you?"

He bent down. "Is the manager here?"

He appeared to be few years older than me—maybe even over twenty—and was unshaven, with dark, shaggy hair that almost reached his shoulders. I leaned forward to get a better view and was momentarily distracted by startling green eyes framed by long, black lashes.

"We won't be open until later," I told him, "but I still have a couple of tickets for tonight's show."

He held out a scrap of the local paper. "I don't need a ticket, kid. I'm here about the job."

Kid? Ten seconds into the encounter and he'd already pissed me off.

"Hang on a second."

I slammed the window shut and went to unlock the front door. He stepped into the cool darkness of our lobby. With as much authority as I could muster, I directed him to a chair and went to get my mother.

She followed me back out, wiping her hands on her apron and wrapping a stray curl behind her ear.

He rose to his feet, held out his hand, and grinned.

Damn, he was cute when he smiled.

"I'm Jake Morganstern. I saw your ad in the *Daily Californian* on campus." He waved the clipping as proof.

They shook hands as my mom replied, "Nice to meet you, Jake. Welcome to the Folk Scene. I'm Blanche Garfield, and this is my daughter, Madeleine."

"Is the job still available?"

"It is, indeed! Let's go inside to talk."

We went into the main room, and I grabbed my backpack off the table. My mother and Jake sat down opposite each other, while I stood behind her, a few feet away from the stage, with my camera strap over my shoulder, and studied him.

The single, bright work light, mounted on a raised tripod behind me, cast just enough shadow to define his strong bone structure and illuminate those extraordinary eyes. I was totally dazzled until I realized I had missed hearing the beginning of the interview.

That kind of tunnel vision normally only happened when I was taking photos. I would get so wrapped up in watching for that special moment when my subjects revealed themselves—a laugh, a reaction to a riff, a clear shot with no microphone in the way, a meaningful gesture, a moment of exceptional beauty—that my other senses shut down, and all my consciousness centered in my eyes. As a result, I hadn't actually heard most of the music as it was performed live by the artists I'd photographed in the club. That was kind of sad to contemplate, but since I was pleased to have captured so many memorable moments visually, it was well worth the tradeoff. Up until now, that intense focus had never happened when I wasn't looking through a camera lens.

I forced myself to pay attention to the conversation.

"...so, after I graduated from NYU, my buddy Bill and I took a long road trip across the country. He's gone ahead to L.A. I'm joining him at UCLA in the fall to work on my master's, but in the meantime, I could use a summer job." He smiled at her again.

Oh, my God. He even had dimples, almost hidden in several days' growth of beard.

A pleased expression crossed my mom's weary face. "Sounds like you're having a great adventure. When is your birthday, Jake?"

He looked a bit surprised but answered, "November thirtieth."

She appeared even more pleased. "Ah! Sagittarius."

He looked at me and raised an eyebrow.

I just shrugged in response. I'd always thought her astrology stuff was pretty cool.

According to my mother, Sagittarians made good associates. They tended to be knight-in-shining-armor types, galloping around rescuing people, but flexible enough to deal with anything. My dad was a Sagittarius, so I knew she was already predisposed to like Jake.

Apparently, he had no local references or even a permanent address—just a pack, a sleeping bag, and that killer smile. But it didn't matter to Mama. She had an uncanny bullshit detector—an ability to ascertain a person's character instantly that had never failed us—and I could tell that she had already adopted him.

"I think you'll be perfect for the job," she told him. "Where are you living currently?"

He looked a bit embarrassed. "Actually, I slept in the park last night."

"Oh, dear! Then you must stay with us. We have a spare room in back. Maddy, show him where to put his belongings."

As he rose, he glanced at me and grinned again, and my stomach did a strange back flip. Trying to maintain my composure, I led him past the kitchen and down the rear hallway.

"Your mom sure makes decisions quickly."

"She has good instincts… usually."

"You have your doubts?"

I shrugged. "I'm reserving judgment."

He laughed.

I showed him where he could stash his pack and sleeping bag.

"Thanks, kid."

"Don't keep calling me 'kid.'"

"Well, you aren't exactly a grownup."

Jeez, he was exasperating.

My expression must have clued him in on how pissed I was.

"Okay, okay. My apologies, Miss Garfield. But it's not an insult. Bogie called Ingrid Bergman 'kid' in *Casablanca*, y'know."

I crossed my arms and gave him my most intimidating steely stare.

"Got it. I'll just call you Garfield."

I wasn't sure why that pleased me, but it did.

* * *

Just before I opened the house for the show, I noticed Jake looking at the photos hanging on the theater walls. Feigning nonchalance, I asked what he thought of them.

"They're all amazing. Who took them? Who's *M. Garfield*? Your dad?"

"The *M* is for *Madeleine*."

"Wow. You shot these? You captured some terrific moments."

"Thanks."

My surge of pride had no follow-up. Flustered, I scrambled for a way to continue my end of the conversation. "My dad took some of the ones in the lobby—shots of the club back in the late fifties. Some poets… a few jazz musicians."

"Oh, yeah. I saw those. It had a different name then?'

"When they first came out here from New York, it was called Greenwich West. They were beatniks," I told him proudly. "I grew up surrounded by musicians, poets, comedians..."

He finally discovered the portrait of my father.

"Wow. That's a beautiful shot."

"My dad. He's gone now." My throat tightened as I fought down rising tears.

"I'm sorry. You sure took a great photo of him."

I nodded, but words deserted me. After his death, it had been months before I could speak at all.

He kept reviewing the rows of labeled photos, and since I figured that my pictures spoke for me, certainly better than any feeble attempts at witty banter, I left him alone with the images.

During the show that night, I couldn't stop staring at Jake as he made the rounds, delivering cups of coffee, clearing tables, laughing and interacting with patrons. Even in an apron with a tray full of dirty dishes, he seemed effortlessly masculine and endlessly appealing. When he glanced up at me, his amused expression embarrassed me down to my toes. My cheeks started to burn, and I turned away abruptly to concentrate on photographing the performance.

It was really unnerving. I'd never reacted to a guy that way before. I was always much more interested in books than in a bunch of immature high school boys. But Jake was no pimply adolescent.

After the final set, when all the cups and plates had been

bussed, tables cleaned, and chairs stacked, I kissed Mama goodnight before she headed upstairs and I turned off the lights. Then I wandered to the back room to see if our new lodger had settled in.

He was sitting on his well-worn sleeping bag in a T-shirt and jeans, with his boots kicked off into a corner, reading *Siddhartha*. For some strange reason my stomach seemed to be doing more gymnastics. I took a deep breath to calm myself.

"That's a good one," I said as casually as I could.

"You've read Hesse?" He seemed skeptical.

I lifted my chin, feeling defensive again. "Sure. I read a lot."

He looked as if he were laughing at me for a moment and went back to reading.

I tried again. "So, you like folk music, huh?"

He glanced up from his book. "It's okay. I actually prefer rock 'n' roll and rhythm 'n' blues."

"You must be kidding. They're so boring and repetitive."

"You're obviously listening to the wrong stuff. There's nothing boring about what I listen to."

"Oh, yeah? Like what?"

He closed his book, crossed his arms, sighed, and gave me a quick list.

"Del Shannon, Everly Brothers, the Drifters, Buddy Holly, Sam Cooke, the Shirelles, and all the Brits: Beatles, Animals, Kinks, Zombies…"

I shrugged. "Not what I would call socially relevant."

"Socially relevant?" His eyebrows rose. "Are we talking music or politics here? I've got nothing against folk music, and

I care deeply about politics. Hell, I sang 'We Shall Overcome' right along with Odetta, Dylan, and Baez at the March on Washington last year. But there's more to music than that. You shouldn't be a snob about it, Garfield. It's a big world. And a lot of it is electric. Keep an open mind."

The heat rose to my cheeks again. I'd never thought of myself as a snob. Chastened, I watched him as he put down his book, stood, and stretched.

"Maybe you could teach me?" I was impressed with my own boldness.

"Sure."

Amazing how a single word could cause a surge of adrenaline.

"I'll see you tomorrow," he added.

As he passed me heading for the bathroom, he gave one of my braids a tug.

Oh, my God—the braids! That had to be why he thought I was a child.

I retreated to my room, where I assessed my face in the oval mirror hanging above my dresser. My eyes were a nice color. *"Deep twilight blue,"* Mama called them. They were probably my best feature and certainly my most useful one. But the braids had to go.

I decided on the spot that from now on, I'd wear my long, brown hair loose, like Joan Baez or Mary Travers. I wished I could also do something about my nose, which I hated, despite what my mom had always said: *"Cleopatra and Nefertiti were considered the most beautiful women in the world, and they didn't have tiny, upturned, candy-box noses, either."*

I fell back on my bed and hugged my pillow, pretending it was Jake, who was going to introduce me to all kinds of new things. As I drifted off, I dared to imagine what it might be like to kiss him.

* * *

The following week Doc and Rosa Lee Watson were playing at the club, and I was shooting their last set when Jake whispered in my ear.

"Look at the back table on the left. That's Bob Dylan."

I lowered my camera and glanced at the slight, curly-haired young man sitting alone, barely illuminated by the single candle at his small table. As he watched the show and jotted notes, I grabbed a few shots of him.

Later, Jake handed me a crumpled napkin with something scrawled on it.

"Your mom might want to hold on to this."

The scratchy writing read, *I was so much ~~wiser younger~~ older then, I'm ~~so much~~ younger now than that now.*

* * *

When I got my proofs back, I printed one of the photos of Dylan in candlelight. I gave it to Mama, and she had it framed along with the scrap of napkin. I showed the results to Jake, who looked as pleased as I felt.

Jake came with us to the Hearst Greek Theater for the Jubilee concert at the Berkeley Folk Festival. Between sets with Mississippi John Hurt and the New Lost City Ramblers, he and Mama discussed the current wave of up-and-coming singer-songwriters and the inevitability of more music going electric.

I expressed my disgust with a snort.

He elbowed me in the ribs. "Come on, Garfield. Don't be so rigid. There's some great popular music out there. Don't you even like the Beatles?"

"I'd be embarrassed to be one of those screaming girls. So juvenile."

Mama patted him on the arm reassuringly and whispered, well within my hearing, "I wouldn't take that too seriously. Aquarians tend to be rather opinionated and stubborn. Fixed signs—not easy to persuade—and with Leo rising, she takes fierce pride in her opinions."

I glared at her behind his back.

He turned to me. "I bet you'd love the stuff I listen to."

"Yeah? Then let's go to the record store tomorrow. You can play me whatever you think is worth hearing."

I leaned across him to address my mother. "See? I'm open to other opinions and tastes."

* * *

The next afternoon I showed up in the back room—no braids this time, my hair flowing freely to my waist—to remind him of his promise.

"Oh, yeah. I forgot about that. You want to go now?"

"That's why I'm here."

He made a big show of sighing as if he were much put upon,

but he pulled on his boots and took me to the local record store to play some of his favorites in one of their glass-enclosed listening booths.

He selected a stack of records to sample, and I slipped the headphones on.

It was a truly electric revelation. I couldn't stop swaying and dancing to all the amazing sounds, including Del Shannon's "Runaway," The Kinks' "You Really Got Me," Martha and the Vandellas' "Dancing in the Street," a Patsy Cline medley, and the recently released Beatles hits.

I hadn't realized how long it had been since I'd danced. I could see him watching me with what might have been a smile of triumph, since his taste in music had been vindicated. But I decided to interpret his pleased expression as appreciation of my dancing skills. Either way, I was elated.

CHAPTER THREE

Love and Loss

1964, Summertime, Berkeley

Everything was so much more fun when Jake was around. With the summer speeding by, I did my best to hang out wherever he was. Despite my continually racing pulse, I managed to maintain an air of indifference. This was not an easy balance to achieve, but since he never told me to go away or leave him alone, I figured I was succeeding in disguising my motives.

Hanging out with Jake was easy and natural. He fit right in with our small family, treating me like a little sister, letting me tag along everywhere, teasing me when I got strident about anything—even though I was sure he recognized that I did actually know what I was talking about. During our discussions I chalked off my constantly speeding heartbeat as simply a normal response to the wealth of intellectual stimulation Jake was providing.

* * *

On Sundays we only had a matinee show at the club, which made me happy, since there were so many great TV programs on Sunday nights, including *Maverick* and *Have Gun, Will Travel*. Jake joined me and my mom on the sagging couch and stretched out his long legs. He reminded me of a cowboy—tall, lean, and lanky. I loved the way his dark hair fell into such beautiful, natural disarray. And his eyes! Those laughing eyes made me forget to breathe.

We also shared the same sense of humor. On Mondays, when the Folk Scene was dark, my mother, Jake, and I watched *That Was the Week That Was* in our tiny living room and laughed over the political jokes and commentary, and especially Tom Lehrer's sardonic songs.

Jake and I even sang a duet of "I Hold Your Hand in Mine," Lehrer's gruesome ditty about love and dismemberment, which had my mom chuckling and applauding.

We caught discount matinees at the local theaters at least once a week. Jake knew practically everything about movies and politics, my favorite subjects, so dinnertime always provided lively conversations. Over a meal of my mother's famous meatloaf, we all agreed that *Dr. Strangelove*, with its outrageous political satire, was the best movie we'd seen so far that year.

An important presidential election was coming up in the fall, and Barry Goldwater had won the California republican primary. Mama and I shared Jake's horror of what could happen if he were elected. Visions of mushroom clouds exploded in political TV commercials and in our imaginations. Goldwater had the support of the most racist elements in society, Nazis and Klansmen, and was opposed to the Civil Rights Act, which had just been passed to end segregation.

Berkeley was even more liberal than NYU, so to entertain Jake I started collecting political buttons that were sold at card tables set up where Telegraph Avenue ended at the campus. To his delight, I found one to counter the Goldwater campaign slogan—*In Your Heart You Know He's Right*—with one that read *In Your Guts You Know He's NUTS!* His laughter gave me a huge rush of pleasure.

I spent twenty-five cents on a small peace-symbol button for him, which he pinned to his denim jacket, promising, "I will wear it forever." I knew he was kidding, but the idea still made me insanely happy.

During a discussion about civil rights, he told me about one of his closest friends, who was a voting-rights activist.

"Andy Goodman was my neighbor on the Upper West Side when we were kids. We went to the same high school, joined the same political groups, and marched in protests together. He headed to Mississippi to register voters. I admire him so much. He's putting his life on the line to do what's right, to make the world a better place. That takes so much courage. But I just heard that he's disappeared, along with two of his buddies who went there with him. God, I hope he's okay…"

Mama and I hoped so, too. During the following weeks, we collectively held our breath, waiting for some news.

In July we all went to see *A Hard Day's Night*, and I had to admit that I really liked the Beatles. I even bought their albums and started playing them on the club's sound system when we were prepping for shows. Jake and I would sing along as we worked. He had a lovely, deep voice, and we harmonized perfectly. As August rolled around, *Another Side of Bob Dylan* was released, and we were all excited to hear the lyrics he had penned in our club for the song "My Back Pages."

On August 4th we were setting up for the evening show at the club, with the radio tuned to the CBS Evening News, when Walter Cronkite announced that the bodies of missing civil rights activists James Chaney, Andrew Goodman, and Michael Schwermer had been found in Mississippi in shallow graves, evidently murdered by the Ku Klux Klan.

As we all listened in horror, Jake started trembling, and tears filled his eyes. "I should have been with him. Maybe I could have saved him. Maybe he would still be alive."

I couldn't bear seeing him in pain. Mama and I hugged him and did our best to comfort him.

"Jake, honey," Mama said softly, holding his hand. "Listen to me. Your friend made a difference in the world with his courage and dedication. Just know that you will, too, but in your own unique way."

* * *

About a week later I was feeling restless and couldn't sleep. I tiptoed downstairs to get a midnight snack from the kitchen and heard laughter.

As I descended toward the living room, I could hear Jake saying, "Aw, what a cutie."

To my dismay and embarrassment, I realized that they were looking through our family album and had apparently begun with my baby pictures. I cleared my throat, and Mama turned around. I gave her my most scathing look, but she just waved me over.

"Come join us, Maddy. I'm telling Jake the family stories."

I leaned over the couch and quickly flipped the pages to well past my infancy.

Mama told Jake that Dad had shot most of the photos of me when I was little and that I had inherited his talent for photography. Despite her praise, I was not ready to forgive her for showing Jake my naked baby pictures.

Jake pointed to a photo of my dad in an RAF uniform, standing near an airplane. "He was a pilot in the war?"

"Yes," Mama replied. "Fifty bombing missions over Germany during World War II without a scratch. He was quite a hero, my flyboy."

"Wow. That's impressive! What happened to him?"

A familiar shadow fell across Mama's face. She straightened her back. "Gabe passed away several years ago." She rose from the couch. "If you'll excuse me... I'm exhausted, so I think I'll hit the sack. Maddy can show you the rest." She gave me a quick kiss on the top of my head and went upstairs.

Jake turned to me. "Did I upset your mom? I'm so sorry. Should I not have asked about what happened to your dad?"

"It's okay. Mama never really got over it. He came away from the war unscathed after all those bombing missions and then got killed by a drunk driver when I was ten." Tightness gripped my throat, and I tried to swallow it away. "He was the gentlest, kindest man on Earth."

I turned the page to two portraits I'd shot—one of just him, a copy of the lobby shot, and one with Mama's arms around him. That session was the first time my dad had let me use his camera. Mama had joined us and stood behind his chair, her head leaning against his, the light from the window behind me reflecting the love in their eyes. He looked contented and handsome, with his long, shaggy hair, worn that way years before it became popular. He was so smart, so funny, so strong—and our happy Bohemian life was completely shattered when he died.

"I remember that Mama cried all the time and wouldn't eat. We were on our own and had to keep the coffeehouse going to survive, so I had to be strong to help her."

I was sitting next to my father when the drunk trucker slammed into the driver's side of our car. I was freaked out, but not injured. But my father's face was covered with blood, and I could see his final concerned glance at me before his eyes glazed and dimmed. The last time I saw him, he was being lifted into the ambulance. I still have nightmares about it. For a long time, I couldn't talk about it at all. I was afraid that if I spoke, I'd completely fall apart, and I had to be strong for my mom.

The memory of that night over five years earlier was still too vivid. My chest constricted, and tears began to well up, but I fought them back.

"Wow, Garfield. That was a lot for a ten-year-old to handle." Jake wiped an escaped tear from my cheek with his thumb. "You're a hell of a lot stronger than you look."

Then he sat with me quietly as I composed myself, which I truly appreciated.

* * *

On a Sunday morning late in August, I caught Jake as he headed for the door.

"Where are you off to?"

"I found out you can go horseback riding in the hills."

"Can I come?"

"If you know how to ride."

"I had a few lessons when I was younger."

"You're not all that old now."

"Cut that out! I'm not a child."

I enjoyed his teasing most of the time, but my youth was still a sore spot.

"Come on, Garfield, where's your sense of humor? Yes, you can come along."

The hills above Berkeley were lush with pines and junipers, still green and fragrant from a rare summer rain. Birds sang and the sun broke through the clouds as we rode the trails through the shady woods.

After we had ridden in peaceful silence for a while, I asked Jake about his ambitions.

"I'm going to make movies."

"Yeah? Like, be a movie star?"

He laughed. "No. Like writing and directing movies."

"That's cool. Ooh, you should make a Western!" It was so easy to imagine him in a cowboy hat and a fringed leather jacket.

"I'll keep that in mind."

"I'll definitely come see your movies."

"Wow. I haven't even started, and I already have a fan."

He grinned at me and took off at a gallop, and I raced him back to the stable.

* * *

There was something else I really wanted Jake to teach me. The next evening, I decided the time had come for bold action. I took a deep breath to calm myself.

He was standing on our wooden back porch when I wandered out and leaned on the railing next to him. The full moon was rising, etching his high cheekbones with shadow.

"Hey, Jake?" My heart was pounding, and my voice wasn't as steady as I'd hoped.

"Yeah? What's up, Garfield?"

I tried to seem nonchalant. "I suppose you've kissed a lot of girls…"

He grinned and shrugged. "I suppose I have."

I would have loved to get in a jab about his cockiness, but there was too much at stake not to go on with my mission.

"Well, I was wondering… if maybe… maybe you would…" I was completely mortified at my incoherence. "…if maybe you would teach me…"

"How to kiss?" His eyebrows rose.

"Yeah. Just so I won't feel like a totally incompetent idiot when I need to know how."

He laughed.

Wounded and on the verge of tears, I punched him in the arm. Hard.

"Hey! Ow!"

"Don't laugh at me! It's not funny."

"I'm sorry, Garfield. I wasn't laughing at you… just at the idea of kissing lessons."

"Well, will you or won't you?" I moved closer, looking up at him in the moonlight. "After all, *'a kiss is just a kiss.'*"

He leaned down and whispered, "'*Here's lookin' at you, kid,*'" then gently touched his lips to mine.

My breath caught in my throat.

He slid his arms around me and kissed me again, slowly this time, lingering.

A powerful bolt of adrenaline rushed through me, and I thought I might actually faint. His arms were strong, his lips were soft and warm, and I melted against him. Completely swept away, I kissed him back. It was ecstasy. Better than anything I'd dreamed of. I wanted that kiss to last forever.

Suddenly Jake groaned and backed away abruptly, holding me at arm's length.

"I think you'll do just fine when the time comes." He paused, then took a deep breath and gave me a quick kiss on the forehead. "Just do me a favor, Garfield."

"Anything, Jake."

"Take your time."

He walked back into the house, leaving me on the porch, breathless and baffled.

* * *

I woke up so happy the next morning, I could have tap-danced on the ceiling. I relived the kiss over and over in my mind—the way his gentle lips felt against mine, the warmth of his skin, his arms around me in a perfect fit, if only for a moment.

I jumped out of bed, brushed my teeth, combed my hair, added a touch of smudged eyeliner, and bounced down the hall to the kitchen. Mama was taking some cinnamon buns out of the oven, but Jake wasn't at the table for breakfast. I went to the back room to wake him up, but he was gone. No pack. No sleeping bag. All gone.

I rushed back to the kitchen. "Where's Jake?"

Mama sat me down next to her at the table and took my hand. "He felt it was time to go."

I tried not to show the physical pain gripping my heart, but I couldn't hide it from my mother. She could always tell when I was upset and insisted that I talk.

Trying not to fall to pieces, I wiped a traitorous tear from my cheek with the back of my hand and told her about the kiss. Despite my efforts, I totally lost all composure, crumbling in front of her.

"Why? Why did he leave?" I choked back a sob.

"It's just timing, sweet girl." She hugged me. "It was just too soon. You haven't even started dating yet. You need more experience in the world before you'll be ready for a serious relationship. Of course, I understand how you felt about Jake. There was a lot to like."

"No kidding," I muttered.

"He actually reminded me of your dad when we first met. But I had already finished school by then and had traveled enough to truly appreciate him. I was ready."

"I appreciate Jake! I don't think I'll ever feel like this about anybody else. Dad was the only one for you—and you never found someone else to love like that."

"Maybe I haven't been ready to let someone else in my life. When I lost him I didn't know how I would survive. Thank God I had you, my beautiful child, and you kept me going. But…" She lifted my chin with the edge of her hand so I would look her in the eye. "…we don't need men to be complete people. Of course, it's lovely when you connect with someone as deeply as I did with your father. Then it truly enhances your life. And, sweetie, I promise you, when you have grown into who you are meant to be, sharing your life with a kindred spirit will be much more satisfying."

"Jake is my kindred spirit."

"That may be. But you need more experience to know for sure." She pushed my hair back behind my ears and wiped the tears off my cheeks. "I guarantee you will encounter many men throughout your life. Some will be charmers, some will be bad boys, and some will be frogs trying to convince you they are princes. You'll learn a great deal about what you want and what you don't want in your life."

I refused to be consoled. "But I only want Jake. What am I supposed to do with all those other guys?"

"I know you, my Maddy. You're smart and kind, and you'll know how to deal with them diplomatically but honestly. Trust your instincts. And take your time. Just remember, you don't have to kiss every clever frog."

CHAPTER FOUR

Rebels and Suaves

1965, Berkeley

I applied and was accepted to attend UC Berkeley. Since the campus was just up the block, I lived at home, which meant I could continue to help my mom with the club. I enrolled in basic-requirement classes, as well as a few electives, including Introduction to Psychology and their only class about cinema—an academic course on analyzing current releases.

I was hurrying around the corner of Dwinelle Hall to get to my English class when I ran smack into a picket line. My mother had taught me never to cross a picket line and to always inquire about the injustice being protested, so I decided to ask a marcher who was passing by with a sign that read *Save the First Amendment!*

"Hey! What's going on?"

"They've banned the card tables from Sproul Plaza and the sidewalks. They won't let us distribute any political pamphlets for candidates or anything!"

No card tables with political buttons and information?

But that was a tradition. It was where I'd gotten Jake's peace button and learned about the war.

I pulled out my camera and started documenting the protest.

"I think they're still surrounding the cop car at Sproul!" the girl shouted, pointing me back toward the plaza.

I ran toward Bancroft Avenue and saw hundreds of students sitting on the pavement around a police car. Everywhere I looked were students in action. I wanted to shoot it all.

So much to document!

I took my new Pentax OM1 from my shoulder and photographed the student speakers, who carefully removed their shoes before climbing on the immobilized police car so as not to damage it.

The crowd began chanting, *"Let him go!"*

I turned to a nearby student and asked, "Who's in the cop car?"

"They've got Jack Weinberg in there. They arrested him for handing out civil rights literature from the Congress of Racial Equality."

Horrified, I thought of Jake's friend who had been murdered for registering voters and fighting for racial equality. As I saw it, the university had no right to arrest anyone for exercising their free speech, but especially when it was to further the cause of civil rights. I was determined to preserve such a historic moment forever—my generation in action!

The cops wouldn't relent. They kept Jack, a graduate math student, locked in that police car as the hours rolled by and the crowd grew.

Students occupied the administration building and dropped flags with the initials *F S M,* for *Free Speech Movement*, from the three balcony windows on the upper floor. I slipped inside and captured images of the protestors playing guitars, singing songs, and dancing in the corridors.

Someone shouted, "The cops are coming!" and they all adopted Mahatma Gandhi's method of passive resistance, sitting down and preparing to go limp when the police dragged them out.

Heart pounding, I shot it all.

Back in the plaza I recognized Joan Baez walking through the crowd to the Sproul Hall steps, and I followed her. Her long, straight, dark hair curtained her face as she tuned her guitar. I climbed on the steps behind her and, keeping her in the foreground, shot the steadily growing crowd. I didn't hear what she sang. I was too focused on what I was seeing: her beauty and intensity against the background of ever-expanding multitudes of protesters and observers. All of them hushed to listen to her voice, joining in on familiar choruses.

Watching so many people allowing themselves to be dragged out and arrested by the police, putting themselves on the line in defense of free speech and civil rights, inspired me to my core. I'd never shot anything journalistic before, but the FSM introduced me to the addictive rush of documenting dramatic historical events.

And the protests had an impact. By January, the chancellor was replaced, First Amendment rights were restored on campus, and classes finally resumed. But I was deeply aware of how important those protests had been in protecting our rights and freedoms and reversing injustice.

When the term began, my favorite class was Introduction to Psychology. The professor was entertaining, and the subject held my interest most of the time. I wrote a paper on phrenology—an archaic and thoroughly disproven study of cranial bumps to determine personality—and even included a hundred-year-old Fowler and Wells pamphlet on the subject that I found in a used bookstore. But Berkeley was lab oriented, and a career studying Pavlovian responses in rats was not the future I envisioned for myself. I craved something more creative.

With only one class about cinema offered, I chose it as one of my electives. One of our first assignments was to see Richard Burton's *Hamlet*, playing for only two days at the local art house.

After class, a tall, gangly, pimply-faced guy approached me. He wore a black turtleneck and a Beatles haircut.

"Madeleine, is it?" he said with a slightly British lilt.

"Yes. And you are?"

"Geoffrey," he replied and bowed, making a circular flourish with one hand. "I have acquired two tickets for tomorrow night's screening of Mr. Burton's *Hamlet*. I was wondering if you might possibly be interested in using my extra ticket?"

"Definitely. How much is it?"

"I intended to give it to you as my gift. Perhaps I might escort you?"

"That's very kind of you."

"Splendid."

"Sure."

I didn't know what to make of him, so I described the encounter to my mother that night.

"Ah," she said. "A *suave*.'

"A what?"

"When I was in college, my girlfriends and I referred to posers as 'suaves.' It was a type we'd all encountered. The label seemed appropriate because of their pretenses. They put up a sophisticated front to impress you with how important they are."

"Should I turn him down?"

"That's up to you. If you think he's harmless and you can handle the situation, go. But watch him through the *suave* lens, and see if I'm not right."

During the movie, when Richard Burton began reciting, "To be, or not to be…," Geoffrey grabbed my hand, as if transported by the brilliance of the performance. I was not particularly impressed by his display… or the performance. Burton was at least forty—too old to be a credible Hamlet, in my view.

Afterward, over coffee, Geoffrey waxed enthusiastic about "Mr. Burton's exemplary oration." He also claimed to be an aspiring poet… and fourteenth in line for the British throne, though his accent slipped now and then. He spent a great deal of time smoking Gauloise cigarettes and staring off into space, as if contemplating great thoughts.

By the end of the evening, I could barely contain my amusement When he walked me home, I thanked him but dodged his attempt to kiss me.

Later I described the date to my mother, and she couldn't stop laughing.

"You have successfully identified and dodged your first frog."

After that, I politely avoided Suave Geoffrey, but I loved the class and wished I could study cinema at UCLA's film school, which sounded amazing. And I knew that Jake had gone there to complete his master's degree, an additional endorsement and incentive, but it would mean leaving Berkeley and my mother. I couldn't imagine that.

When I told her about the film program in Los Angeles, she said, "Maddy, my darling girl, if that's what excites you, then go. Follow your dreams."

"But what about you? How will you run the club without me? I can't leave you. You need me."

"Don't worry, sweetie. I will miss you terribly, of course. But you can always call or write and visit on holidays. And there are plenty of students here who can use the part-time work. I promise, I'll be fine."

When I received my acceptance letter, we celebrated, but I couldn't help worrying about leaving her alone. Ever since Dad died, I'd been her right arm, her companion, her friend.

I knew she would need plenty of help, so I plastered flyers all over campus and on local bulletin boards. I was relieved when she interviewed an undergrad student who had often frequented the club and was a devoted folkie and a tech wizard—perfect for setting up sound systems and lights—and who was efficient at the box office, as well. We also found two girls willing to waitress just for tips in exchange for hearing the shows for free. By the time I was ready to head south in late August, she had found several additional volunteers from among the new students arriving for the fall semester, which definitely eased my reluctance to leave her.

It was the end of summer, and I was ready to tackle life on my own, with a new major in a new school and a new city.

And maybe, the little voice in my head whispered, *you might even see Jake again.*

CHAPTER FIVE

Friends, Movies and the Summer of Love

1967, Los Angeles, California

Feeling overwhelmed and a little lost on the nearly four-hundred-acre UCLA campus, I finally located Heddrick Hall, where my assigned dorm room was located. I dragged my suitcase into the elevator and pressed the button for the seventh floor.

When I got to Room 714, the door was ajar and I peeked in. A barefooted redhead was standing on one of the twin beds, hanging a Beatles poster on the wall. She turned and saw me in the doorway.

"Come on in! You must be my new roommate—Madeleine, right?"

She hopped down from the bed and hugged me, which took me by surprise but made me feel a little less lost.

"I'm Darlene. Welcome to our new home!"

Her grin was infectious.

"You can call me Maddy."

"Cool name. So, what kind of food do you like? What's your major? Do you have a boyfriend? Tell me everything!"

"Uh… I eat pretty much everything, as long as it's not too

spicy. I think maybe motion picture production. And no... no boyfriend yet."

"Me, too. Except I do like spicy food. The film department is definitely the coolest place to be. And it's better to start the year unencumbered. There are definitely a lot of cute guys around. We're gonna have a blast this year. Pull up a bed, girl!"

I hauled my suitcase onto the other twin bed and plopped down next to it. Darlene sat on her deep green coverlet, twisted her legs into a yoga position, and continued her enthusiastic interrogation.

"So, where are you from?"

"Berkeley."

"Ooh, I've heard so much about Berkeley! Wow, were you there last year during the Free Speech Movement? Are you a political activist?"

"I was there. I shot it. And I'm absolutely against the war in Vietnam."

"Shot it? Are you already making movies?"

I laughed. "No. I'm a still photographer. I just want to work on movies someday. So, where are you from?"

"A ridiculously small, uptight town in Iowa that you've never heard of. Its big claim to fame is that John Wayne was born there." She rolled her eyes. "But I'm against the war, too." She spread her arms wide. "I've thrown off my Midwestern shackles!"

I chuckled as her questions continued.

"What kind of music do you like?"

"I like most music, but especially rock... Beatles, Stones..."

I thought of Jake watching me in the music store and singing Beatles songs with me while setting up in the club, and I tried to suppress the small pang of longing.

"Me, too!" She gestured toward her posters. "Who's your favorite Beatle?"

"John. I like intellectuals."

"I like the cute ones, so... Paul. But I would gladly make out with any of them."

That thought had never occurred to me. *Who would I be willing to make out with?*

Darlene's voice pulled me back to the conversation.

"So many great bands play in L. A. Are you going to photograph them?"

"That's a really good idea. Yeah, I plan to shoot everything."

"What a great excuse for us to go to the rock clubs on Sunset together! We can look out for each other... and UCLA always has really cool guest speakers on campus, like politicians and authors." She paused in thought for a moment. "Do you ever shoot any glamour photos?"

"I've never tried, but I bet that would be fun."

"If you want to practice, I can help. I'm really good with hair and makeup. Maybe I could model for you, and we could shoot some classic Hollywood-style glamour photos!" She piled her flaming locks on top of her head and struck a pose for my imaginary camera.

"Absolutely!"

I zipped open my suitcase and started hanging clothes in one of two tiny closets. Though it was almost impossible to keep up with her flood of questions, by the time I had unpacked and sat back down, we knew almost everything about each other, and I knew I had found a friend. I even told her about Jake and my first kiss and first heartbreak. She was very sympathetic.

"Older guys are so much cooler than high school boys. And they know how to do it. Teenagers just fumble around."

Do it? As in go all the way?

"Uh... so you've... done it?"

"Yeah." She shrugged. "The first time was not all that great, to tell you the truth. But it sure makes the guys feel full of themselves. I actually lost my virginity in the backseat of the quarterback's ancient Chevy. I was just lucky that he didn't knock me up."

She reached over to pat my hand before going on. "But college guys are smarter and better at it, and you'll find the right guy in no time. Ya gotta live your life. Which reminds me, there are a lot of mixer parties coming up, so we gotta be prepared." She glanced at my now-filled closet and shook her head. "I think we have to go shopping. Trust me. We're gonna be irresistible!"

That afternoon we went to the local import emporium, where we found Indian bedspreads in a lightweight cotton with gorgeous patterns and elaborate borders. Darlene bought one in shades of blue and green, and I bought one in blue and purple.

"We are going to have the coolest dresses in the city," she said with a shimmy.

When we got back to the dorm, she folded my bedspread in half and spread it out on the floor. She had me lie down on it with my arms outstretched along the folded edge. Then she cut around me, leaving a wide margin. Next, she cut a scoop out of the center of the folded area to become a neckline. She then cut the wide decorative borders from the discarded material and turned them into belled sleeves, which she attached to the dress extending from the elbows. We did the same with her bedspread. When we added belts, our full-length dresses were fabulous, and I was truly impressed.

"Where did you learn to do that?"

"I had to make all my own clothes at home, so this is a piece of cake."

"You made all your own clothes?"

"Not everything. I had store-bought underwear… plus hand-me-downs from my older sisters. But I was always pretty resourceful about making cool dresses."

The next day, after we had finished enrolling in our chosen classes, we took off to visit a shoemaker in Westwood Village, a block south of the campus. We both had our feet traced for patterns to have custom moccasins made. Then we hit a fabric store where we bought a yard of half-inch black velvet and some Velcro strips, which Darlene planned to turn into choker necklaces.

Back in our room, she scooped up the top layer of my long, brown hair and wove skinny braids on each side, with the rest of it hanging straight as their backdrop. We also discovered that there was no lipstick on Earth that looked good on me, but she showed me how to apply black eyeliner, and I loved that look. It felt like me.

* * *

In the back of my mind all this time, I was well aware that Jake had left Berkeley to attend grad school at UCLA, which was one of the reasons I had chosen to be here. Despite nearly forty thousand students on campus, and not much interaction between undergrads and grad students even in the same departments, I still harbored hopes of running into him.

I was on the way to my favorite class—every Friday's all-day triple feature of classic movie musicals—when I spotted him standing on the steps of the film studies bungalow. His hair was still shaggy, his dimpled grin still heart-stopping.

I took three steps in his direction before taking in the full picture. He was with someone.

The tall, skinny blonde at his side wore thigh-high boots and a miniskirt that left several inches of sleek thigh exposed. Her lustrous golden tresses fell in a silky sheet down her back, ending just short of the broad belt around her tiny waist.

She took Jake's face in her hands and kissed him, which stopped me in my tracks.

I made a quick mental comparison: *Taller than me. Thinner than me. Obviously a few years older and more sophisticated than me. More beautiful than... well, almost anyone I'd ever seen.*

I didn't think my heart could sink any lower.

I swiveled around and ran to my class.

After a little sleuthing, I turned up some information about the woman named Christine Blake. A part time student and part-time model, she was also the daughter of a British financier, one of the richest men in England.

No way I could compete with that.

A few weeks later I quite literally bumped into Jake, and my stack of books went flying. We both knelt to gather them before he glanced at me with the luminous eyes I remembered so vividly.

"Garfield?" He looked genuinely pleased to see me. "I didn't know you were here."

His surprised expression held something more that I couldn't define. All I could think about was being in his arms again, his lips on mine. The intervening three years dissolved. My cheeks burned, a battalion of butterflies took flight in my belly, and I momentarily lost the ability to speak.

I somehow managed to stutter, "Uh… yeah. I'm going to film school here."

"That's great! I'm sure you'll love it." Our eyes met, both of us speechless for a few moments, as we stared at each other grinning awkwardly. "It's really good to see you again."

I resisted the impulse to throw myself into his arms, but it was all I could think about.

He glanced at his watch and grimaced. "Damn. We seem to have terrible timing. Forgive me… I have an appointment with my advisor, and I'm already running late. We definitely should catch up soon."

He piled my books back into my arms, gave me a quick peck on the forehead, and hurried off.

Damn.

* * *

What to do about Jake? It was either give it up as a lost cause or come up with some dramatic gesture to let him know how I felt. After conferring with Darlene and with the benefit of her cheerleading and emotional support, I chose the latter course.

Valentine's Day was coming up, and I came up with an idea to capture Jake's attention. I gathered some chicken wire, a bunch of old newspapers, and a bucket of paste, and I constructed a gigantic three-dimensional heart out of papier-mâché—four feet across, four feet high, and two feet thick.

After painting it bright red, I attached a note that read:
For Jake,
My heart is yours.
From your secret admirer

In the middle of the night on Feb 13, Darlene helped me carry the absurd art project to the film bungalow, where we left it sitting on the porch while we went home to get a few hours of sleep.

The next morning, I located a grassy area nearby where I could keep watch to see if he found it and how he reacted.

When Darlene joined me at lunchtime, she could barely contain her curiosity.

"So? Did he find it?"

"Yeah."

"Did he laugh?"

"Yeah."

I had expected laughter. It was an outrageous thing to do, and I knew he'd find it funny. But it hadn't turned out as I'd planned.

"He was pleased, right?

"Yeah. He loved it."

I was on the verge of tears.

"For God's sake, Maddy. What aren't you telling me?"

"He wasn't the first to find it. Christine got there before he did. When he arrived, he assumed that she was the secret admirer. And she, apparently, didn't deny it. He laughed and kissed her."

"No!"

"Yes."

We shared a moment of silent mourning.

I tried to shrug it off. "It's just as well, I suppose. He'd probably be disappointed if he knew it was from me."

But it hurt.

* * *

When the spring quarter started, Darlene and I found a small apartment three blocks from campus and moved in. I was fortunate to be accepted into the very selective Film Production division. I signed up for Project One, the first filmmaking class, where small groups of students would crew for each other as we each made an 8-millimeter film, supervised by a teaching assistant.

The film production teacher for my group turned out to be the notorious Bill Branigan, an ex-marine from North Carolina and former New York City cop who had returned to school, grown his hair and beard, and become a counter-culture cowboy. Billy was the oldest, hardest-living, and most profane member of a group of young rebels who had gotten undergraduate degrees at NYU and then migrated west. He outraged nearly everyone he met, and I couldn't quite figure out how he had landed a job teaching impressionable novice film students, but our whole class adored him.

My film was an anti-war metaphor, in which a mysterious toy tank makes its way down a residential street as children from each house run to follow it in a long line. It leads them down an ally, where they line up. The tank then turns and shoots them all down, leaving a pile of bodies in its wake as it moves back out into the street to find more victims. I recruited local neighborhood kids, distant cousins, and younger brothers and sisters of all my fellow students until I had more than twenty children under age ten. After the initial march down the street and lineup in the alley, I took close-ups of each one screaming. I edited the slaughter scene like the "Odessa Steps" sequence in the silent film *The Battleship Potemkin*, with brief shots of agonized faces and falling bodies.

During my next weekly phone call with my mom, I was thrilled to tell her that my first film had been selected to screen in the annual showcase, a big deal for a first-year student. Her voice radiated pride.

At the end of the quarter, before summer break, Billy invited me to a special meeting in the film department. A select few gathered in a small circle around him, and he told us what he had in mind.

"Here's the deal, kiddies. For my master's thesis, I'm gonna shoot a documentary about all the stuff happening this summer, all over the state—festivals, celebrations, peace marches… the counterculture in action. I've rented a Winnebago, and I need a crew."

He chose Terry, a skinny young grad student, as his camera operator, and Danny, a senior who reminded me of a hobbit, as his sound man.

"And you, kiddo," he said to me, "you're gonna be my third-unit camerawoman. For part of this movie, I want you to shoot eight-millimeter—which is actually sixteen-millimeter sliced down the middle—and we'll tell the lab not to cut it, so we will have sixteen, with four images to each frame. It means shooting the second side with the camera upside down so that all the images will be right-side up. You up for it?"

"Absolutely!"

At almost nineteen and about to begin my junior year in the fall, I was the youngest of the bunch. I was thrilled that he believed in me enough to invite me to join his little band of filmmakers documenting the summer of '67.

We piled into the Winnebago and drove north.

In San Francisco we headed to the Haight-Ashbury district, where the RV jerked to a halt on a steep street in front of a slightly shabby Victorian house.

Billy pulled up the creaking hand break. "We're here, kiddies. Everybody out."

He waved his black cowboy hat to usher us to the sidewalk.

"Hey, man!"

A young Santa Claus with a wild mane of black hair, a full beard, and merry eyes ambled down the front steps to greet Billy. I immediately recognized Jerry Garcia, the Grateful Dead's amiable lead guitarist and patriarch.

"You made it!" He pulled out a large joint and lit up, and I noticed the missing digit on his right hand, which made his well-regarded musicianship even more impressive. "Okay to turn your crew on?"

Billy swiveled to us, eyebrows raised.

Terry shrugged, and Danny replied, "It's your movie, Bill. Your call."

Billy rolled his eyes. "Yeah, sure. Just don't fuck it up."

Jerry took another hit before passing the joint to Billy. "That's Acapulco Gold. Mighty fine weed," he croaked, smoke streaming from his nose and mouth.

Billy passed it on to Terry, who took a hit and passed it to me. I inhaled the acrid smoke and exploded in a coughing fit.

Jerry laughed and patted me on the back. "Easy does it!" He turned back to Billy. "We're just about to head out for the park. There's plenty of extra room on the truck for your crew."

We all piled on the band's flatbed truck and rode into Golden Gate Park to document the celebration of the summer solstice, which promised to be the largest and most colorful "love-in" to date. The day was warm and sunny, and the park was already full of celebration. The aroma of incense and cannabis filled the air. Naked children ran across the meadow, blowing giant bubbles.

The Dead were not the only band playing the free concert that afternoon. Flatbed trucks around the periphery hosted Quicksilver Messenger Service and Janice Joplin with Big Brother and the Holding Company, and each played sets.

I'd never heard anyone throw herself into a song like Janice. I was sure her vocal cords were being shredded… but she laughed and swayed and belted, "Take another little piece of my heart now, baby!" Arrayed in feathers, fur, and layers of colored beads, she gave me footage filled with intensity and joy.

Ecstatic flower-children clad in tie-dye, lace, and leather (and a few in just their own skin) danced to the music, celebrating the glorious day. Longhaired, topless girls crowned with flowers twirled across the vast expanse of lawn. I scanned Speedway Meadow with a long lens, isolating small groups, smoking, laughing, dancing… and a couple who sat facing each other, the girl's legs wrapped around her long-haired companion's waist, joined in motionless and ecstatic tantric union as they gazed into each other's eyes.

A bearded guy in a ragged shirt near our truck was freaking out, waving his hands in the air yelling, "Get away, away!"

Jerry asked one of his roadies to lead the guy to the Free Clinic nearby, where they could talk him down from his apparent bummer. "Avoid the brown tab acid," he told the crew. "I don't know what it's cut with, but we don't want anybody else having bad trips."

After several hours of documenting the colorful mob, we rode back to the Dead's peeling mansion, shared a final joint, and said a fond goodbye to Jerry and his band-mates with hugs all around. We piled back into the Winnebago and headed down the 101 to Monterey to cover the International Pop Music Festival.

Billy had arranged for press passes and ideal seats right in front of the stage. Saturday night I was able to shoot the Who, destroying their instruments in a blaze of neon violence. When I ran out of film on the first side of the roll, I cranked it back, rewinding, and shot again, double exposing the exuberant guitar-smashing.

On Sunday, Ravi Shankar played his sitar in serenity and near-stillness, as devotees tossed flowers from the front row. I shot the second half of my reel holding the camera upside down, to capture the performance so it would run right-side-up opposite the Who footage—the perfect contrast of East and West. As usual, I was so focused on the action and framing that I didn't hear very much of the performances, but I was enjoying myself immensely.

When the festival ended, Billy hustled our crew back onboard to head down to L.A. again. The last thing on his documentary checklist was a peace march close to our campus a week later, near the new Century City Hotel, where President Johnson would be attending a fundraiser. We all promised to gather in a nearby park just before the march was to begin.

* * *

Laden with gear and searching for our group on the day of the march, I made my way through the crowd in the park not far from the new hotel. I dodged families picnicking on the grass and various contingents preparing protest signs emblazoned with such slogans as *Get out of Vietnam, Senior Citizens for Peace,* and *War Is Not Healthy for Children and Other Living Things.*

I finally spotted Billy's familiar black cowboy hat and American-flag shirt, which led me to our ragtag crew. I nodded hello to Terry, who was loading his camera. He resembled a very pale beanpole with a mop of wheat-colored hair. Danny, our soundman, was tying back his dark, stringy locks and adjusting his small, round, John Lennon eyeglasses.

Darlene had volunteered to be our assistant-everything for the peace march. Surrounded by notebooks, camera report forms, and film cases, she was too busy touching up her stylishly pale lipstick to notice my arrival until I found a spot on the grass next to her and started loading the sixteen-millimeter Bolex. Happy to have been promoted from eight-millimeter, I cleaned the three rotating lenses on the heavy camera as Billy briefed us on the upcoming march and demonstration.

"You guys know what I want. Make it come alive for me, kiddies. Show me who's here—show me the faces, the passion, the signs, the families, the old ladies—and document everything. And don't forget, Maddy, a Bolex is as good a weapon as it is a camera. So if ya come up against some asshole givin' ya a hard time, just whack him across the head with it."

"Ha! Then I guess you better watch your back, Billy," I replied, which cracked up the entire crew.

Billy waved to someone behind me who was apparently threading through the picnicking family groups to join us. He stepped forward and grabbed the man around the shoulders, pummeling him affectionately and pulling him into our circle with his back to me.

"Hey, compadre! Did you come out to protest or just to pick up idealistic, nubile young women?"

Billy's "compadre" laughed and shrugged, then replied, "Just taking a break from writing. I'm leaving for London at midnight, and I thought, 'What the hell, I might as well affect the course of history while I stretch my legs.'"

I recognized Jake's voice instantly, and every cell in my body began to vibrate. Completely flustered, I was reduced to an insecure fifteen-year-old again. I turned away, trying to appear occupied with cleaning the camera's already spotless triple lenses.

Jake peered at me from several feet away, a slow smile growing. "Garfield?"

"Hiya, Jake."

Darlene's head whipped around, eyes wide, and she whispered to me behind her hand. "Is that *the* Jake?"

I nodded, tongue-tied and holding my breath.

Jake came closer. "Are you on this crew? How great to see you again!"

I nodded, trying to maintain my cool, despite the lack of oxygen in my system.

"Hey, man." Billy looked surprised. "You know Maddy?"

"We're… um… old friends. Almost got each other in trouble once."

Trouble? So that's how he viewed our first kiss?

Billy laughed as he herded his brood toward the front of the gathering parade. "Well, it wouldn't be the first time old friends got in trouble."

As Darlene fell into line behind Billy, she whispered in passing, "Okay. I *so* get it. Wow."

CHAPTER SIX

After the Police Riot

1967, Century City

Darlene plopped herself down next to me, still pulling leaves out of her hair but with composure restored. "Terry's going to take me with him to follow Danny's ambulance to the hospital. Are you okay?" She glanced at me with Jake's bloodied head in my lap, as I stroked his hair, and she grinned. "Uh, never mind. I can see you're doing fine."

Terry flagged down the approaching ambulance, and paramedics gently lifted Danny onto a stretcher.

Billy offered Darlene a hand up, saying, "I'll be checking on Danny later, too." He cleared his throat to get my attention. "And Maddy, be sure to drop that film off at the lab tonight. I can't wait to see what you got!" He turned to Jake. "Hang out for a second, man. I'll be right back."

As Billy led Darlene to Terry's car, Jake rose and helped me to my feet. My hands felt small enveloped in his.

"I'm really glad to see you again, Garfield."

He bent forward and kissed me lightly on the forehead, and memories of our summer and my first kiss came flooding back like a tidal wave. I tilted my head back to look at the face I loved looming above me and, on impulse, kissed him on the lips. His eyes widened momentarily and I could feel his smile against my mouth. He murmured deep in his throat, a purr of pleasure, and put his arms around me and kissed me back, taking his time. Heat flooded my entire body, and I turned to liquid. Pure joy.

He pulled back enough to look into my face with that familiar amused expression. "You've certainly mastered kissing," he whispered. "I knew you would."

"And I'm legal now."

Jake grinned, but before he could say more, Billy was hauling him out of my arms.

"Goddamn, Jake! We damn near get the shit kicked out of us, and you're busy charmin' the pants off Maddy. We've got just enough time for a quick toke before you get on the plane, you lucky asshole. You're gonna make out like a goddamn bandit in London."

"We can go back to my apartment," Jake told him, then turned back to me. "You want to come?"

Standing on the grass in Jake's bloodstained jacket, I watched the tall, lean figure and the broad, bearlike one heading down the street and made an important decision. He wasn't going to walk away this time.

I ran to catch up with them.

* * *

I was impressed with the way Jake rolled the joint. He licked the glued edge of one rolling paper and attached it to another, then sprinkled the sticky, gray-green leaves evenly across them and rolled them up with his thumbs. He wetted the free edge and sealed it, then licked the whole joint and lit it, taking a deep drag and holding his breath before handing it to me. I followed his example, drawing a deep inhalation of the acrid smoke, and exploded into uncontrollable coughing.

"I'm sorry," I croaked. "Relatively new to this…"

Jake brought me some water, the joint dangling from the corner of his mouth. When my coughing subsided, he leaned closer.

"Here, this will make it cooler."

He turned the joint around with the glowing end inside his mouth, leaned to within an inch of my lips, and blew a steady, thin stream of white smoke into my mouth. I inhaled and closed my eyes, then felt slightly dizzy.

Billy chuckled. "Okay, I get the picture, compadre. Give me a hit, and I'm outta here." He took a long toke, gave Jake a bear hug, and with his arm around Jake's shoulder, they walked to the door.

"Have a ball in London, man." Billy lowered his voice conspiratorially, though not enough to be out of my hearing. "And don't seduce my student, you asshole. Maddy's a really sweet kid, and…"

"Don't worry, Billy. I know. We're just really good friends. I wouldn't hurt her." Jake opened the door for him.

"Hey, man, I know that. Shit. Never mind." He thumped Jake on the back. "Make a kickass movie!"

He took one last deep toke, handed back the joint, and walked off into the night.

I was still hung up on *"just really good friends"* and yearning to be so much more than that.

Jake rejoined me on the couch and held up the joint. "Want some more?"

I nodded, only this time he took a deep hit, drew my face close to his, gently pressed his parted lips against mine, and slowly exhaled as I inhaled. I let go, languid from the smoke and the warmth of his lips, as his mouth caressed mine, savoring the moment. When I finally opened my eyes, there was Jake's face, a few inches from mine, observing me, his expression a mixture of amusement and intensity. He slipped his arm around my waist and drew me closer, leaning in to kiss me again. My heart soared.

The phone rang, shattering the moment.

"Oh, God." Jake glanced at his watch as he rose from the couch. "I have a plane to catch." He reassured the apparently angry owner of the voice on the other end of the line. "Yes. Yes, I know. Jesus, Christine, I get it. I'm on my way."

He hung up and turned to me, his face tense and his brows knit. "Forgive me, Garfield. I have to go. I'm so sorry. Bad timing again."

As I readjusted the clip in my disheveled hair, he grabbed his duffel bag and walked me down the steps to the sidewalk. Despite my deep disappointment I feigned a cavalier attitude. I wanted him to remember me fondly as the girl with "balls of steel."

"Don't worry about it, Jake. Do what you need to do. I know your movie will be great."

He rturned briefly to call back to me. "Thanks, kid. It was great seeing you again."

He disappeared into the darkness and was gone. Again.

Damn.

CHAPTER SEVEN

Film School and Bad Boys

1968, Los Angeles

Darlene shook me awake.

"Come on, Maddy! It's Tuesday. We have to get down to the induction center before they load the buses."

I leaped out of bed and pulled on one of my handmade Indian bedspread dresses and my comfortable moccasins. We grabbed the bunches of flowers we had gathered the day before and took off.

The Vietnam War was so controversial, it hadn't surprised me to learn that Jake's feature film script about coming of age during that debacle had to be produced by an English company. Meanwhile, the rest of us were doing everything we could to change hearts and minds about it, and weekly trips to the draft board had become a mission for Darlene and me.

At the Center we located the area where the young inductees were boarding to leave for basic training before being shipped overseas, and we handed flowers to each recruit, trying to convince them to resist the war and refuse to go.

Many of the young men looked subdued as the buses drove them away, but I was astounded by the shouts and hostile looks we received from some parents.

"*Get lost, hippie freaks!*"

The jeers were coming from a small group of mothers who were there to cheer their sons on as they left. *How could they so enthusiastically send their children to die or be maimed in a senseless war?* I knew that my own mother would never for one moment consider anything like that.

As we walked back to the car, I told Darlene about my mom's latest letter.

"My mother says she took a course on how to coach young men on avoiding the draft."

"You have such a cool mom. Isn't she worried she'll get arrested?"

"She learned exactly what you can and can't say, within the law, to get the information to them. And she says she can always tell who the undercover cops are—by their brown shoes."

We shared a laugh before continuing on to another of our usual topics of discussion: men. Of course, Darlene knew about my crush on Jake, but she was adamant that I should try dating other guys.

"So…when are you going to start dating? Jake's not the only guy in the world, y'know. How do you know your dream-boy isn't out there if you don't even dip your toe?"

I shook my head. "I did try. I went out with a poser who tried to charm me with his fake British accent. And I went out for burgers with a guy from my English Lit class who called me a frigid bitch because I didn't want to sleep with him. Dating has not been fun at all. I have better things to do."

The next week, Darlene posed for me by candlelight—ten candles in front, to one side, and another few behind her, to halo the rim of her vibrant red hair and render the flowers in her wreath translucent. She wore a low, scoop-necked peasant blouse, pulled off one shoulder, with a strapless bikini underneath. From a three-quarters angle, seeing only her face, her bare shoulder, and bare back, she looked as though she could be naked, though nothing was revealed.

When the rest of the girls on our dorm floor saw the results, they lined up to get their own free glamour shots. I learned how to find the best in each one, bringing out their most beautiful features with my choice of lighting and angles. And I learned how to put my subjects at ease by joking, listening to what they were hoping for, and offering props like feather boas or crowns. They gave me their trust, and I gave them my growing skills.

Running late for my film history final, I was trotting uphill on the long sidewalk bordering the campus when a large Harley Davidson pulled up and kept pace with me. The rider looked like a modern version of a Viking marauder in black leather.

"Need a lift?"

I paused to catch my breath, looking dubiously at the chopper and noticing the hand-drawn cycle-club insignia on the back that read *VIPERS*.

"Thanks, but I don't think so. Almost there."

"Film History 103B, right? I'm in it, too, and we're both going to be late, so you might as well hop on."

Clutching at the stitch in my side and looking at the half-mile uphill grade still ahead, I realized it was a reasonable solution to the problem.

"Maybe I will, after all. Thanks." I climbed on the seat behind him "I'm Maddy."

"I know. I've been watching you all semester. I'm Eric. Hold on."

He took off so fast that I almost flew off the back. I threw my arms around his waist and hung on, my cheek pressed against the back of his leather jacket. He gunned the bike and ran it straight up the steep, grassy slope next to the road as I held on for dear life. Then he hopped the curb on the other side, spinning out to halt in front of Melnitz Hall.

He looked back over his shoulder. "We're here."

I emerged tentatively from my cringe and squinted up at him. "And still alive?"

I released my grip and jumped off as he laughed. He turned off the ignition, swung his leg over the seat like a cowboy dismounting, and parked. He was easily six-foot-three, with straight blond hair hanging just past his shoulders and a nose that had probably been handsomely chiseled before it was broken.

"Definitely still alive," he replied as we hurried into the building. "It's the rush that reminds you."

After class, Eric gave me a ride back to my apartment, but I insisted that we stay on the road the entire time and that he keep his speed under fifty miles per hour.

He walked me to the door and leaned against my doorframe,

very close, towering over me. He smelled like sea wind and leather.

He asked if I was planning to attend the Kubrick film on campus that night. As he looked down at me with gentle eyes in a dangerous face, I could not deny that I found him very attractive.

"I was thinking about it."

He leaned a little closer." How about if I come by to get you at 7:30, and we can go together?"

"Only if you go slowly."

"I'll go as slow as you like."

He leaned down and gave me a light kiss on the lips. It gave me a pleasurable jolt, taking me completely by surprise. Then he swaggered to his Harley and roared off, and I went inside, still feeling somewhat breathless.

"Wow!" Darlene emerged from behind the curtains where she'd been peering through the window at us. "What a hunk! Where'd you find the bad boy?"

I tried to sound blasé. "He gave me a ride."

Darlene laughed out loud. "Yeah, I bet he did!"

* * *

After the movie later that night, I invited Eric in. We smoked a number, and he followed me into the kitchen.

"Got the munchies, huh?" he teased.

He came up behind me as I made cinnamon toast and cocoa. He lifted my hair and drew it to the side, baring the back of my neck, then brushed his lips across the nape, sending a little quiver down my spine. He slid his arms around my waist and pulled me against him. I sighed and leaned my head back against his chest. He buried his face in my hair and inhaled deeply, his body pressed against mine.

I enjoyed the sensations for a moment before turning toward him, my hands on his chest to create a few inches of safety zone between us. I took a deep breath and asked, "So what made you join a motorcycle club?"

"A couple of the guys were in the army with me in Nam. Their friendship was the only good thing to come out of that place." He leaned down between sentences and brushed my lips lightly with his. "They figure that I look dangerous enough to prevent fights, so they like me to hang out with them, but the truth is"—he kissed me again—"I'm a very peace-loving guy. I'm a lover, not a fighter." He took my hands from his chest, kissed them, and wrapped them around his waist as he pressed me against the kitchen counter.

Considering the series of disastrous dates with other fellow students that had ended in unwanted messy kisses, I hated to admit that I was enjoying Eric's skill immensely. He wrapped my hair around his hand and pulled me gently to his mouth, his tongue subtly probing the inner edges of my lips, sending little sparks through me. I returned the kiss with equal ardor. A deep growl rumbled in his throat as he lifted me onto the kitchen counter and started to unbuckle his belt.

"Just what do you think you're doing?" I raised an eyebrow and crossed my arms.

"Uh… getting ready to make love to you?" Eric's self-assurance seemed to waver.

"I don't think so. I'm not ready for this." I hopped off the counter and handed him some cinnamon toast. "But you sure are a good kisser."

Eric broke into laughter and took the toast. "Thanks, I guess. So what's the problem? You're not a virgin, are you?"

"What's wrong with that??"

"Wow," Eric looked genuinely impressed. "I don't think I've ever kissed a virgin before." He took an awkward step backward. "No liberation for you? You waiting for marriage, or what?"

"I just want to be in love when I make love. But that doesn't mean I don't like kissing and stuff."

He followed me back to the living room couch. "And 'stuff,' huh? That's cool. I like 'stuff' too."

* * *

It was late afternoon on a Friday, and Darlene was away for the day. Eric had been coming over almost every evening for weeks, often taking me out to the movies or sometimes just watching TV. Darlene usually ate dinner with us before discreetly retiring to the bedroom while Eric and I made out on the living room couch late into the night.

I could tell he was restraining himself, respecting my boundaries, but with great effort. He had won my trust so far by never pushing things beyond kissing and touching, gradually reaching the point where I was comfortable when we were naked together. He'd taught me how to get him off, which kept him satisfied. It was an opportunity to explore his male body and learn what pleased him, without pressure to do more.

With Darlene away, Eric and I were lying naked on my bed and stroking each other. He suddenly rolled on top of me, his knees pushing my legs apart.

"Don't go in." I put my hands against his chest.

"Yeah, I know… but you are so ready. I just want to feel you against me."

He reached down between us, his hand around his shaft, moving it up and down in my wetness. He rubbed against me, hard between my thighs, and I was enjoying the sensation but worried that he might have forgotten his promise. He lodged between my swollen folds, and I stiffened.

"Just relax, Babe. You know this feels good. Jesus! I can't play this game anymore."

He took his hand away and thrust to the hilt.

A flash of brief pain, and I was suddenly invaded, his hardness inside me, filling and stretching me to the limit. It was unexpected and uncomfortable, and I tried to pull away. He thrust once more, and I felt him expand and flood me with heat. He groaned and abruptly pulled out and rolled on his side, liquid pulsing across my belly and the sheets.

The realization hit hard.

I'm not a virgin anymore.

A deep sadness welled up, and I had to bite my lip to avoid breaking into tears.

"Whoa! Oh, man, that felt so good!" He looked very pleased with himself. "I'm so glad we don't have to hold back anymore. No more blue balls." He lay back, eyes closed, his breath calming. "No more games. Now we can fuck all we want."

I stared at the ceiling.

I should have realized there were limits to Eric's restraint. This was my own fault.

It wasn't what I had imagined as my first time, but it was done, and there was no taking it back. Of course I was glad it didn't hurt badly, but I felt a tremendous sense of loss. I drew my legs together and curled up on the edge of the bed.

"I'm sorry I came so fast… but don't worry, babe. Next time, I'll make it last longer."

Next time? He seemed to think that we would be doing it regularly now.

Eric glanced at the bedside clock. "Oh shit… I have to go." He gave me a peck on the shoulder, jumped up, and pulled on his jeans and T-shirt. "I'll see you tomorrow."

After he left, I dressed silently. The realization that Jake would never be my first felt like a fist around my heart, and I couldn't hold back my tears.

* * *

The following day, Darlene sat down next to me on my bed.

"Hey, Maddy. Are you okay? You seem really down today."

"I know." I sighed.

"Lay it on me. That's what friends are for."

Darlene's concern was a comfort.

"I finally did it."

"With Eric? Really? So, how was it? Was he a lousy lover? You seem really upset."

"I didn't really mean to do it. It just happened… but it was my fault for not stopping him." Tears rose, and I wiped them away. "And now he expects us to do it all the time, and I know he's not the one… that I don't want to spend my life with him."

"Oh, Maddy. He's just a boyfriend. It doesn't have to be forever. It's okay to have some fun and move on. Guys do that all the time."

"But he's getting serious. And the longer we drag this out, the harder the breakup will be. What should I do?"

"What do you want to do?"

"Turn back the clock."

She laughed and patted my hand. "Short of time travel, what do you really want?"

"I don't know. I don't want to hurt him, but I don't love him, and my heart's not in it. I don't want to be his old lady, and I don't want to do it again. A breakup is inevitable, so why make things any more difficult?"

"You shouldn't have to do anything you don't want to do. He doesn't own you…" She paused. "Did he use a rubber?"

"No. He pulled out while he was coming."

"Oh, boy. When's your monthly due?"

"In a few days. Oh, God. I'd better not be pregnant. I really don't want a permanent connection. He's not the one I want as the father of my children!"

I thought of Jake and burst into tears.

"No need to panic, hon. One step at a time. If your period is late, you can go to the med center. They can give you a pregnancy test… and check for any diseases he could have given you. It will all be okay." She hugged me. "I'll go with you, if you want."

* * *

I had promised to go to the movies with Eric the next evening but hadn't discussed what we'd see. He didn't know about my history with Jake, so I was very surprised when we pulled up at the local art house where Jake's first film was playing in a limited run. The movie had made Jake the hero of the film school but had also received a lot of criticism for its antiwar stance, and it hadn't occurred to me that Eric would want to see it, maybe because of his history in the service.

It was even better than I imagined. I felt humbled and proud to know Jake. I was inspired by his clarity of vision and the humanity of his characters, mesmerized by the skillful filmmaking, swept up in the story, and feeling both sad and exhilarated when it ended.

I was quiet when we emerged from the theater, still immersed in Jake's heartfelt statement about the loss of innocence, both sexually and politically. It touched me deeply, especially in my new circumstances. Meanwhile, Eric was rambling on about the heroine in the film and insisting that she reminded him of me, but I was too wrapped up in thoughts of Jake to pursue that line of discussion.

Back at my apartment, Eric started to unbutton my blouse, and I stopped him. "I don't want to."

"Come on, babe. It'll be so much better this time."

"No. Seriously. I don't want to do it."

"Jesus, Maddy. Not this again." He raked a hand through his hair and took a deep breath. "Okay. Maybe later, then. So… my buddies are having a party, and I promised to drop by. They all want to meet you."

"I don't know. We need to talk."

"After the party we can talk… and stuff."

He swung onto his Harley and offered me his hand to hop on behind him. At that point I didn't know what else to do but acquiesce and try to discuss it all later in the evening.

As we entered the mostly bare, ramshackle house in Culver City, I felt all eyes assessing me. Mattresses and crates stood in for furniture, and the walls were covered with drawings, poetry, and commentary. On every surface empty wine bottles served as candlesticks, and in one corner a plaster skull had become a base for colored candles that dripped wax into fanciful designs.

As Eric's friends pummeled him in greeting, I wandered around the room, reading the bits and pieces of graffiti on the walls—some of it humorous, some of it simply crude.

A barrel-chested man with long, black, thinning hair cornered me. "Is this the little chick that's got Eric pussy-whipped without the pussy?"

He loomed over me, flashing a smile full of stained teeth. He leaned close enough for me to smell his foul breath before he was suddenly jerked away.

"You can't talk about my old lady like that, you cocksucker!"

Eric spun him around, punched him in the belly, and

dropped him to the floor with a hand-chop to the back of his neck. Two other guys in scuffed leather joined the fray, fists flying.

"What are you doing?" I screamed at them. "This is stupid! I thought you're supposed to be friends. Stop it. *Stop!*" I yelled, but my voice was lost in the din.

I found my way to the kitchen, located a dented cooking pot, filled it with cold tap water, and returned to the living room, where I flung it on the battling bodies. Drenched, they stopped abruptly, turned to face me—their small attacker—and burst into laughter.

"Takes things real serious, don't she?" The bleeding hulk at Eric's feet rose, dripping and laughing.

I headed straight for the front door, slammed the screen open, and crossed the porch in a fury. Eric followed me out.

"Come on, babe! They're just a bunch of assholes." He lengthened his stride to catch up with me. "They spend most of their time fighting. It's their idea of a good time."

I spun around to face him in defiance. "Well, it's not mine! I hate that! I hate that stupid, violent behavior. And these are your friends?"

Eric looked as though he was suppressing the urge to smile as I stood in front of him—barely up to his shoulder, my fists clenched at my sides—but he held up his hands and conceded, "You're right. You're absolutely right. Come on… I'll take you home."

He led me back to his motorcycle, and we drove back to my apartment.

He sat on a kitchen chair as I washed off his cut lip and bruised eye and lectured him. "You didn't have to start a fight. I could have taken care of myself."

"Yeah. Sometimes I forget what a tough little chick you are." He reached around me, hands sliding over my bottom as he pulled me between his legs, biting gently at my nipples through the thin material of my shirt. I caught my breath at the rush of unwelcome sensation and tried to pull back, but he held on.

"Come on, baby. No reason to hold back anymore. Now we can fuck whenever we want. You know you were ready."

"Cut it out, Eric. I don't want to do it again." I struggled out of his grip and put some distance between us. "I'll decide when I'm ready."

"Is it because I came too fast? But you're my old lady now. Now that we're doing it, there won't be so much pressure, and I can make it last longer."

"That's not the problem. I just don't see a future for us."

"So... you don't want me at all?" His body contracted as if punched in the gut.

The moment of truth had arrived. I could tell his feelings for me had been getting deeper, and there was no point in dragging it out. I had to end it now.

"I'm sorry, Eric. You've got to admit that we really have very little in common. There's no place for this relationship to go from here. Maybe we should just call it quits."

Silently he rose, his face dark, grabbed his leather jacket from the back of the chair and headed for the door. His voice was soft, tinged with bitterness. "So after all this time holding back and playing your game, you've decided I'm not good enough for you? I should have known better. Have a nice life, Maddy."

The door banged shut behind him. I watched through the window as he tore a branch off the tree in the front yard before mounting his Harley and speeding away.

When Darlene returned, I told her what had happened.

"Oh, Maddy, I'm sorry. Even if he seemed pretty cool, you shouldn't have to do anything if you don't really want to."

* * *

My period was due the following Sunday and didn't come, which threw me into a total panic. First thing Monday I went to the UCLA Med Center and was seen by a graying doctor with a severe demeanor. He looked at my paperwork and frowned.

"I am so sick of you irresponsible girls, sleeping around and not using protection. Stupid. Just plain stupid. You can't get an accurate pregnancy test until after you've missed a period for at least two weeks, but I'll test for gonorrhea, chlamydia, and syphilis."

I already felt miserable, and his tirade didn't help. "I don't intend to ever do it again." I mumbled.

"Of course. Right." He handed me a prescription for a diaphragm. "It will take a few days to get the results of the blood tests. Try to restrain yourself in the meantime."

"That won't be a problem."

I broke into tears after he left the exam room, then pulled myself together, dressed, and returned to the apartment.

* * *

To my relief, my period started the next day. But I no longer felt as sure of myself and was wary of anyone showing an interest. I avoided eye contact with my fellow students in class, not wanting to attract any attention, especially from the guys.

Eventually Darlene tried to fix me up with one of her classmates, insisting that I at least go out for a meal with him. He was nice enough, but I wasn't particularly attracted to him. After sharing some fries and inane small talk, he walked me back toward the apartment.

Without warning, he pushed me against a tree and shoved his tongue down my throat. I kneed him in the balls and ran home, leaving him curled up and moaning on the grass.

I decided that would be my last attempt at dating. In my mind, none of them could hold a candle to Jake, so it all seemed like a huge waste of time.

I focused my attention on covering campus events and guest speakers—everyone from Dr. Spock, the famous pediatrician, and science fiction writer Ray Bradbury, to the first black congresswomen, Shirley Chisholm.

When Darlene and I went to the Whisky to photograph rock bands and to the Troubadour to shoot singer-songwriters, comedians, and folk-rockers, she ran interference with would-be pickup artists. Her flirt-and-dodge skills were remarkable, and it freed me to focus on the work. I learned to deal with low light levels and colored stage lights constantly changing, how to avoid mic-stands blocking the musicians' faces, and how to maintain a steady shot while everyone around me danced and screamed. When I was shooting, capturing the moment was all that mattered, and I could shut out the rest of the world. My camera was my shield, my barricade protecting me, and it gave me joy every time I preserved an image worth saving.

I graduated *Summa Cum Laude*, but I knew no one in the movie industry, except Jake. But there was no way to contact him, and I didn't have any real experience on film sets.

I had to find a job.

CHAPTER EIGHT

The Underground Press

1969, Los Angeles

Despite graduating with honors, I had no immediate employment prospects, had no contacts in the film industry, and had rent to pay. I applied at major movie studios, but without connections I couldn't even get a mailroom job.

I finally landed some part-time work at the Free Press Bookstore. The people who worked there were intelligent and easygoing; the customers were all book lovers, which created a laid-back atmosphere, and being able to spend time reading while getting paid was a major perk.

Just because I wasn't participating in sex didn't lessen my curiosity. I wanted to be well educated on the subject, so I systematically worked my way through their whole erotica section.

But working for minimum wage didn't get me very far. My mother's weekly letter always included a check for $50, which helped but barely kept me afloat.

I wanted a camera job. I knew getting work on movies was unrealistic, but it only took one person, me alone, to shoot photographs. Perhaps I was meant to be on a team with a reporter, shooting events and pivotal moments in history.

Maybe I should be a photojournalist.

I tried every legitimate newspaper within a hundred miles. The responses were all the same:

"We've already got a guy who shoots for us."

"...you, kiddin'? Go away little girl."

Or, pointing to the camera hanging from my shoulder, they'd ask, "*You know how to use that thing?*" followed by skeptical laughter.

Not a single major newspaper showed any interest in hiring me, so I decided to try the underground press.

With a portfolio under my arm filled with glamour portraits of my dorm friends, folk-singers from my mother's club, rockers from the Whisky and the Troubadour, and a variety of antiwar and political campaign events, I climbed the rickety stairs to the dilapidated offices of *The Alternative*. It was an offshoot of the original *L.A. Free Press*, an underground newspaper covering music, politics, popular culture, and the literary scene.

The paint in *The Alternative*'s office was peeling from walls plastered haphazardly with articles and photos. A scruffy young man, his long legs propped up on the wooden desk was talking on the telephone when I arrived.

"Warhol, huh?" he said on the receiver.

He pushed some papers aside and waved to me to take a seat on the edge of his desk before finishing his phone conversation.

"Okay. I'll be at the Polo Lounge at three. Very cool. Later."

He hung up and grinned at me. "The photographer, right?" His smile revealed dimples above his thick, brown beard. "Let me see what you've got."

I offered my portfolio, which he flipped through quickly.

"Okay. *Nice*. And perfect timing. I've got an interview set up with Andy Warhol at the Beverly Hills Hotel in an hour, and I need a photographer. Wanna come?"

I couldn't believe my luck. "Absolutely!"

"I'm Peter, the editor and main writer for this rag. Glad to have you." He shook my hand. "The job pays fifty dollars a week, when we have it… and all the freebie food the publicists are willing to spring for when we interview their clients. You're going to love the Polo Lounge."

* * *

In the garden lunchroom at the Beverly Hills Hotel, Peter and I greeted Warhol and his companions—a fading, middle-aged, blond actress and a gaunt director. We slid into the booth opposite our subjects.

The room had perfect soft light, and after feasting on eggs Benedict with fresh-squeezed orange juice and listening to a little shop talk about the independent film business, I raised my camera, elbows braced on the table, and began documenting the three of them.

Peter struggled to get coherent responses to his questions, but Warhol was laconic and seemed deliberately enigmatic, rarely saying more than a single word or two. His friends joked, chuckled to themselves, and made their own esoteric comments to amuse each other.

I focused my lens on Warhol, waiting for any change. He sat directly across from me, pale and expressionless. After an hour my arms began to ache, but I waited patiently. It seemed as though his standard deadpan was the only shot I would get, but a comment by one of his friends made him smile for a fleeting moment and stick his tongue in his cheek. I clicked and grinned at Peter. We had our cover shot.

Two nights later I shot a Doors gig at the Kaleidoscope, a local "floating" club that changed locations each week. Wild Bill ran their light show, and a few former students helped.

Billy recruited me to "play" the lighting keyboard for the opening act. The keys were hooked into the entire system of lights and effects, so hitting a note would trigger a given moving visual image on the walls or the stage.

Before the Doors set began, Jim Morrison wandered backstage and stumbled toward the light board I'd been operating. He sat beside me on the bench, awkwardly leaned on the keys, and jerked in surprise at the explosion of lights, staring in stoned wonderment at the swirling designs changing around him. He rose and stumbled into the light-show paraphernalia as he headed to the stage.

I turned the lighting master-board over to Billy so I could go down front to shoot.

Morrison, looking like a wasted angel with his shoulder-length dark curls and half-closed eyes, hung on the microphone stand as if it were the only thing keeping him vertical. Several times he nearly collapsed into the audience. A small group behind me took bets on whether this was the night Morrison would keel over and die. At the end of the set, his band-mates led him off stage.

The following week I shot a shy, soft-spoken singer named Jimi Hendrix poolside at a West Hollywood motel during one of Peter's interviews. He had just come back from making a splash in London, but he was unknown here. An upcoming performance at the Shrine Auditorium downtown was to be his West Coast debut.

As Peter asked questions, I rested my elbows on the table to steady my camera, and shot a frame each time Jimi reacted or responded. Periodically he would glance at me across the round table and smile, which gave me some lovely informal portraits.

As we rose to leave, Jimi stopped me. "Would you like to come backstage Saturday night?"

"I'd love to."

He borrowed Peter's legal pad, jotted a note and handed it to me. "Give this to the guard at the stage door."

Peter watched Jimi depart, then turned to me with raised eyebrows. "Wow. You made quite an impression on him," he said. "He was flirting with you."

"You're kidding." I was completely oblivious. "You think so?"

"I know so. Being cute opens doors. And I bet you got some great shots."

On Saturday evening, an hour before the show, I located the artists' entrance and presented the note. The guard told me to wait a second, ducked inside for a moment, and then nodded me in. I found the backstage area, noted the low light level, loaded my camera with Tri-X black-and-white film and set the normal 400 ASA to 2400. The higher the ASA, the less light was required to capture a photo. The lab could "push" the film while developing it to accommodate the change.

Music echoed from the stage, and I followed the sound. The curtains were closed, and Jimi was jamming with musicians from all the other bands on the bill. Buddy Miles played drums near the rear of the stage, looking like a vast, dark mountain. David Crosby sat on the floor in a fringed jacket and cowboy hat, strumming along on his guitar. Harvey Brooks leaned close to Jimi to follow his chord progressions. I photographed them all while fending off pickup lines from their roadies.

The bass player from the headlining band came up behind me, close enough to feel his breath against my ear. "Hey, baby. Wanna party after the show?"

After a quick glance and polite smile, I returned my eye to the viewfinder. "Gee. As tempted as I am by your charming invitation, I'm afraid I can't. I'm on assignment with a short deadline. But I do appreciate the offer."

He shrugged and moved on.

Being "cute" had its drawbacks. I had to become adept at rejecting crude attempts at seduction with a smile. I'd learned that rock musicians are a notoriously horny lot and will generally flirt with any girl in their immediate vicinity, so I was often a target. Usually it was flattering, and I was able to flirt back while keeping them at bay. Sometimes it went beyond flirting to blatant sexual propositions.

After a few awkward episodes trapped in crowded backstage corridors or private hotel rooms, I learned to tap-dance gracefully out of potentially difficult situations, bantering my way free without inflicting too much ego damage on my pursuers, who apparently assumed they were irresistible. My camera gave me a physical barricade and provided the detachment I needed to observe and capture the moment. I learned never to let superficial attraction override my good sense or my imperative to get the shot.

Peter was thrilled with the pictures from the informal sessions and concerts and featured them prominently. I hoped it would be the beginning of a very productive association.

I loved sitting on Peter's desk like a reporter in a forties movie, ready at any moment to dash off to cover a political event or shoot a portrait of an author promoting a book. As time went on, I spent several days a week shooting interviews with assorted writers, performers, and politicians, and I covered every major rock concert in Los Angeles.

My photos became a main attraction of the paper, and Peter made sure I received my fifty dollars a week, even if there wasn't enough to pay the entire ragged staff. Our circulation grew modestly but steadily.

Peter always let me set up the interview space, so I could position the subject in the best possible light. Then I would choose the ideal spot to shoot from. My subjects seemed to be at ease with me, and I would click away happily as Peter conducted the interviews. When his questions got them talking about the things they cared about most, I always got expressive, personality-revealing pictures.

The Alternative was giving me a showcase for my work. Combined with my part-time job at the Free Press Bookstore and my mother's checks, it was just enough extra to keep me going. The downside was that I was working constantly but barely making ends meet.

* * *

The postmark on the envelope was from Berkeley: my weekly letter from my mother. I tore it open and discovered a charter airline ticket and a Eurail Pass, along with a note.

Dear Maddy,

Happy 21st birthday, my darling girl. Here is my gift to you. It is time for you to have your European adventure, a must for every educated young woman. It was in London after the war that I met your father, when I had my European sojourn. The charter flight will take you to and from London, but I've arranged to make the return open-ended, and I've purchased a Eurail pass for you so you will have unlimited train access. Perhaps you can combine the pleasure trip with some work for your newspaper.
I hope you will send me regular letters recounting your experiences, which I will save for you as a journal.
Have a wonderful time, my darling. I'm very proud of you.

Love,

Mama

I read it to Darlene, who squealed with excitement and volunteered to drive me to the airport.

"Oh, Maddy, you are going to have a blast! Make the most of every minute. I can't wait to hear the stories about your adventures!"

CHAPTER NINE

Colin and Purple Harry

1970, London

The charter made a forced stop in Pennsylvania because of a series of storms, and they kept us on the plane for five hours, without air-conditioning to preserve fuel. Sweat condensed and dripped down the inner walls of the cabin, and several people passed out and fell into the aisles before we were finally cleared to take off again. Many more hours later it was a relief when we finally touched down at Gatwick Airport.

I loved London from the moment I arrived.

Armed with a student guide and a map book entitled *London A to Z* (pronounced "zed" by the Brits), I checked into the cheapest Kensington bed-and-breakfast hotel I could find and set off to explore the city. History filled my senses. I doubted that anything in Los Angeles was older than the 1920s, so seeing block after block of buildings hundreds of years old made me feel like a time traveler, a tourist in another age.

The friendliness of the people was astounding. Anytime I looked the slightest bit lost, strangers on the street spontaneously offered directions and assistance, pleased to be helping a "Yank." Even the "bobbies" were a revelation—not the helmeted, faceless enforcers I was so accustomed to fearing and avoiding in California, but charming, polite, and helpful policemen—and they didn't carry guns.

I discovered how easy it was to get around the city on the subway "tubes," exploring at will with no effort at all. And every few blocks I encountered another park lush with grass and trees. It was like seeing the color green for the first time in my life—a green so rich and deep that it took on new dimensions in space.

My portfolio opened doors, and I landed a freelance job for *Time Out* magazine, the local counterculture guide for activities in London. My first assignment from Editor Clive Martin was to photograph a rising rock band, Purple Harry, in the recording studio.

The studio receptionist pointed the way, and I slipped quietly into the control booth, where I found an empty corner to load my cameras and stash my equipment. The walls of the dimly lit room were painted black. The area was large enough to accommodate a huge control panel, stretching nearly wall to wall, with knobs and sliders and meters to register sound levels. A door on one side led into the recording studio just beyond it, and windows in the wall provided a clear view of several musicians jamming inside, trying out various riffs before recording.

The balance of the control booth held a dark leather couch facing the windows, where a young blonde woman was hunched over a narrow coffee table, chopping up lumps of white powder with a razor blade. She formed several long, thin lines on an unframed mirror lying on the table's surface and then glanced at me briefly before returning to her task. I recognized her, both from the covers of several fashion magazines and tabloids… and from UCLA. It was Christine Blake.

The engineer was just finishing a playback, and a couple of band members were engrossed in fiddling with the sliding knobs on the mixing board as they listened. I waited for a break between songs to introduce myself to the musicians.

Derrick, the band's charismatic lead singer, noticed me.

"And 'oo is this tasty morsel? A lit'le Yank bird? Very far out." He gave me a crooked-toothed grin. "You just shoot away, luv, while we go about our business."

Christine inhaled a long line of powder through what looked to be a rolled up pound note and sat back on the couch. "How much longer, Derrick?" she called out, pouting and crossing her arms in obvious annoyance.

"Patience, swee'art. This cut's almost done. Then playtime."

He herded the band back into the studio.

"Cor…!"

The deep, throaty sound of Cockney appreciation coming from behind me made me turn away from the control board. The voice had come from a tall, pale, extremely skinny fellow with hair vaguely resembling a pale orange haystack.

"Very nice, indeed." He looked me up and down and nodded. "Come to 'ang out wi' the band?"

I smiled politely and extended my hand. "I'm here on assignment for *Time Out*. My name is Madeleine. And who are you?"

"Name's Colin Jones, 'ead roady and lorry driver for the band. Where in the States are you from, luv?"

"California." I tried to extricate my hand from his grip, but he held on. "I'm going to need this to work with," I said, and finally pulled it free.

"Oh, sorry. I love birds from California."

"So you know other girls from California?"

Colin looked embarrassed. "Well, not exactly. Not yet. I plan to, though. The band's getting so big, we'll get to tour the States eventually, and I've 'eard that California birds just love English musicians."

"So you're a musician, too?"

He grimaced. "Not as good as the band yet, but I write songs sometimes. And working for the band is close enough for now, don'tcha fink?"

I smiled. "I wouldn't worry about it, Colin." I returned to focusing my camera on the band and added, "I'm sure the girls in California will adore you."

"Yeah? Really? Ya fink so?"

I glanced back at him. He looked so pleased and hopeful, rather like an excited sheepdog, that I had to stifle a laugh.

Colin crossed his arms and leaned against the wall to watch me work.

The musicians returned to the mixing board to listen to the playback, and I got good shots of them adjusting the knobs, debating the merits of the take, and joking and laughing with each other.

I asked Colin about the origin of the band's name.

"Derrick's real name is 'arry Gump…, and Purple 'arry refers to his old man."

"His father?"

Colin broke into a giggling fit. "Not 'is da. 'is John Thomas."

I was baffled.

"His prick… dick… private, manly parts."

"Ah. Thank you for that clarification." We both burst into laughter.

At four o'clock they packed it in. Derrick and Christine had a brief argument in the hallway. She stormed off as Derrick shook his shaggy mane, swore under his breath, and called after her, "Bollocks! We can fuck later, Chrissy."

He reentered the control booth, muttering about the hazards involved with "shagging posh birds."

"We've got a football match against another band," Colin told me as he locked up the equipment for the day. "Want to come along?"

"I'm not very experienced at sports photography, but I'd like to give it a try."

Colin gave me a lift to the soccer field in the band's truck. It was drizzling, but that didn't seem to faze the players at all. They barreled up and down the field, somehow always too far away when I used a wide lens and too close when I had a telephoto lens. I was cold, wet, and frustrated by the time the match ended.

"Okay, you guys," I yelled. "Line up for team pictures!"

The bands cheered and took turns—soggy, muddy, and dripping—posing for team photos. The photos ended up not just in *Time Out* but on the cover of Purple Harry's new album.

Despite Colin's brash come-on, he went out of his way in the following days to help me find a flat in Belsize Park near Hampstead, which would cost less than the Kensington bed-and-breakfast where I had originally landed. I loved wandering on Hampstead High Street, visiting the antiquarian bookstores and the pubs and the poets' hangouts on the way to Hampstead Heath.

The heath itself was my favorite place in the whole city. It was an untouched natural wonder in the heart of northwest London, four miles across, and included every type of native English terrain imaginable, from meadows and streams to hills and forests. I found an ancient oak tree not far from the late poet Keats's house, which could comfortably accommodate at least four people in its branches. I would take my camera and a book and sit in the tree, quietly enjoying the company of others who did the same.

Colin soon became my personal guide to London and my friend. He hungered for tales about life in America.

"It's the greatest bloody country on the face of the earf," he insisted. "No bloody fuckin' class system to treat you like you're… like you're…"

"Inconsequential?"

"Wot's that word mean?" Colin drew back momentarily, looking defensive.

"It means not important, worthless."

"Wot a great, large word to mean wurfless.' Yeah. I got

sick and missed taking my Eleven-Plus exams when I was a lad, so I'm a lorry driver. And treated like I'm completely… inconsequential." He beamed with pride at his new word. "That's wot's so great about America, y'see. You went to University, and yet you're my friend, and I can ask you wot a word means, and you don't put me down for it like some upper-class English twit would. You just tell me wot it means, wif no judgments."

"You mean, your whole life is determined by how you do on an exam when you're eleven years old? That's so unfair!"

"Yeah. Idnit? But I'm not gonta let it stop me. The music business is the one way a poor English lad can make it big in the world, and the band's gonta be big. And maybe someday they'll record one of my songs, and I'll be rich and famous and go live in America."

I patted his hand. "I know you will, Colin. You've certainly got the energy and the perseverance."

"Percy-verance?"

"Determination."

"Ah. Yeah! I do. I've got Percy-verance. And I'm not inconsequential, nythah." He gave me a proud, lopsided grin. "That would make a great name for me own band: *Percy Verance*."

* * *

After shooting the opening act for Purple Harry, I wandered backstage. The lads had piled their jackets on a table near their guitar cases before heading onstage.

"Come on, Maddy-girl. Showtime!" Derrick waved to me

as he entered the stage to the screams and cheers of the crowd. I glanced back and noticed an unfamiliar man rifling through the coats. He took a small bag out of his pocket. I lifted my camera to my eye and snapped a shot of him as he appeared to be stuffing the bag into Derrick's leopard-print coat. He turned and spotted me. I shot again and caught a clear image of his face.

"Hey, you. Did you just take a photo of me?"

I rewound the film canister and stuck it in my pocket.

"It's a public venue. I can shoot what I like."

"Give me that roll of film, girl, or I'll arrest you." He pulled out a badge and waved it at me.

I raised my hands as if in surrender. "I haven't done anything wrong. But if you are so upset, just take it."

I reached into my pocket and grabbed a canister with a roll of unexposed film in it and handed it to him. He snatched it from my hand and disappeared out the artists' entrance door.

I reloaded my camera and went down front to shoot the Purple Harry set. Though I didn't hear much of the musical performance and managed to tune out the steady screaming of the fans and groupies behind me, I captured each leap and grimace, and every proud grin after an acknowledged great riff.

Afterward, sweaty and elated, the band gathered backstage.

"You blokes up for a pint?" Derrick was already out the door, donning his coat as everyone followed him into the alley behind the theater before I could tell him what I'd seen. We hadn't walked more than a few feet when we were suddenly surrounded by men in dark suits.

"Scotland Yard," said the man I recognized from backstage. "Line up against the wall."

Two of his men began patting down the band members.

"What's this?" One of his men pulled the small bag from Derrick's pocket. He dipped his pinky into the white powder and tasted it. "You are under arrest for possession of cocaine."

"Wha...?" Derrick's jaw dropped. "That's not mine. I'm not that stupid."

"Come with us. The rest of you lot, stay back, or we will arrest you as well."

They hustled Derrick away.

Colin rushed to the nearest telephone booth to call Derrick's advocate—his lawyer. "They've tried this before," he said as he waited for the barrister to pick up. "Bust a big star, and you get lots of press and promotions."

"I think I can help. I just have to get a roll of film developed."

The next day the front pages of the tabloids showed Derrick's mug shot and photos of him being hauled into jail. I developed my roll of film and made several prints of the police detective planting the evidence. When I gave them to the band's barrister, he shook my hand, and Colin kissed my forehead.

"Well done, Maddy," the lawyer said. "We'll have him out before teatime."

The next day, my photos were on the front page, and Derrick was a free man.

Colin drove the van to pick him up outside the court, with me and the band crammed in the back.

Derrick smothered me in a hug. "You fuckin' saved me, Maddy, old girl! You are now and forevah my favorite photographer!"

* * *

I began to stop at Colin's flat on Saturday afternoons, followed by picnics on the Heath. I always brought sandwiches—not the flat, anemic, white-bread kind sold in the English tea shops, but hearty ones on rich brown bread.

After having been up almost all night at a gig, Colin greeted me on a bleary Saturday morning with a fresh pot of strong English tea to help wake us up, and I searched his kitchen in vain for sugar to make the brew palatable. At last I found a few sugar cubes on the mantelpiece and popped one into my cup.

Colin and I had been talking and joking for about twenty minutes, gathering up our picnic supplies, when I noticed that the walls were melting.

"Colin…?" My voice was quavering slightly. "Colin, was there something in the tea?"

"No, luv. Why, what's the matter?"

"Maybe the sugar cube…?"

Colin's eyebrows rose and his eyes got very round. "Sugar cube? Where did you get it?"

I pointed to the swiftly dissolving mantel.

"Oh, bollocks!" Colin grimaced. "Okay…" He furrowed his entire face in thought. He looked like Deep Thought personified, a cartoon of those words made flesh.

I started to laugh.

Colin brightened. "Oh. Good, then. Yeah. It'll be just fine. First of all, I fink you ought to know you've had some excellent acid, and fortunately you seem to be properly enjoying it so far. But for safety's sake, we probably should continue on wif our picnic to 'ampstead 'eaf." He grabbed the sack of food, handed me my camera, and led me outside. "A nature trip is always the best kind. How ya doing, luv?"

The house seemed to melt away as I stepped outside. The world around me was taking on bizarre designs, and I felt uncomfortable in the pit of my stomach. The building to my left was shimmering, and its visibly shifting molecules glittered, dancing in patterns. The path below my feet undulated, so I took a surfing stance to keep my balance. I looked down, and each individual blade of iridescent grass was distinct around my moccasins, waving me forward. I took a photo of my feet.

I sat on the curb, overwhelmed by the patterns and fluidity around me, and looked up, trying to find cool blue air to breathe. Swirling, spiky clouds curved into blue and white paisley swirls, pulsing like cerulean arteries.

"I'm not ready for this, Colin." My voice was still quavering, and I was afraid to move in the suddenly unfamiliar surroundings.

"It's okay, luv. It's very mellow acid, and it's only one tab. Honestly. I'll look ahfta you and protect you, and I'm a good guide, so you can just relax and enjoy it. Come on." He helped me to my feet, gently coaxing. "Let's go to your tree."

He led me carefully across the road to Hampstead Heath.

My tree had changed. Larger, more majestic, ancient, and wise, it had become the first primordial tree, with dozens of gnarled branches spreading wide and low. It reached out to me as I climbed into its arms.

In perfect comfort, I melted into my tree, its bark my skin, its limbs my own. I felt the spirits of everyone who'd ever inhabited this tree, poets and lovers and children who read books and dreamed in its branches. I observed the seasons coming and going, extended my roots in the rich soil, and enjoyed the warmth on my leaves.

As the sun set, the intense backlit illumination turned the leaves above me into glowing emeralds, slowly fading. Suddenly, Colin's voice rose from beneath the tree, where he was lying spread-eagle on the grass below. He grinned.

"'ow you doin', Maddy-girl? Startin' to come back?"

I nodded. "I was part of the tree!"

"I was part of the earf."

He reached up and helped me down from my branch. We inhaled the sweet, cool twilight air, and he led me back to his flat.

"Nature trips are always the best," he said as I fell asleep in his arms.

* * *

I was at home in London, enjoying my independence, shooting the music scene for Clive and having adventures with Colin. When the band was on tour, I fed his cat, Lucy, and when they returned, he hung out at my flat. By the following summer, however, I could tell that his feelings for me had grown beyond infatuation.

"Marry me, Maddy!" he said one afternoon before leaving with the band for the Lake District.

I was deeply touched, and I paused to think of how best to phrase my refusal. Colin beat me to it.

"It's that 'unrequited love,' idnit?" he said, looking gloomy.

"Not really, Colin, because I do love you… just not in that way. But it was very sweet of you to ask me, and I'm deeply flattered."

"I guess perseverance wouldn't help?"

"I'm afraid not. I treasure your friendship, and I always will, but I don't want to get married. I'm very content with my life the way it is."

"Yeah. I'm sure you're right, luv. Don't know what got into me. Lost me 'ead for a moment."

He smiled, but his cheeriness didn't ring true. He bowed his head, and the corners of his mouth turned down as he disappeared out the door.

CHAPTER TEN

An Encounter with Jake

1971, London

Time Out received notices about press screenings and film festivals periodically, and when the invitation to view Jake Morganstern's latest film showed up on Clive's desk, I could barely contain my excitement. I practically tore it out of his hand.

"This one's *mine*!" I grabbed the card and hid it behind my back, dodging his attempts to retrieve it. "You'll have to kill me to get this away from me."

Clive laughed and shook his head. "You Americans are so bloody violent," he said, relenting and plopping back down behind his desk. "If it means so much to you, come along. I'm not ready to start killing my staff."

I attended the private press screening with Clive. The film was about a young man swept up in a local miner's strike. It was funny, stirring, and deftly constructed, so the audience would be drawn into sympathy with the laborers just as the protagonist was. Jake was not at the screening but was scheduled to attend the official premiere three days later at the British International Film Festival.

At the festival event, I flashed my press pass and was allowed into the special section in front of the cinema where the stars and filmmakers paused for interviews before entering the theater. I paced impatiently, watching celebrities go by, until I spotted Jake. He had the lead actress from the film on his arm, a striking brunette in a tight blue mini-dress. They paused in front of the press area so she could pose for the sea of photographers.

I couldn't take my eyes off Jake. He looked happy, relaxed, confident. He waited patiently as the starlet finished posing, then offered her his arm again. As they turned toward the theater, I caught his eye, and his brow furrowed for a moment, followed by a noticeable flash of recognition before he was hustled into the lobby. I stood outside the theater until the crowd had dispersed, then walked all the way back to my flat, oblivious of my surroundings, my mind filled with Jake and the beautiful woman who was with him.

I talked Clive into setting up an interview with Jake for the magazine and taking me to shoot the photos. We were granted an hour within the course of a full day of interviews scheduled by the film's publicist. As we waited in the hotel room for Jake and the publicist to arrive, my stomach was so full of butterflies that it required all my concentration just to load my camera and take light readings without revealing the trembling of my hands.

Jane Hampton, the production company's English publicist, breezed into the room, her layered blond bob falling into her eyes as she checked her clipboard. Her accent gave away her upper-class origins.

"Our director, JT Morganstern, is on his way. I'm terribly sorry we're running a bit late. We've got just an hour here before we must to get to the next interview." She checked her watch. "Well, almost an hour. Ah. Here he is. I'll leave him with you and be right back."

She gave Jake a peck on the cheek and tapped on her watch with a cautionary look as she swept out the door.

Clive introduced himself and then turned to introduce me.

Jake gave me a dazzling smile. "Garfield! I hoped I'd get to see you again," he said, holding my extended hand in his.

The warmth emanating from it radiated up my arm, setting off chain reactions in my stomach. I found myself speechless, a rare condition for me.

Clive cleared his throat politely and regained Jake's attention long enough to steer him to a spot on the couch that would provide me with the best light for shooting while he conducted the interview.

As they conversed, I watched Jake through my camera's lens, focusing on the definition of his long, dark eyelashes and the light reflecting from his beautiful, eloquent eyes. He often looked at me as he spoke, and each glance sent another little spark of desire through me. I was grateful for the camera in front of my face, covering the flush of my cheeks and providing a protective barrier, along with a legitimate excuse to look at him to my heart's content.

When the interviewed ended, I couldn't believe how fast the time had flown. Jane was already back and took Clive aside to ask a few questions. That gave Jake a moment to speak to me alone, and I put down my camera.

"I've seen your photos in *Time Out*. Looks like you really got into rock 'n' roll,'" he said as he rose from the couch.

"You turned me on to… to a lot of great stuff." I felt like a tongue-tied idiot, with so many unsaid words tripping over each other in my head.

He helped me to my feet. "During the premiere I came back outside to find you, but you'd gone by then. Someday we'll really have to get together for more than fifteen minutes."

"I'd love that."

I looked up at him, and our eyes locked for a long moment, connecting so deeply that the world around me disappeared. There was only Jake.

He leaned down and touched his lips to my cheek. I turned my head toward his warm face and impulsively kissed him full on the lips. Three seconds of bliss.

"JT?" Jane's jaw dropped at the sight of her client kissing the photographer. She held up her watch. "We are running quite late, luv." She shook Clive's hand and held the door open for Jake. "We really *must* fly."

Jake squeezed my hands gently. "I can reach you through the magazine, right?" he whispered so only I could hear. I nodded. He turned away to shake Clive's hand, just before Jane hustled him from the room.

Clive turned back to look at me and raised an inquiring eyebrow.

I blushed to my toes. "Long story, Clive. Don't ask."

Clive shrugged. "It's all right, m'dear. I rather fancy him myself."

CHAPTER ELEVEN

Blood and Sand

1971, Barcelona

I daydreamed about Jake for a few days, reliving the brief kiss over and over in my mind before mentally slapping myself and returning my focus to my work. I was disheartened to see the articles in the tabloid press about Jake and Christine Blake, whom I'd seen dozens of times on the covers of magazines like British *Vogue* and *Nova*. I'd also watched her snorting coke at the Purple Harry recording session, but there she was in the press, on Jake's arm for the world to see. I told myself I should let go of my foolish, adolescent crush.

I directed my energy into covering concerts, interviews, and political events all over London. When *OZ* magazine featured illustrations of a popular children's book and TV character, Rupert Bear, having sex, it was shut down for obscenity, and the rallies in support of the underground publication presented me with wonderful images.

Clive was so impressed with the quality of my photo stories that when I announced I had decided to vacation in both Barcelona and Amsterdam, he gave me free rein to cover whatever appealed to me while I was abroad. He made a brief list of possibilities and contacts and even saw me off at the train station.

When I arrived in Barcelona I was struck by the apparent inhibitions of the inhabitants. Under the regime of dictator Francisco Franco, everyone I saw was wearing nondescript shades of beige and gray, trying to blend into the crowd rather than attract any attention.

While American and English hippie tourists generally caught the first available boats to the trendy and popular islands of Ibiza and Formentera, I decided to stay on the mainland to pursue one of my story leads. I had loved reading *The Sun Also Rises* and *Death in the Afternoon* and felt that this trip was a good opportunity to learn more about bullfighting.

The current idol of the Spanish-speaking world was a charismatic young matador named Miguel Cortes, known as Miguelito, and he was going to be fighting in the bullring that Sunday. I arranged to interview him and take his portrait the day before.

On Saturday, as I was ushered into his presence by members of his extensive entourage, Miguel rose to greet me. With jet black hair tied in a small *coleta* at the nape of his neck, he was only a few inches taller than I and very slim, but his undeniable charisma made him seem larger than life.

"Senorita Garfield?" He extended his hand and lifted mine to his lips in a courtly gesture.

"I'm afraid my Spanish isn't very good," I said. "Do you speak English?"

"Fluently. I went to school in England for a while." He offered me a chair. "Do you know much about the traditions of the *corrida*?"

"I've read my Hemingway, but I'm not sure I understand why one would want to fight a bull."

He thought a moment before replying. "It is an ancient ritual in which death is challenged. The tradition stretches back over a thousand years, and every action in it has a purpose. The bulls selected to fight are powerful beasts, bred and born to kill. A man has only his brain and his grace with which to convince death to pass him by."

"It seems... cruel."

"You Americans are so sentimental. You imagine that the bulls are like pet dogs and cats, yet you love to eat beefsteak. These fighting bulls are very dangerous creatures and are bred to be so." He smiled and continued, "If I were a bull, I would rather have a day of glory in the ring, being true to my nature, than simply being shipped to a slaughterhouse to be hit over the head or electrocuted before bleeding to death. Sometimes these bulls are spared for exceptional bravery, to breed, but usually their meat is given to local orphanages to sustain the children. It is not wasted. And if I do my job properly, at the end, they die instantly, without pain."

"So the bull is your enemy?"

"No, no! My enemies are time and the wind."

"Not the bull?"

"Not at all. The bull is a noble creature, absolutely true to its nature. It will charge at and kill whatever moves. It will fight until it dies. The best bulls are fearless but predictable, not capricious like the wind." He rose and walked to the window. "I prefer to fight in Madrid. Barcelona is too close to the sea with its breezes, and death can come quite unexpectedly here."

I began the session by photographing Miguel as he stood at the hotel window gazing toward the bullring, his expression grave, the light deeply etching his sharp cheekbones and reflecting in his dark eyes.

I documented everything he displayed for me—the gold-encrusted "suit of lights" he would wear the next day, the odd black hat called a *montera,* and his sword and capes. He showed me how to hold the large cape and then stood behind me as he held my hands and demonstrated how to move the cape in basic passes.

Then he kissed the back of my neck.

I turned to look at him in surprise.

"Would you stay with me tonight?" he whispered.

He certainly exuded a powerful magnetism, and I had found the brief physical contact quite pleasant. I was tempted, if only for the great tale it would make, but Miguel's picador, an older, heavyset man standing in the doorway, gave me an unmistakable warning glance.

I smiled and shook my head. "Thank you for the invitation, but I think I'd better not."

"Perhaps you would grant me one kiss, then? In my profession, one truly never knows if it might be the last."

He gently took my face in his hands and kissed me—a long, sweet kiss. It felt like a kiss goodbye.

"You are a very beautiful woman, Miss Garfield. It is probably just as well you will not stay, as my entourage would be very upset if I did not spend the evening in prayer. I would personally rather celebrate life as intensely as possible, but I suppose I should not tempt fate, lest you prove to be as dangerous to me as the wind."

He smiled and kissed my hand once more, lingered for another moment, then left the room. His picador heaved an audible sigh of relief and escorted me to the door.

* * *

I noticed two things when I first arrived at the Plaza de Toros the next day: the armed soldiers everywhere, as there always seemed to be in Franco's Spain, and the brisk sea breeze.

There were two distinct sets within the vast crowd—those in the sun and those in the shade. The poorer citizens of Barcelona and the rowdier tourists sat in the cheap seats in the direct sun, drinking *cervezas* and squirting wine directly into their mouths from leather *bota* bags. I sat in the more expensive section in the shade, which provided protection from the brutality of the afternoon sun and allowed the aficionados to see without having to squint. Fortunately, it also prevented the sun from flaring into my camera lenses.

The corrida began with the blare of a trumpet and the parade of the matadors with their entourages, crossing the ring to the tune of a lively *pasodoble* march. Three matadors would fight a total of six bulls that day, chosen by lot. As the headliner, Miguelito would fight third and sixth.

His first bull was gigantic and powerful, splintering the wooden barricade with the impact of his mighty horns as the *banderilleros'* capes lured him around the periphery of the ring.

The massive beast was single-minded, running as if on rails.

Miguel made the most of the drama, using his large cape with great skill to attract the bull's charge. Despite the horns passing within inches of his chest, his feet remained planted firmly on the ground until the huge animal had moved by, when he gracefully spun away. He lured the bull into lunge after lunge, exposing more and more of his body and less and less of his cape. The crowd cheered in chorus with every pass, exploding into deafening applause at the end of each series of movements. I used my longest lens, the sharp image intimately compressing the dangerous dance between the man and the beast.

The *picadors* entered the ring to boos from the crowd. Those men on protectively padded horses carried long lances designed to pierce and weaken the bull's powerful neck muscles. That procedure was intended to lower the horned head in preparation for the final act, in which the matador would face the "moment of truth," as it was called. He would have to fling himself directly over the bull's horns to sink his sword into a tiny spot between the bull's shoulder blades, which would result in its instant, painless death.

Much to the surprise of the crowd, Miguelito waved away both the *picadors* and *banderilleros* to move on to the next phase. Throwing his cape to his men, he personally took the colorful *banderillas* to place into the beast. Completely unprotected, he ran at an angle toward the bull, deftly placed the barbs neatly in the hump on the bull's back and twisted away untouched by the deadly horns.

When the traditional three sets had been placed, Miguel

stood in the center of the ring. He took off his hat and held it up, slowly turning to dedicate the bull to the entire crowd. The audience cheered their approval.

Then he took the *muleta*—the small cape supported by his sword—for the closest, most dangerous moves. He lured the bull closer and closer with each pass. He rocked the cape back and forth behind his body, placing himself at the center of that pendulum.

The crowd roared, *"Olé!"* in unison with each pass.

Miguel knelt, with the cape on the ground beside him, tempting death as he reached out and touched the bull's horn with his bare hand. The crowd screamed in approval. He then rose and completed one spectacularly controlled pass after another, closer and closer, with the crowd going wild.

I could barely breathe. As I clicked away, the frames captured images of danger, the deadly horns coming within inches of Miguelito's chest with each pass.

At last exhaustion lowered the bull's head, and Miguel prepared for the final moment of truth. He removed the sword from the edge of his cape and held the crimson muleta low across his body with his left hand, as he sighted along the blade he held in his right.

Just as Miguel threw himself over the horns and sank the sword to the hilt in the tiny spot that would kill instantly and painlessly, the wind rose. His cape lifted, guiding the bull's head upward with it, and its left horn hooked deep into Miguel's ribcage, hurling him through the air with blood gushing from his chest.

Seeing it all through my telephoto lens somehow made it seem unreal and removed from the moment. My finger kept clicking automatically for some time before I even realized fully what had happened

Miguel's entourage rushed into the ring to distract the bull with their capes, but his sword had landed cleanly, and the bull had dropped to its knees, already dead. As the crowd fell into a hush, his men lifted Miguel to their shoulders and hurried him out of the ring and through the side doors to the *enfirmeria* below the plaza. I had a momentary vision of my father after the accident, covered in blood, on a gurney, heading toward the ambulance.

My hands shaking, I stopped shooting and rushed out of the stands to the labyrinth beneath. At the end of a wide corridor, shafts of light streamed down from high windows and glittered off something on a table, with people in the shadows nearby. Reflexively I lifted the camera to my eye like a pair of binoculars, and as I focused its long lens, I realized that it was Miguel's body in the torn suit of lights, lying on the table in a pool of blood, his weeping friends and associates gathered around him. The play of light and shadow on that tableau reminded me of a painting by Rembrandt or Caravaggio, and I took a final picture to capture it.

The click of the shutter was like a gunshot in my ears. A wave of guilt washed over me as my tears fogged the viewfinder, and I lowered the camera with trembling hands. Suddenly horrified at my invasion of their overwhelming grief, I turned and ran back down the hallway and out of the bullring.

When I reached my hotel room, I went through the motions of packing and, after stuffing the film into an envelope addressed to Clive in London, caught the first train out of Barcelona.

I wept all the way to Amsterdam, riddled with remorse for shooting such a painful, private moment and mortified by the detachment that had allowed me to release the shutter.

I began to question my calling as a journalist.

I kept remembering Miguel alive… and then dead… and the swiftness of the change. I could still hear his voice saying, "I would personally rather celebrate life as intensely as possible."

A voice inside my head echoed, *"Carpe diem!"*

I was still in emotional turmoil when I arrived in Amsterdam.

CHAPTER TWELVE

Vida and Stephen

1971, Amsterdam and London

Amsterdam belonged to my generation. Travelers in their teens and twenties poured into the town square from all over the world, camping out in the open or staying in cheap, government-sponsored housing. Hashish was available for purchase at any of the clubs, and live bands played each night in venues all over the city.

It was a counterculture paradise, but I was not emotionally ready to start photographing anything. I checked into a student crash pad along one of the canals. It resembled a giant army barracks, with rows of bunk beds on each side of the cavernous room. For less than a dollar a night, each arriving student was assigned an arbitrary bunk, male and female housed together. The room was so full of smoke from groups of kids sharing joints and water pipes that it only required taking a deep breath to get high.

"Would you like to join us?" a refined English voice inquired from the center of a circle of students seated on the floor. The young woman, her long, straight, light brown hair framing an angular face, offered me a large joint.

"Thanks. I think I will."

I joined them on the floor, took a hit, and burst into a coughing fit. "There's tobacco in this!"

The young woman laughed. "We always roll our hashish in tobacco. You're obviously an American. Lovely! I think we must have a veritable United Nations here."

She introduced each member of the circle and the countries they hailed from before introducing herself. "I'm Vida, from London… at your service," she added, nodding her head in a mock bow. "And this," she said, holding up the chocolate-brown lump in her hand, "is the best Afghani hash I have ever smoked in my life. *Gawd,* I love Amsterdam."

The whole group broke into an extended fit of giggles in response.

Soon famished, we all wandered along the canal to a small restaurant, where we left the choice of the meal to the discretion of the plump, rosy-cheeked, little Dutch woman who served us. We feasted on crisp fried fish and dishes of sweet yogurt covered with cherries and sugar, all for the equivalent of a dollar each.

* * *

By the end of the week Vida had become a good friend, and she invited me to return to London with her to meet her family. We made our arrangements and bade farewell to Amsterdam.

When we got off the train in London, Vida hailed a cab and, much to my surprise, directed it to Mayfair, one of the city's most expensive neighborhoods. In the back seat, she leaned over and whispered in my ear.

"Have you ever made love with a woman?"

"No. I never have. I can't say I ever really wanted to." I shrugged apologetically.

"Oh, well. Never mind." Vida settled back comfortably in her seat. "You'll probably love my brother."

We drew up in front of an elegant eighteenth-century townhouse and were greeted at the door by a butler who was obviously surprised to see her.

"Welcome home, Miss Vida!"

"Hello, Moreland. Tell Mother I'm back, would you? And freshen up the rose guest room for my American friend, Maddy."

We turned into an archway and collided with a tall, extremely attractive blond gentleman in a suit and tie.

"Vida! Back again with a new 'friend,' I see." He gave me an appraising look. "Won't mother be surprised."

"Oh, give over, Stephen. She's a really nice girl, and she's straight. I thought you'd like her, actually. She's an American. Very independent, you know. She might even loosen you up a bit. Wouldn't that be a thrill?"

She all but stuck her tongue out at her brother as she dragged me off to change for dinner.

Vida's world was entirely different from the one inhabited by Cockney street kids in the rock-and-roll world I had been covering. She let me know that her mother always wore conservative, flower-print dresses—"like the Queen Mum," as Vida put it—and served tea at four o'clock on the dot, and that everyone was expected to dress for dinner.

After a typically English meal of overcooked beef and Yorkshire pudding, Vida, Stephen, and I adjourned to the parlor and sipped port and talked late into the evening. I entertained them with stories about California and my travels, and I learned that Stephen was entering the British Diplomatic Service and was leaving for Pakistan in a week.

"Gawd. If you're going to start talking about the bloody foreign service, I'm going to bed." Vida kissed me on the cheek and headed for the door. "Have a good time, kiddlywinks. See you in the morning."

"Perhaps I should go up, too," I said, putting down my glass.

"No. Please. Stay. I'd like to hear more about your experiences, if you don't mind."

Stephen's bone structure was very sharply defined, reminding me of a bird of prey, but there was also something very magnetic about him.

He moved to the couch to join me. "I hope Vida hasn't given you the wrong impression of me," he said, refilling my glass. His voice was extremely deep, his speech impeccable.

"As in stodgy and stiff?" I teased.

He rolled his eyes. "Yes. Vida doesn't actually know me very well. She only sees a certain side of me and makes broad judgments. I get along quite smoothly in society... ergo, I must be quite a dull fellow." He reached into his pocket and took out a tiny pipe. "Would you like a smoke?"

"Are we talking illegal substances here?" I was still teasing him.

"Absolutely. If you're a friend of Vida's, I assume you smoke hashish." He loaded a tiny brown lump into the pipe, lit it, and passed it to me.

"I didn't think diplomats indulged in such things." I took a hit and passed it back to him.

He moved closer and rested his arm on the back of the sofa behind me. "I'll have to educate you about the wonders of diplomacy." He leaned forward and kissed me softly on the lips.

I was surprised at my body's immediate response. He kissed me again, his arm around me, pulling me closer. I caught my breath and pulled back from the embrace.

"I hope Vida hasn't given you the wrong impression of *me*," I said.

I attempted to regain my composure and sat forward on the edge of the couch.

"As a point of fact, you're nothing like any of Vida's other friends. Actually, you're not like anyone I've ever met before."

He brushed my hair to one side and kissed me behind the ear. It sent a tiny tremor of arousal down my spine. I didn't move. His lips brushed softly back and forth across the tiny hairs on my nape, and I felt my resistance slipping. I sighed.

He turned me toward him and kissed my mouth again, the tip of his tongue urging my lips apart. He was very skillful, and I was enjoying myself immensely. He began to slide his hand under my skirt, but I put my own hand on his to stop its progress. He pulled back to look at me, raising an inquisitive eyebrow.

"I think it's time for me to make a diplomatic exit," I whispered.

"Ah. I see. Well. Perhaps you would allow me to take you to the ballet tomorrow night?"

"I'd like that very much. Tomorrow, then." I rose from the couch and hurried up the stairs to the guest bedroom.

Deep under the warm covers, I couldn't help but reinvent the evening in my mind as I drifted to sleep, imagining myself in Jake's arms.

* * *

The next morning, I dashed over to the *Time Out* office to check in with Clive.

"Maddy, I hope you don't mind," Clive began, "but the photos you sent with the story about Miguelito…"

"Oh, God, Clive. Please don't tell me they didn't turn out right, or the lab destroyed them, or they got lost in the mail."

"Oh, no! Nothing like that, Maddy, my girl. They were wonderful. More than wonderful. Much grander in scope than anything we could handle. Actually, I thought they might be more appropriate for *LIFE* magazine, so I sent them on to the editor. I hope you don't mind?"

"Mind?" I was in shock. "Mind? Oh my God. What did they say? Are they running them?"

Clive handed me the copy from his desk. "It just arrived."

I sat down, slowly turning the pages of the beautifully reproduced photo spread entitled "Death in the Afternoon." Having sent the exposed rolls of film directly to Clive, I hadn't seen the results until now: the portraits of Miguelito, the moment when he dedicated the bull to the crowd, holding up his montera and saluting the cheering aficionados, the graceful passes with the bull's horns mere inches from his face… the moment of his death, with the horn buried in his chest, his body flying through the air… and then, below the Plaza del Toros, the light streaming down from a high window as he lay on the table with his entourage in mourning around him. It looked like a Rembrandt painting.

How could art come from such tragedy? What was it in me that could detach from my subjects enough to document a death, to see the beauty of the light falling on mourners and on the corpse of someone who had kissed me so tenderly only hours before? Tears welled up again as I relived it all in my mind and considered giving up my profession in penance.

Clive looked uncomfortable. "Have I upset you? I'm so sorry, Maddy. I thought you would be pleased."

I looked up at Clive through my tears. "Don't be sorry, Clive. I'm grateful to you. I wouldn't have been able to deal with it myself. I've always wanted to be in *LIFE* magazine, but never under such tragic circumstances. I guess you need to be careful what you wish for."

A sob welled up in my chest and I couldn't hold it back.

Clive hurried around his desk and awkwardly attempted to comfort me. "Oh, please don't cry, dear girl. We British are not very good with grief. You're a journalist, Maddy. You captured a story, and you did it brilliantly. You couldn't have changed what happened, and you did your job. You mustn't grieve." He patted me on the shoulder.

"I don't know if I want to be a journalist." I dried my eyes and took a deep breath. "I don't know what I want."

* * *

"Good Lord." Stephen's eyebrows rose and his jaw dropped. "You look absolutely magnificent."

Vida was giggling with delight as I paused at the bottom of the stairs, made a slow turn to show off the borrowed blue velvet gown, and finished with as graceful a curtsy as I could muster.

"Really, Vida," Stephen said, his eyes riveted on me. "Who would have thought that a friend of yours could be so exceedingly presentable?"

Vida laughed and punched him in the arm. "I told you you'd like her. You never listen to me."

Stephen took my hand, kissed it, and led me to the waiting car.

* * *

Being at Covent Garden was like traveling back a century in time. I felt elegant and romantic and wished that I had a fan to flirt behind.

I was completely transported by the Royal Ballet's version of "Marguerite and Armand," Fredrick Ashton's retelling of the tragic story of Dumas's "Camille." Though entering her fifth decade, Margot Fonteyn, the prima ballerina, floated across the stage like a sixteen-year-old nymph, a perfect vision of grace and weightlessness. Even though Rudolph Nureyev was fully twenty years her junior, their passion was so believable that when he kissed her hair as she lay "dead" on the stage at the end, I had to wipe away a tear.

"Yes?" I responded to Stephen's thoughtful look.

"You are not at all what I expected." He leaned back in the theater seat and regarded me with half-closed eyes.

After the ballet, riding in Stephen's limo, I watched the energy of Covent Garden change to the elegance of Mayfair. The car pulled up to the family's beautiful townhouse, and he escorted me inside. He removed my wrap, handed it and his coat to Moreland, and turned me toward him, lifting my chin with the edge of his finger. He gave me a brief kiss and then looked at me again, his head tilted slightly as if considering some matter of importance.

"Have you ever been to Pakistan?"

"No. But I'm interested in everything. I like traveling. I suppose I might go there someday."

"Hmm. Have a good night, my dear. Thank you for your company tonight." He kissed me again, fervently enough to make me catch my breath, then turned and walked off to the library.

Vida observed the scene from the doorway. "My word. You certainly have Stephen in a state." She sauntered into the room and plopped down on the couch, shaking her head in amazement.

I was skeptical. "A 'state'? There's a state going on here?"

"Oh, yes, my dear kiddlywink. The lad is a goner. Well done!"

I laughed and shook my head. "I think you've smoked one too many, Vida," I said as I retreated to my room.

* * *

When I returned to my flat in Belsize Park, near Hampstead, I accepted a few interview assignments for Clive.

A month later I received a letter from Stephen, which included a round-trip ticket to Karachi.

My Dear Madeleine,

As the diplomatic community is permitted to fly family members to their foreign stations for free, I thought you might enjoy this opportunity to visit Pakistan. The ticket is in my mother's name, for obvious reasons, but it is intended for you. There are no strings attached to this offer. It would simply afford you the opportunity for additional travel to exotic lands and a chance to get to know me better. Just call the British Embassy upon your arrival, and I'll send the car to pick you up.

Most sincerely,
Stephen Smythe-Davies

CHAPTER THIRTEEN

Karachi and Holy Men

1972, Pakistan

I was more than a little intrigued. Stephen was intelligent, handsome, and a sophisticated member of the British aristocracy, and we obviously shared a physical attraction. Perhaps he was my Prince Charming.

Evidently the trip would cost him nothing, and he had assured me there were "no strings attached." It was a chance to explore a country and a culture completely foreign to me, and I couldn't resist.

After receiving a half dozen inoculations against various exotic diseases, I packed a bag, grabbed my camera case, and went to the airport, not realizing that it was customary to first get a visa. Eight hours later I stepped off the plane into a blast of heat and dust and was immediately detained by two burly, mustachioed security guards and transported to the police station in Pakistan's largest city.

The Karachi Police Department looked like something out of a 1940s foreign intrigue movie. The room was dark in contrast with the intense daylight shining through the slats of the barred windows. The beige walls were stained, and the ceiling fans revolved so slowly that they had no effect at all on the stagnant air and oppressive heat. Various policemen sat around the room in their tan uniforms, staring at me. Fortunately, I'd had the good sense to wear a long skirt but had no idea what a stir a barefaced Western woman would make in a strict Moslem environment.

A fly strolled across the desk of the inspector who was questioning me.

"Your ticket says you are Eleanor Smythe-Davies, but the name on your passport is Madeleine Garfield. You are *not* Eleanor Smythe-Davies, and you have no visa. Who are you, really, and why are you here?"

"As I have already told you," I repeated for the tenth time, "if you will just call Stephen Smythe-Davies at the British Embassy, this can all be straightened out."

A commotion in the next room ended abruptly as Stephen burst through the door and moved toward me in long, determined strides. He took my arm and led me toward the exit.

"May we have Miss Garfield's passport and bags, if you please?" His politeness did not conceal the contempt in his voice.

An officer with a huge black mustache dumped my camera case, pack, and purse on the desk. They had obviously been thoroughly rifled.

Stephen's jaw tightened, and his eyes narrowed as he grabbed my bags and led me out to the waiting limousine. He fumed as the driver pulled away from the building and into the streets of Karachi.

"I'm terribly sorry that this was your introduction to

Pakistan." His controlled diction and elegant tone poorly concealed his fury. "Unfortunately, it's typical of the bureaucracy, ignorance, and corruption of the Pakistani government."

His anger sent a wary chill down my spine, despite the oppressive heat. I tried to diffuse the situation.

"Thank you for rescuing me." I tilted my head and gave him a tentative smile in an attempt to change his mood. "It was certainly an interesting adventure."

"Ah. Well. Yes. Not a problem." He gave me a quick kiss. "I'm just very sorry you were detained. It was not the welcome I had hoped for." He sat back and loosened his tie.

The streets were narrow, lined with wood-frame buildings with rickety, open wooden balconies. Stephen told me there had been a market held that morning. Garbage from it was heaped in the center of the road, and people walking in the street were forced to step into stinking piles of rotting vegetables to avoid our car as it passed.

We drove to Islamabad, the capital city and center of the diplomatic community. The driver stopped the car in front of a huge, white, colonial-style house in the center of a baked-earth plain. The chauffeur opened the door for me, and a slim young man took my bags and gave me a shy smile. I extended my hand to him.

"Don't do that, Madeleine." Stephen guided me past the young man. "That's my manservant, Haneef. It would not be proper to shake his hand."

"Why not?" I gave Haneef an apologetic smile as Stephen steered me into the house.

"Because he's a servant… not an equal… and unmarried women should avoid physical contact with Moslem men."

"He's still a human being, just like we are, Stephen. He just does a different job."

"This is a very different society from the one to which you are accustomed, Madeleine." He removed his suit jacket and handed it to Haneef. "You do need to learn to adopt a country's mores and customs in order to get by. I'm sure you'll realize that in time."

"Some things are worth learning, and some things aren't," I muttered under my breath as Stephen led me up the stairs to his palatial bedroom.

"Do you have everything? Did they take anything from your bags?"

While he waited, I looked through my backpack and camera bag. My camera and five rolls of film were still there, but my forty English pounds, the equivalent of about a hundred dollars, were missing.

Stephen shrugged it off. "Typical. The police undoubtedly stole it. That's about half a year's income to most Pakis. Not to worry, though. I can provide whatever you need. With more than twenty rupees to the American dollar, it doesn't require much to get whatever you want. On the black market the exchange rate is even better."

He retrieved an ornately carved wooden box from the dressing table and opened it, sighed audibly, then slammed it shut.

"Haneef!"

The dark-eyed young man appeared at the bedroom door.

Stephen railed at him in Urdu, and Haneef looked apologetic and took the box with him as he retreated.

"He's been instructed to keep a supply of joints rolled and at the ready." Stephen shook his head and forced a smile. "I had imagined that after your long trip, you might like a smoke and a nice bath. I'm afraid the smoke must wait until later." He directed me to the adjoining bathroom. "You must forgive me, my dear, but I have some paperwork to finish. Please make yourself at home for the next few hours. Then we can have a pleasant dinner."

After a refreshing bath, I spent the afternoon exploring the house and grounds. All the interior walls were white, punctuated with paintings of hunting dogs and horses against the verdant, rolling hills and meadows of the English countryside.

I slipped into the kitchen and watched Haneef as he made *chapatis*, which looked like Pakistani tortillas. He showed me how to work the flour and water into dough and how to slap it back and forth between my hands until it was the right thickness. My chapatis were crude compared to his, and we both laughed at the results.

Stephen walked by the kitchen and frowned.

"I've been called to our offices for a while. Duty before pleasure, unfortunately. Stay here and relax for the rest of the afternoon, and I'll take you to the bazaar in Rawalpindi tomorrow. Do try to maintain some distance from the servants." He looked to Haneef with a warning glance before leaving for the embassy.

Wandering around the estate grounds late in the day, I

discovered a marijuana plant about five feet tall growing in a drainage ditch. I ran to the house for my camera and dragged Haneef out to see it. He seemed dumbfounded at my delight. He looked thoughtful for a second, then held up a finger to tell me to wait.

He returned with a bicycle. He patted the handlebars, and I hopped on. After a wobbly start, we sped down the dirt road toward a small row of mud houses in the distance.

He pulled up in front of one of the tiny whitewashed huts, and I jumped off. Once inside, Haneef used hand gestures to introduce me to his mother and sister. I shook their hands and smiled apologetically when Haneef dragged me outside and around to the back. Growing in the drainage ditch that extended behind the entire row of houses was a forest of cannabis about eight feet tall. He presented it with a flourish, his palm up like a ringmaster at a circus, and I laughed and picked a huge bouquet of the massive, fragrant stems and leaves. Handing him my camera, I showed him how to take my photo surrounded with fragrant shrubbery.

I took a portrait of Haneef's mother and sister together before hopping back on the handlebars for the ride back to the mansion.

"Thank you, Haneef," I said, as he put his bicycle away. "That was great."

"Teach English?" Haneef asked, pointing to himself.

"Doesn't Stephen speak any English with you?"

Haneef shook his head. "For good jobs I need English. Mister not teach."

I nodded, and he gave me a shy, grateful smile and hurried back to the kitchen.

When Stephen returned, I asked about Haneef. Stephen shrugged it off.

"He's nineteen. This is his first legitimate job, I would imagine. I need him to practice and improve my Urdu."

"But couldn't it be an exchange? You help him with English, and he helps you with Urdu?"

"Whatever for? So he can run off and get a higher-paying job? I'm not here to be his teacher. He's my servant, Madeleine. You still don't seem to understand."

"No, I guess I don't." I suppressed the desire to point out the injustice of this stance and privately resolved to speak English with Haneef as often as possible.

After a delicious dinner of lamb korma, Stephen escorted me upstairs.

"There is a guest room down the hall, if you wish," he said as he took me in his arms. "But you are welcomed to join me in my bed, if so inclined." He kissed me with consummate skill, but I was not yet ready to go farther.

"The guest room will be great, thank you."

"Ah. As you wish." His disappointment was evident. He walked me to the door of the guest room. "Let me know if there's anything you need. And feel free to join me, if you should feel the urge."

"No strings attached, right?"

"Of course not, my dear. But I do hope we can explore our… compatibility. Foreign service can be a lonely life without companionship. But by all means, take your time. My hope is for you to experience what life is like here, with me. But without undue pressure."

"I appreciate your understanding." I kissed him again before I retreated into my room.

* * *

The next day Stephen took me to the bazaar at Rawalpindi where I purchased some appropriate Pakistani clothes. I bought lightweight white cotton *shalwar*—long, loose, comfortable drawstring pants—and several *kurtas*—gauzy cotton shirts with long sleeves that hung to mid-thigh, embellished with hand embroidery around the collars. Much to the shock of the seamstress, I placed a custom order—a pair of shalwar to be made in pale-blue, transparent chiffon, which was my idea of Arabian Nights harem pants. The seamstress took the special order with wide eyes and asked me to return in a week for them. To accommodate local proprieties, I also purchased a chiffon veil to drape over my head and across my face, and silver ornaments to dangle in my hair.

That evening, when I modeled my traditional Pakistani garments for Stephen at a candle-lit dinner in his elegant dining room, he raised an eyebrow. "Hm. I hadn't actually intended for you to... um... go native. But it is quite charming on you, my dear."

Haneef grinned from the edge of the kitchen door.

That evening, there was a soft knock on the guestroom door. Stephen stood just outside in a maroon silk dressing gown.

He held up his hashish pipe.

"Care for a nightcap?"

"I would." I welcomed him into the room and we sat on my bed. He lit the aromatic brown lump and passed it to me. I inhaled deeply, suppressing the urge to cough, and grew dizzy. "Very nice."

"He smiled and took another hit. "It is quite good. There's a government sponsored opium shop in the city where they sell excellent hashish from Afghanistan under the table."

"Under the table?"

"Yes. Absurd as it might be, opium is legal here, while non-addictive hashish is internationally illegal. It makes no sense, I know. But at least it is available."

He placed the pipe on the end table and took me in his arms. All of my muscles relaxed and I melted into his embrace. His kisses were skillful, coaxing, teasing. We lay back on the bed and he stroked my face, his hand sliding down to cup my breast through my sheer nightgown. His hand was warm, his thumb adroitly stroking my hardening nipple. I moaned against his lips as my arousal grew. He guided my hand down under his robe to the evidence of his own arousal.

"If you would like to join me in my bed, you would be most welcome," he whispered. "I would like to give you pleasure." He lifted the edge of my nightgown and slipped his hand up my inner thigh. I arched involuntarily against his exploring fingers before placing my hand on his wrist to stop him.

"I will keep that in mind. A tempting invitation." I lowered the hem of my nightgown as he withdrew.

He nodded in acceptance and rose. "It is an open invitation. You know where to find me." He kissed my hand and retreated.

I lay in bed, aroused, restless, and curious.

If he is my Prince Charming and wants to give me pleasure, perhaps I should join him in his room for the night.

I rose and tiptoed up the hall to Stephen's bedroom and knocked softly.

Stephen answered the door, wearing only his dressing gown. His sharp features softened when he saw me.

"I'm glad you chose to come to me." He led me to his bed. 'I wish only to please you. Please be direct with me about what you like and what you don't like."

He was systematic, focused, and thorough in his exploration of my body—from my inner wrist to the curve of my hip. He turned me, embracing me from behind, pushing my hair to one side to access the sensitive nape of my neck. He slipped the nightgown from my shoulders, and it slid to the floor. His hands cupped my breasts, gently pinching my nipples until my knees began to buckle. I turned toward him, and he gripped my hair in his fist and kissed me until I was breathless. He sat me on the edge of the high bed, pushed my thighs apart and, standing between my legs, reached down to stroke me.

"Lie back, Madeleine. Let me give you pleasure."

I lay on the bed, my legs dangling over the edge. He knelt and lifted them over his shoulders as he kissed my inner thighs and explored my hidden recesses with his skillful tongue and hands until I was deeply aroused and moaning, my hips lifting to meet his mouth and probing fingers.

Even as my body recognized and responded to pleasure, my mind remained detached—an observer of his skill and its effect on me.

He reached to the side table and retrieved a small packet, pushed off his robe, and rolled a rubber onto his erection. Rising with my ankles on his shoulders, he guided himself to my entrance and entered with a single deep thrust. Reaching between us, he teased me with his fingers as he pumped hard and fast until I lost control and cried out as I came in a brief, intense release. With a few more thrusts he found his own satisfaction, lowered my legs, and fell forward on his hands above me. As he withdrew, he leaned down to kiss me.

"I hope you enjoyed that as much as I did," he murmured as he rose, threw away the condom, and joined me on the bed.

I could not deny that his skills were remarkable. But something was missing that I could not define.

"Your hospitality is greatly appreciated," I said, still breathless as I recovered and attempted to stand.

He laughed at my formality. "Stay the night," he said as he pulled back the covers and held out his hand.

I retrieved my nightgown from the floor and covered myself. "Perhaps another time. I think I need a good sleep… alone."

His brow furrowed and he was silent for a moment, then nodded. "As you wish, my dear."

In the privacy of the guest room I relived the evening but, as always when I was alone, imagined myself in Jake's arms instead.

The following day, Stephen had business to attend to in Nurpur, a local village. I put on my cool, comfortable Pakistani clothes and accompanied him.

After we arrived, he left me standing near the car as he walked off with the village headman, so I began to stroll along the winding dirt road that led through the tiny village.

A lovely young girl, with a pink veil draped loosely over her head and shoulders, was watching me from a nearby crumbling wall. She appeared to be no more than eleven or twelve years old.

I smiled at her, and her face lit up in response. She beckoned me to follow her between the whitewashed mud houses to a large, walled enclosure. Inside were women of various ages, most garbed in shapeless black, some old and bent and others with young children and babies in their arms.

The girl indicated that her name was Firzana. She ushered me to a carpeted area with high-backed, hand-carved, wooden chairs, their low, woven seats only inches above the ground. One of the women brought me pale amber tea, fragrant with the aroma of jasmine.

I took out my camera, and the women hesitated for a moment, glanced at each other warily, then nodded permission. I took several photos of groups inside the women's quarters before Firzana caught my eye, pantomiming taking photos and shaking her head *no* as a warning signal to hide my camera. I stuffed it back in my bag just as her father and uncles entered.

"Mr. Smythe-Davies is waiting for you outside," the heavyset patriarch told me, as all the women dropped their gaze to the ground and hurried back to their routine activities.

Firzana led me back out to the winding dirt road and walked on my right side. Stephen joined us on my left as we proceeded through the village. Everywhere I looked, children's faces appeared. Responding to my smiles, they flocked to accompany us. By the time I had reached the far end of the village, Firzana, Stephen, and I were surrounded by a sea of beautiful, laughing children. Some reached out to touch the hem of my kurta, as if I were in some biblical epic by C.B. DeMille. I felt exhilarated, welcomed, accepted, even loved.

When we had settled back into the car, Stephen snorted in disgust. "Don't delude yourself, Madeleine." He brushed the dust from his sleeve and loosened his tie. "They would have given exactly the same reception to Jack the Ripper."

My euphoria ended abruptly. Was I completely deluded? Perhaps my perceptions were not as clear as Stephen's... but I found that hard to accept. Then again, he had been here awhile and knew the place much better than I. Stephen explained that the Pakistanis judged beauty entirely by the fairness of one's skin and so, of course, with my blue eyes and light skin, I would be treated well. But he insisted that there was no genuine emotional exchange going on between me and the people I encountered.

As we drove away, I wondered if perhaps Stephen was right, and my feelings of connection and acceptance could all be attributed to my fertile imagination. My confidence deflated, I felt subdued for the rest of the evening. I retreated to the guest room and spent the night alone.

The next day, in an attempt to raise my spirits, Stephen took me horseback riding. I was not accustomed to a tiny, uncomfortable, English saddle, and the borrowed pith helmet kept slipping forward over my eyes as I bounced along.

We rode through a field of hemp growing more than ten feet high and as far as the eye could see. My horse kept stopping to nibble at the leaves, and soon it began to ignore me altogether, running free and frisking through the field. I held on for dear life, the helmet covering my face, until Stephen finally grabbed the reins and led my rowdy steed back to the stable.

Late in the afternoon we attended a garden-party gathering of the diplomatic community's families. The food was entirely British, with not a chapati in sight, and all the guests were dressed for a formal English tea.

I made the mistake of giving my honest and decidedly negative opinion of the state of American politics, including my disgust with Richard Nixon and my opposition to the war in Vietnam. Several of the wives looked shocked. Stephen took me aside and suggested I steer clear of controversial subjects, if only for the sake of diplomacy. I took a deep breath, gritted my teeth, and made polite small talk for the rest of the evening.

The next day, Haneef took me into Rawalpindi and pointed out the government opium shop. I found it astounding that deadly, addictive opium was sold legally here but that hashish could only be purchased "under the counter" by request. For the equivalent of about three US dollars, I bought a ten-ounce slab of excellent, chocolate-brown, Afghani hashish. In London it would be worth hundreds of pounds, perhaps thousands in the US, but despite any risk, I could only imagine the delight on Colin's face when he saw it and the pleasure of being able to smoke it in the evenings without tobacco mixed in. I considered ways of shipping it back to London in secret and soon devised a plan.

At the local bookseller, I bought an old, rather poorly made, extremely thick but relatively lightweight book. I spent a whole evening attempting to hollow out the book to turn it into a box for shipping my stash back to London. This turned out to be much more difficult than I imagined.

To prevent mangling it, I had to cut with great precision no more than a few pages at a time. By midnight I managed to hollow out a perfect rectangle, one inch from the edges of the pages all around. When I was done, the book looked unchanged when held tightly closed.

I wrapped the block of hashish in plastic and sealed it with tape, hoping that would prevent the pungent, earthy fragrance from seeping out. Then I fitted it neatly into the hollow book and wrapped it thoroughly with brown paper, tape, and string. I addressed it to Colin's cat at his flat in London.

The next afternoon I put on my native Pakistani best, including the silver decorations to braid into my hair, and brought my package with me when I accompanied Stephen to the Agency for International Development. I asked the American secretary, Yulanda Washington, where to find the post office. She sighed and rose from her desk.

"You might as well come with me. I have to get some stamps. I just hate going there by myself. I don't like to be out on the streets too late in the day."

She took me out to her car.

* * *

The post office was in a British Raj-era building. We walked between white columns and over marble floors and joined the end of the line. By the time we approached the counter a deepening orange glow was streaming through the front windows.

Yulanda purchased her stamps and stepped to one side. As I handed him the package, the postal official smiled at me and quoted a price for mailing it. I was sure the price was too high and that he was waiting for me to bargain with him.

I smiled back at him. "Don't you have a book rate?"

He flashed very white teeth and raised an eyebrow.

Yulanda began to tap her foot. "Could we speed this up, please?"

The postal employee ignored her.

"Ah, so this is a book? If that's true, we indeed have a book rate." He picked up a pair of scissors and began to cut open the end of the package. "Do you like it here in Pakistan, miss?"

I felt a flash of cold fear rip through my stomach as I watched him cut away all the wrapping paper from one end of the package. "Yes," I replied as casually as possible. "I love Pakistan. Such kind and friendly people."

I gulped as he separated the pages at the end of the book. From my angle I couldn't tell if he could see in, past the inch of paper, to where the hollow held my contraband. My heart was pounding in my ears.

"You should stay here for a long time," he said, showing more teeth than I thought could coexist in one mouth. "Just one moment, please."

He went behind a wall into the back of the post office.

'Stay... a long time?' I thought to myself. *As in, spend the rest of my life in a Pakistani dungeon?*

I tapped my fingers on the counter and smiled wanly at Yulanda. I imagined the postal worker calling the authorities in the back room. I was tempted to run.

"Could you hurry up, *please*?" Yulanda yelled after him. "It's getting late, and I don't want to be on the streets after sundown."

We may never see the sun again, I thought, expecting Pakistani police to flood through the door at any moment.

The post office employee returned, tossed my book into a pile of packages, and quoted me a more reasonable price, which I immediately paid.

"You are a very lovely girl," the postman said as he lingered to touch my hand while taking the money. "I hope you enjoy your visit."

Overwhelmed with relief, I gave him a big smile as Yulanda dragged me out the front door.

That night, I pleaded exhaustion and took to my bed, again alone.

The next afternoon, well wrapped in my veil, I accompanied Stephen on a return trip to Nurpur. There was a religious festival in progress, and men had traveled from all over Pakistan to worship at its shrine.

There were hardly any women in the crowd except some who apparently lived in Nurpur, and they were covered from head to toe in long, black clothing intended to conceal them completely from view.

The sun was setting, and torches were lit throughout the village. Men were drinking *bhang*, a heady liquor brewed from cannabis, and smoking water pipes. The air of the village was filled with smoke, diffusing the light.

I was offered many things to eat and drink, and I politely sampled everything offered. I took a few photos in the smoky half-darkness, though I expected many of the slow-shutter, low-light-level frames would be blurred because strange men kept bumping into me, unused to having a Western woman in their midst.

"The holy man will see you now."

Firzana's father, the village headman, led me and Stephen to the shrine and whispered etiquette in my ear: "Keep the bottoms of your feet facing away when you sit before him. Only speak when addressed."

I nodded. I had been told, (though I wasn't sure if the translation was accurate), that this Moslem holy man had been crippled from a self-imposed twenty years sitting in a stream while contemplating Allah. He now sat in the shrine, surrounded by his followers.

I knelt next to Stephen on an embroidered cloth in front of the holy man. His head was shaved except for a single, braided lock hanging down one side, and his body was severely twisted. His eyes were huge, round, and black, shining with fanatic fire.

I felt a presence behind me. Looking over my shoulder, I spotted Firzana in the crowd. I waved her forward to sit next to me. We exchanged grins. The holy man's eyes narrowed for a moment. Then he looked from me and Firzana to Stephen and gestured for his interpreter to translate his words.

"You," he said pointing to Stephen, "are not the lucky one. These two," he said, inclining his head toward me and Firzana, "are the lucky ones, because they know how to love instantly and honestly."

My heart lifted. I had certainly never expected my emotions to be validated by a Moslem holy man, but I felt vindicated. I could trust my own instincts.

The holy man permitted me to take his photograph with his attendants all around him. Before we left the shrine, he gave me a blessing.

"He says your firstborn will be a son," the interpreter told me, obviously impressed by the pronouncement. I bowed my thanks as I politely backed away.

* * *

Over the next several days, I avoided Stephen's bed. He had meetings with various headmen from local villages, culminating in a trip into the foothills of the Himalayas—to the Swat Valley and the villages of Madyan and Bahrain. He invited me to accompany him, though his temper seemed short, snapping at Haneef and his chauffeur.

From the backseat of the car, I watched the baked plains turn into a deep valley, with paths zigzagging upward and waterfalls ending in a river below. In the village of Madyan we were greeted by Sultan Zareen, the headman, a tall, distinguished gentleman with gray hair. He directed Stephen to a Raj-era house down the road, to meet with some officials, and offered to escort me to the local market, accompanied by an interpreter.

The open market was fragrant with spices: cardamom, cinnamon, cumin. He assisted me in buying fruit and helped me find some Afghani mountain hats to take home for my friends. He observed my good-natured bargaining and noticed the tip I subtly slipped to the vendor at the end of the lively session. He nodded his approval.

He guided me to the local shrine in Bahrain, a cave built over a series of waterfalls, the cool darkness of the rock-hewn holy place and the sounds of running rivulets providing instant relief from the intense sunshine outside.

An old holy man in a saffron robe studied my palm and intoned, "I see honors and respect. I see a great love and children." I thanked him, left a bowl of fruit by his knee, and backed away.

I turned to step carefully over the streams of water that flowed through deep crevices in the flat rock floor leading out to one of the thousand tiny waterfalls of Bahrain, which splashed down to the distant river that had created the Swat Valley. Sultan Zareen bowed to the old man and gestured me toward the sunlight outside.

He led me across the narrow, baked-red-earth road to a wooden building. Its lacy, carved-wood doors were open to the street. Zareen greeted his dignified, gray-haired friends, and we were ushered to elaborately hand-carved wooden chairs, with woven hemp seats supported by stubby, five-inch-long legs.

A woman with her face covered and her eyes cast downward brought a tray with glasses of pale amber liquid to refresh us. It was cool and aromatic, redolent with sandalwood. After drinking it, and for the rest of the day, the moisture on my skin surrounded me with the scent of incense.

Stephen ducked in the door, the backlight creating a bright halo around his sandy hair. "Come along, Madeleine. The car is waiting."

I rose and turned toward the bearded men and nodded politely. "Thank you for your hospitality." I extended my hand to Sultan Zareen, who fervently held it in both his hands and spoke to me in rapid Urdu.

His friend laughed and translated. "He wishes to know if you might consider becoming his second wife and staying in our valley forever."

I gently withdrew my hand. "Please tell him I am very honored, but I must regretfully say no." I smiled sympathetically at his slightly exaggerated show of disappointment at my refusal.

Stephen took my arm and led me outside to where the driver waited at attention, and we entered the car.

"Enchanting the natives again, I see," he snapped as he slammed the door.

* * *

I awoke in the middle of the night, fierce pain tearing through my stomach. I ran to the bathroom barely in time for the deluge. I was in agony as I retched violently. My body seemed to be trying to turn itself inside out, and by dawn I was semiconscious but still retching uncontrollably, with nothing left but bitter green bile.

I could hear Stephen calling me to come downstairs, but I couldn't manage to reply. Finally he knocked on the bathroom door. "Oh, for God's sake, Madeleine! What nonsense is this? I mustn't be late, so if you aren't ready, I must go without you."

He left me in the bathroom and went to the embassy. By the time he returned that evening, I was barely conscious and was wrapped in a blanket, lying on the couch where Haneef had carried me. Stephen called the local English doctor.

"Good Lord, man," the doctor reprimanded Stephen. "Why didn't you call me right away?" He gave me an injection and shook his head. "Terrible case of gastroenteritis. Badly dehydrated. Were you just planning to let her die?"

"I had no idea it was so serious."

Stephen was subdued. He stood back against the wall as Haneef glared at him silently from the shadows.

For the next four days and nights, all I knew was darkness and the glittering sound of a million crickets singing an epic oratorio outside on the arid plain. At one point I dreamed of my father, who kissed my cheek and murmured, *"Not yet,"* before fading back into golden light.

Haneef stayed by my side, giving me sips of boiled water whenever I drifted into consciousness. On the fourth day I was able to hold down the broth he had made, and by the fifth I was able to stand and wobble to the bathroom.

I was shocked by the image in the mirror. I had lost so much weight in less than a week, I was absolutely gaunt, down to skin and bones, with dark shadows under my eyes.

When I packed for my return to London the following week, I was still painfully thin, but the color had begun to return to my cheeks. I made a point of saying goodbye and thank you to Haneef. I would have hugged him, but I knew it would be considered too intimate between unmarried people of opposite sexes, though I did shake his hand before heading for the car.

Stephen rode with me to the airport. "I'm terribly sorry about the way this all turned out, Madeleine. Perhaps I had unrealistic expectations."

"What was it you expected?"

"I admit I was dazzled when you wore that blue velvet gown at the ballet, and I imagined you on my arm, enchanting my circle of friends—your Grace Kelly to my Prince Rainier. I believe I was infatuated with the rebellious glamour of dating an American. I thought perhaps you might be able to foresee abandoning your dabblings in the counterculture to adapt to the requirements of foreign service. But I now realize you are too unconventional and exotic to fit into my life and its necessary guidelines. I'm sorry if this visit was not what you had expected."

My jaw dropped. "Seriously, Stephen? You must know that we are not at all suited to each other. We have very different world views. And I love my career."

In my mind, I launched into a self-righteous rant: *What you refer to as my "dabblings" are my heartfelt commitments to humanism and the arts, not some fad to be discarded like last year's fashions. I could never be happy in a world mired in a class system that devalues so many, in which I would have to keep my opinions and perceptions to myself.*

Instead I added, "Please don't apologize. This trip was very enlightening for me, and I have no regrets about it."

I knew that my mother would be proud of my diplomacy and the fact that I had recognized another frog masquerading as a prince. I couldn't wait to write to her about… most of it.

* * *

On the flight back to London, I could not stop thinking about Stephen's sense of entitlement, his lack of empathy, his arrogance and disdain for those he perceived as "beneath him," especially compared to Jake's attitudes about brotherhood and justice, so effectively communicated in his films. The comparison only increased my admiration for Jake.

The gastroenteritis had left me lacking my usual curves, but since I could fit into the tiny, Twiggy-inspired London fashions (even if temporarily), I treated myself to an afternoon of shopping on King's Road. Happy to be in England again, I looked forward to settling back into my flat at Belsize Park and resuming work for Clive

CHAPTER FOURTEEN

Colin and Canna-bliss

1973, London

The day after I arrived in London, Colin turned up on my doorstep with a package wrapped in torn brown paper. He was absolutely gleeful.

"Somefink arrived in the post for my cat!"

We opened the ragged package together, and I thought he would faint when he saw the quantity of excellent hashish the book contained. I gave him a good chunk and kept the rest to smoke in the evenings throughout the next year.

While I was away, Colin had formed his own band with a few friends from his old neighborhood, all genuine Cockneys born within the sound of the Bow Bells. He had named the band Percy Verance, and they had started playing gigs in local clubs.

All the lads in the band were sweet and funny, and I truly adored them. They came to my flat regularly to rehearse and relax, and when I picked up a guitar at a local flea market, they taught me basic chords and let me play with them during informal rehearsals. The illusion of being in a band was one of the most enjoyable things I'd ever experienced.

Over the next few months my days were filled with the sights and sounds of the city and regular assignments covering concerts and interviews. But when I drifted off to sleep at night, Jake's face was always in my mind's eye, smiling above me in the darkness. I kept every article about him I could find in the press, from *Cahiers du Cinema* to the local British tabloids, but he was still often photographed with Christine Blake, whose father was both Jake's film producer and one of the wealthiest men in England.

Christine had frequently been touted by the English press as the "Most Beautiful Girl in the World," and I didn't doubt it for a second. Her looks, whether genetic or acquired, were spectacular. In addition, she was fashionably emaciated, which she jokingly attributed to the "crab meat and cocaine diet" that briefly became all the rage among those who could afford crab meat and cocaine.

She was already a notorious part of the English music scene, a fixture at the most popular nightclubs and outrageous parties, and in addition to her association with Derrick from Purple Harry, had often been linked with other major rock stars. She was best known as the blond ice queen on the arm of the darkly handsome director whose latest film, rumor had it, would open the Cannes Film Festival in the coming year. When the tabloids began to print conjecture about their engagement, I felt as if something inside me was dying, and I decided it was time to leave London.

Clive showed several of my photos to his old friend Neville, the director of publicity for Paradise Records, who decided to send me to Jamaica to shoot stills of all the label's reggae artists. Of primary importance were shots of the trio who comprised The Righteous, a band on the verge of international recognition.

I spent one last afternoon photographing Colin's band on the front steps of their flat and then bid him goodbye.

Colin was on the verge of tears. "I'm gonna miss you, Maddy, luv. I'm writin' a song about you, so you'd better come back."

"I don't know what's next for me, but I know it's not here." I tried to lighten Colin's mood, adding, "I promise I'll be there when the band plays in Los Angeles, though… when you're all rock 'n' roll stars."

I hugged him and the other band members and headed for the airport.

CHAPTER FIFTEEN

I and Eye

1974, Jamaica

The change of scenery was exactly what I needed. Stepping off the plane in Kingston felt like walking into a warm hug. The gentle air caressed my skin, and the scent of flowers surrounded me. I checked into a hotel and hired a car to take me to Tommy Chow's recording studio.

Tommy, a stocky fellow with the beginning stubs of dreadlocks, greeted me cheerfully, gave me tea, and took me out into the yard to introduce me to the session musicians lounging under a spreading *ackee* tree. I posed them, photographing them as a group and individually, then asked Tommy about Ras Bembe one of the three legendary and notably reclusive recording artists Paradise most needed me to photograph.

"He knows you're here," Tommy tried to reassure me. "Soon come."

I quickly discovered that Jamaica functioned in its own unique time frame. The response to *"when?"* was always *"soon come,"* which could mean anything from a few minutes to a few days.

One of the musicians shook his dreadlocks in disbelief. "Mi woulda suhprize if dee mon truly come fahward," he said in lilting patois. "Dee laas photographa weh come ya no get no pikcha ah Ras Bembe. Him is a powahful obeah-mon, enoh, an' him tell dis photographa, seh, 'I don' let dead men take my pikcha'… and, sure enough, diss mon dead a few days fahward ah that time."

A disembodied voice rang out, "*This* one can take my pikcha."

A short, slim man, with very black skin and an impressive mane of almost waist-length dreadlocks, emerged from the shadow of the trees. His dark eyes glittered as he studied me for a moment. Then he nodded and turned to talk with the gathered musicians.

I photographed Ras Bembe as he socialized with his fellow musicians. He would periodically gaze directly at me with intense eyes that seemed to pierce right through the lens, and he would shift positions to give me better shots, as if he could read my thoughts. Someone passed him a spliff measuring almost a foot long, and he took a deep hit, clouds of smoke circling his head. Then he handed it to me with a slight smile. I grinned and took a substantial hit, gagging slightly to hold down the acrid smoke. The Rastas under the tree murmured approval and smiled and nodded at me as I passed it on.

I turned at the sound of Tommy's voice calling me from the door of the recording studio.

"Robbie Jobson is here. Come in to take his pikcha, too."

I turned back to say goodbye and thank you to Ras Bembe, but he had vanished.

Robbie was a member of "The Righteous," along with Ras Bembe and his charismatic half-brother, Johnny Cole, the superstar of the group, whom I was scheduled to photograph the following day. Robbie was dressed in army fatigues and a red beret with a gold marijuana leaf pin on the front.

Robbie was, by turns, angry, militant, charming, and funny. As we shot photos, he regaled me with stories about "gun court," where anyone caught with a weapon could be detained indefinitely behind barbed-wire-topped walls, and about his run-ins with the local police. He was highly animated in his descriptions, leaping to his feet periodically to reenact parts of his story, creating sound effects of guns blasting, his fingers pointing like pistols at my camera. The time flew by, and I felt enlightened, entertained, and immensely pleased with the day's work.

Early the next day I drove out to what was known as "James Bond Beach," where Ursula Andress had emerged from the water in her iconic white bikini a decade before in the first "007" film, *Dr. No.* Incredibly lush jungle opened out to a white stretch of sand, where a spectacular waterfall splashed icy clear streams down to meet the warm, blue-green sea.

Several other reggae bands showed up unannounced to have their photos taken, and I posed them on the beach and among the trees and waded out into the water so I could use the waterfall as a backdrop. Then they took me to Bongo Syllie's house for "herb tea."

Syllie's home was entirely woven in an earth-tone rainbow from what appeared to be dried vines or fine tree twigs, with carved wooden lions above each arched doorway. His delicious tea gave me a mellow buzz for the rest of the day.

My flight to Los Angeles, to deliver the photos to the Paradise Records' West Coast office, was scheduled for the following day. Only the legendary Johnny Cole remained to be photographed. I had received word that *People* magazine wanted to run a story about him, and this would be my chance to be published there.

I was taken to his old colonial-style house that afternoon. Johnny had been told I would be coming, but he and a half dozen of his friends were already piling into a car to go play soccer when I arrived.

"It won't take very long," I pleaded, but he just shrugged and drove off. I leaned back against a tree, frustrated, discouraged, and fighting tears. The Rastas lounging on the porch gave me sympathetic looks.

A young woman with her hair wrapped up in a multicolored turban joined me under the tree. She held a beautiful child in her arms, and she patted me on the arm and said, "Don't be sad. Tomorrow will be a betta day." She turned to the child and added, "I and I will have a talk with Papa about this."

"Are you Johnny's wife?"

The woman laughed. "Johnny has a wife already… and many other children with many other women."

"Doesn't that bother you?"

"Not at all! Johnny loves us all and loves his children. We can have children with other men we love, as well. We are an extended family… 'One Love,' y'know. Jealousy is a foolish emotion and accomplishes nothing but unhappiness. You come fahward Sat'aday, and I'll make sure Johnny will be here."

I rescheduled my flight and returned on Saturday to find Johnny engaged in a lively ping-pong match. He ignored me as I photographed the morning's activities, shooting him playing games, jamming with the other musicians, and joking with friends in a patois so thick that I could barely understand a word, which was doubtless the point of that choice.

At long last, I asked him if there were any places in the house that he would like included in the photos. Without replying, he led me to a wall where a picture of "Ras Tafari"—the revered emperor of Ethiopia, Haile Selassie—was prominently displayed. Johnny stood near it in the archway and lifted his chin in my direction. I photographed him full length and shirtless, his lean and muscled torso well-defined. I asked him to stand in front of an Ethiopian flag, where he stared into my lens, unsmiling, the green, red, and yellow design making a perfect backdrop.

I peeked out from behind the camera. "You know, many people seeing these pictures will be people who already love you."

Johnny burst into a spontaneous smile. The ice finally broken, I snapped the photo that I hoped would end up in *People* and on his next album cover.

As I sat on the wooden steps of the house, rewinding and labeling my film, the young woman I had seen the day before approached me. She was strikingly beautiful, with skin the color of milk chocolate and luminous black eyes in a perfectly oval face.

"Irie!" she said in greeting. "So, Camerawoman, did you

get good pikchas?"

"Yes, thank you. I believe I did." I smiled at her with gratitude. "Thank you for making him come back."

"Rastaman *nevah* comes 'back.' I and I only come *forwahd*," she said as she sat next to me on the step.

I understood the use of "I and I" in this case, rather than "you and I," as an acknowledgment of our sisterhood.

"Ah, I see." I finished packing up my gear. "And are Rasta men also forward thinking? Or do they consider themselves superior to women?"

The woman smiled slightly, looking at me from the corner of her eye as she considered the question. "The Rastaman *is* a superior man…," she said, holding up her hand to stop my protest. "…and therefore must have superior women!"

We shared a laugh.

"I, myself, am Johnny's lawyer. I and I are both superior women." She tilted her head back at an angle studying me. "I have the "sight," y'know, and I can foresee a superior man in your future."

She rose and walked off.

For a brief moment, the image of Jake's face as he held me in his arms filled my mind. Then I mentally chided myself again for clinging to adolescent fantasies, and I turned my mind *forward* to the business at hand.

CHAPTER SIXTEEN

Hollywood and Horror Films

1974, Los Angeles

After I got settled in L. A., I met Darlene for coffee and told her all the details of my travels and my work as a photojournalist. The photos from the trip had provided Paradise Records with all the publicity pictures and album cover shots they needed to launch their American reggae campaign and had earned me enough to rent a tiny apartment near the beach in Venice, California, but I needed another gig and asked if she had any ideas. She suggested an independent producer who had just hired her to do hair and makeup on a low-budget horror movie.

"Honestly, Maddy, this is a natural for you. You'd have a blast! Come over while we're in prep, and I'll introduce you around."

Darlene's enthusiasm was contagious, so I brought my portfolio to the production office and was hired to shoot the production stills for *GHOSTNIGHT*. The film starred Robin Brock, the teenage daughter of two very prominent Hollywood stars. It was to be her first starring role in a feature film.

On the set I found a natural camaraderie with the entire cast and crew, but every time I turned the camera in Robin's direction, she would turn away or hide her face. Finally, I asked Darlene if she knew the source of the problem, and her answer was perceptive.

"Well, despite starring in this movie, maybe being in the celebrity limelight and assaulted by the press since she was born might have made her a little still-camera shy."

To show Robin my work and reassure her that I was not a paparazzo, I made a point of leaving my portfolio in her dressing room trailer. It was filled with portraits of rock 'n' roll stars, as well as dramatic pictures from Pakistan and Jamaica.

From that point on, her entire attitude changed, and she became my ally in getting the best possible photos. She posed for me off the set whenever the light was good, reenacted scenes to give me great shots, and faked screams for dramatic portraits. When the director realized how important the photos would be to pre-selling the shoestring-budget film, he gave me a few minutes at the end of each scene to get the shots I wanted.

Although I sometimes worked as many as sixteen hours a day, six days a week, I enjoyed the atmosphere on the set and found the work challenging and satisfying. I invested in another camera, a sturdy Nikon F2, and two "blimps"—soundproof casings for my cameras—so I would be able to shoot silently during takes.

The resulting photos were published everywhere. The pictures were so dramatic and evocative that the film received a lot of attention and publicity before it was even released, and subsequently it did very well at the box office.

That experience helped me score a job on a low-budget sequel to another horror film, but this time with an insecure, first-time director who neither trusted the crew nor understood my job. Before each scene, when every crew member found a spot to stand out of sight, I had learned to check with the camera operator to make sure I was not reflected in any windows or glass on the set. But in this case, each time the director heard the operator tell me to shift one way or another, he would kick me off the set. When one of the actresses had to disrobe for her death scene, he automatically banished me from the sound stage, not trusting my discretion. Even when members of the camera crew approached him and tried to explain that I was just doing my job, he continued to dismiss me on an almost daily basis.

As time went on, the shoot became almost intolerable, but I toughed it out, getting what I could and doing my best to maintain my sense of humor and self-worth. Fortunately, the production company was satisfied with the results, and I breathed a huge sigh of relief when it finally wrapped.

Luckily, I was able to get ongoing work on a few additional independent feature films, and as my reputation among the various indie companies started to grow, I found myself more and more in demand. Shooting on low-budget motion pictures might not have been my ultimate dream, but I was grateful that it was paying the rent while I tried to work my way up to studio films with bigger budgets and higher salaries.

I wanted to join IATSE Local 659, the Cinematographers Guild, the union that represented directors of photography, camera operators, assistants, and still photographers who worked on big studio films, but there was a "Catch 22." Only union members could work on a union film, but no one could join the union unless they had already worked on a union film for thirty days.

When Robin Brock requested me as the still photographer for her next movie, the production company signed a contract with me before they signed their union contracts. Because the union could not invalidate a legal, preexisting contract, I was finally allowed to shoot my first union film… and after thirty days I became eligible to join and qualify for bigger productions.

At last, I was admitted to the prestigious International Cinematographers Guild. I was ready to work for the major studios. After an almost ten-year journey, beginning when I first documented the campus demonstrations and continuing with photos for the music industry, alternative press, newspapers and magazines, and serving my time on various low-budget, independent feature films, I had finally come of age professionally.

CHAPTER SEVENTEEN

Union Work

1975-76, Hollywood

After my first union feature with Robin Brock, my next union gig was on a television pilot for a situation comedy. It starred Rick Hunter, a former action star, and Hildy Spitz, an actress famous for playing ditsy characters. It was an intimate shoot on a sound stage, with four cameras on rolling dollies and hundreds of tape marks around the floor to guide them and the actors into position.

The director of photography, a sweet man in his eighties, welcomed me to the set and warned me never to stand on any of the tape marks, or the dolly-grips would not know where to put the cameras. He advised me to work out a signal with the grips so I could jump out of the way if a dolly was about to head in my direction.

I was ready. Or so I thought.

Before I could even focus, Rick Hunter halted the first take to tell me to stay out of his eye-line… which meant shooting only from far off to the side with a very long lens.

When Hildy Spitz came onstage, and the cameras were about to roll, she suddenly swiveled off of her tape-marked position and held up her hand.

"Stop!"

Everyone froze.

She walked straight to me and said, "You aren't planning to shoot this, are you?"

I smiled as ingratiatingly as I could and replied, "Uh... yes, I was, actually. That's my job."

"No. No. You must *never* shoot while I am acting. You may shoot rehearsals only."

The producer, who heard this exchange from the stands behind me, rushed down to the floor and accosted me. He looked haggard and tense, sweat beading on his brow.

"When Hildy comes on the set, you are to put your equipment down and back away from it, or you will be fired."

I quickly discovered that shooting rehearsals would be useless because Hildy invariably had her eyeglasses on, a script in her hand, and pieces of paper stuck in her collar to prevent makeup stains on her wardrobe. Still, I knew better than to contradict a direct order from the boss, so I spent the day backing away from my equipment.

The combination of not being able to shoot the male star from the front or the female star at all left me with little to do. I watched in frustration as one ideal production shot after another slipped by undocumented. I covered the antics of the supporting players, but nothing I photographed could serve as the key art necessary to promote the show.

Much to my surprise, since I had managed not to offend anyone, they called me back to cover the remaining six episodes. At the end of their short season, the producer thanked me for not shooting, and I thanked him for not firing me. The show flopped, but at least I paid my rent.

Fortunately, I soon received a call to photograph a science fiction anthology series at Universal, with well-established directors for each episode. Although the job was only for one day per week, it was a chance to work with a variety of exceedingly talented people. In this case I was allowed to shoot at will, and the studio was very pleased with the results.

When the show ended, I got a call from Pinnacle Pictures about a possible job on an unidentified feature film. I was excited to have finally arrived at the brink of a major goal.

I pulled up to the elaborate, double-arched, Melrose Avenue gate at Pinnacle Studios. The guard searched through his stack of drive-on passes for the one with my name and then waved me onto the lot.

I was genuinely thrilled about becoming part of the glamorous history of the home lot of directors like Sturges, Lubitsch, and Coppola. I drove through the large parking area, numerous sound stages visible in the distance on each side. To the right were pathways leading past patches of lawn surrounded by charming bungalows that had once housed Marlene Dietrich, Jean Harlow, Gary Cooper, and Cary Grant. To the left, behind a row of massive stored backdrops and set sections, were the former offices of Lucille Ball and Desi Arnaz, surrounded with stages used to shoot sitcoms.

I rolled my car down several feet into what was known as "the tank," most of the time used as a recessed parking lot but which periodically became a lake or an ocean—most famously the Red Sea that had parted for Moses in Cecil B. DeMille's *The Ten Commandments*. Its giant painted blue-sky backdrop blended into the vast, genuine L.A. sky beyond it, with the Pinnacle logo on the water tower looming to the left.

I was surprised to learn that the studio was resurrecting *Star Trek,* a cancelled science fiction TV show, and turning it into a feature film. As I parked the car and walked back past the commissary, background actors in stylized uniforms and space-alien costumes were returning to their stages to finish the afternoon's scenes for the motion picture version.

This was my first call from a major studio, and my stomach was churned with anxiety as I climbed the steps to the publicity department. After an agonizing twenty-minute wait, I was finally ushered into Harris Dunworth's office.

Sitting behind a massive desk that nearly dwarfed him, the short, thin man with neatly coiffed red hair and an impeccably tailored suit, barely glanced up at me.

"I'm Madeleine Garfield," I volunteered politely.

I extended a hand, which he ignored.

"Yes. I know," he replied in a dry tone, making me feel like an idiot for stating the obvious. "You've been requested to shoot the production stills for *Desperado*. I can tell you quite frankly that I think this is a huge mistake. This is an action film, a Western, being shot on location in Colorado with a prestigious cast and director, and I personally believe we should be hiring a more experienced, action-oriented photographer."

He leaned back in his chair and crossed his arms, enunciating his list of requirements as if each word spoken to me was a painfully taxing and inefficient use of his precious time. "We need outstanding key art of all the principals—especially our stars, Brett Shaw and Amanda Price—bright verticals, portraits in character, tight twos and threes, and action shots. John Taggart will be appearing in this film, his first performance in twenty years, and will require extensive coverage."

"I understand what's required. I will document the production thoroughly."

He went on with an extra dose of scorn, not deigning to look up at me. "Any pictures of below-the-line crew are a waste of film. I have no pressing need for artful shots of grips sitting around eating donuts."

He pursed his lips and paused, glancing with disdain at me standing patiently at his desk. "As far as I'm concerned, you're on trial here. I have plenty of experienced male photographers in my stable ready to step in and shoot this properly. You screw up, and you're out. Do you understand?"

Heat rose to my face, but I controlled my voice carefully. "I think I understand you very well," I answered coolly. "But you don't have to worry. I'm very good at what I do, and I'll get you everything you need to promote this film properly." I straightened my back and returned his arrogant stare.

"We'll see, won't we?" He raised an eyebrow, then waved me off with a dismissive gesture and swivelled his chair away from me as if I were beneath his contempt.

I tried to keep any trace of sarcasm out of my voice and

replied, "Thank you for your time. I don't think you'll be disappointed in my work."

I departed with as much of my pride intact as I could muster. At the door I turned and asked, "Pardon me. Would you mind telling me who requested me?"

With his back still turned to me he replied with undisguised annoyance, "The director... JT Morganstern. He was most insistent. The studio is apparently willing to indulge him"—he glanced back at me briefly, for emphasis—"for the time being. You can pick up the script and your plane ticket from my secretary."

I quietly closed the door, my heart racing.

JT Morganstern. I would be working with Jake!

After I received an envelope containing my ticket, I picked up one of the scripts stacked neatly on the desk in the outer office. The title page read *DESPERADO—by Bill Branigan.*

CHAPTER EIGHTEEN

Arrival on Location

1976, Denver to Durango, Colorado

On the afternoon flight to Denver, I read through the script. It had initially surprised me that the studio would be financing a Western, a category of film not held in great esteem for many years, but reading the manuscript quickly changed my mind.

It was a work of genius. In the guise of a traditional American genre, it was both a dark allegory exploring the differences between justice and law, myth and reality, and violence and redemption, and it also featured a soaring reaffirmation of the power of the individual to effect change in the world. Over all this time, Jake and his old pal Billy had continued to live up to my expectations—an unbroken record for both of them.

After catching my connecting flight in Denver, I wondered how far it was from the Durango-La Plata airport to the hotel where the crew was staying and if there would be taxis available. Everything had happened so quickly that I'd barely had time to pack. I hadn't even been able to make any arrangements for my arrival, so I was overjoyed to find Billy waiting for me near the gate at the smaller airport. His pale hair, slightly more silver now than gold, was tied back in a low ponytail, with his black cowboy hat still jammed firmly above it. He grabbed me up in a suffocating hug, squeezing the breath out of me and whooping like a ranch hand.

"Goddamn, Maddy! Look at you. All grown up and a pro! Gimme all those bags and come out to my truck. I'm here to be yer personal escort to location."

I immediately told him how brilliant I thought his script was. He swept off his hat in a mock bow, revealing a bit more skin on the top of his head than ten years earlier, and grabbed my suitcase and equipment pack. I shouldered my camera bags and followed.

On the way to the hotel I looked out the window at the spectacular Colorado springtime scenery in the twilight and daydreamed a bit as Billy regaled me with the trials and tribulations of getting *Desperado* off the ground. He'd written the original script years before, when he'd been a student aspiring to be a screenwriter, hoping to be the next Howard Hawks or John Ford. Billy's epic dealt with themes of individualism, responsibility, exploitation, and redemption in a classic Western framework, and it had weathered many incarnations, but it wasn't until Jake had contacted him recently, and they'd done one more rewrite together, that Pinnacle had jumped at it.

"Thank God he's directing this sucker. The studio didn't bite till the famous JT Morganstern came on board."

Hearing Jake's name suddenly snapped me out of my dream state. When I had learned that Jake would direct the film, it had set off a new series of erotic fantasies in my head, inspired by our brief encounters.

It suddenly occurred to me that I had spent the past decade as an unwilling soldier in an ongoing sexual revolution, mostly fending off men who constantly tried to hustle me into bed. My experiences with my pursuers had been educational and bittersweet at best and downright painful at worst, until I had no desire to leave any more disgruntled suitors in my wake.

I had sworn off dating as more hassle than it was worth, preferring to provide my own satisfaction, using my memories of Jake as a catalyst. He had become my enduring fantasy; the image of his face looming above me and the memory of his arms around me were just enough to push me over the edge anytime I cared to conjure him. Now we would be working together on his new project. I was both excited and wary at the prospect of seeing him again, and it was hard for me to think of anything else.

Since that first feature about coming of age in the counterculture had established him internationally as a major talent, Jake had gained a reputation as a brilliant writer-director. Two years ago his last film, a sweeping political and social epic called *Rite of Passage*, had won the Palme d'Or, the grand prize at the illustrious Cannes film festival, an amazing and enviable achievement for a young director.

He had also become a subject of gossip columnists as a notorious womanizer, and perhaps he deserved the label, but the woman who most often accompanied him in public seemed to be the infamous Christine, supermodel of my recurring nightmares. I had seen his picture in the trade papers, attending the Academy Awards last year with her on his arm yet again, and I couldn't help but wonder how he could tolerate her scandalous behavior and not be put off by her particular brand of notoriety.

Billy brought me out of my reverie. "Maddy? You remember Jake, right? Didn't he save your ass in Century City back in '67?"

I tried to keep my tone as casual and conversational as possible.

"Of course I remember him. How is Jake? I just didn't know if he was here yet."

"He's been here about a week, checking out all the locations, taking a breather from his women. Damn, that man's a hound! Lucky asshole. Just can't seem to fight 'em off. I think he needed a vacation. shit, I should be so lucky."

"I thought I heard he had gotten married."

"Jake? *Ha!* That'll be the day. Christine Blake's been trying to nail him down for quite a while, but it sure hasn't slowed him down much." Billy shook his head and chuckled before returning to his enthusiastic commentary about the film. "I've been waiting to do this movie with him for almost fifteen goddam years. I can't believe it's finally happening."

He rambled on about various aspects of the production, but my thoughts were wrapped up in the man in charge, so I missed a good deal of his musings.

"Hey, kiddo," Billy was waving his hand in front of my face. "Come on back to the planet. We're here."

We pulled up before a beautifully preserved Victorian hotel, which was to be the crew lodging for the next ten weeks. The tiny location town had been a product of the Gold Rush, and I felt as if I had stepped back in time.

Billy ushered me into the lobby, all in deep shades of burgundy and gold, velvet and brass, flocked wallpaper and lace. He led the way up the long, curving staircase with its polished wooden banister and deposited me at the door to my room on the second floor.

He handed me the key. "Have a good rest, kiddo. The shuttle will pick you up in front of the hotel at six o'clock tomorrow morning. We writers, however, get to sleep in."

He gave me a wink and strode off down the hall toward his room, calling back over his shoulder as I let myself into my quarters. "We got the whole film-school wolf pack on this floor. Should be one helluva shoot!"

Darlene and I had been missing each other's calls and just leaving messages with each other's services for a couple of weeks, and I couldn't help but wonder if she might be part of the crew, but I was too tired to try to find out at that moment. I unlocked the door to my room and hefted my baggage inside.

The decor was really lovely. There was a wood-burning fireplace with a hand-carved wooden mantel, and a balcony overlooked the street, its entrance hung with lace curtains and red velvet drapes tied back with braided gold cord. The ornate brass bed was dressed in a deep red velvet bedspread, piled high with matching down pillows.

I changed into an oversized T-shirt, brushed my teeth, turned down the light in the crystal sconces near my bed, and slipped under the cool sheets and into a dream.

I was driving in the car with my father.

"We have to hurry! I can't be late for the first day of shooting!"

The crash happened, and I bolted upright with a start in a cold sweat.

I forced myself to lie down again and close my eyes.

As before, I was driving in the car with my father.

"I forgot my camera equipment. We have to go back to the hotel!"

The crash happened again. I woke up shaking.

I tried it once more.

I was driving in the car with my dad.

"I forgot to bring film! We have to go back!"

My father's face emerged from golden light and spoke to me.

"Everything will be okay, Maddy. Take a deep breath. Sleep." He faded back into the light.

I woke up and checked the clock. Only 2 a.m. I took a deep breath, and then double checked my cameras, motor-drive batteries, and film supply to reassure myself that I was prepared.

My last conscious thought before drifting into a deep sleep was *Tomorrow I'll see Jake again.*

CHAPTER NINETEEN

First Days on the Set

Durango, Colorado

My anxiety kept me tossing and turning and checking the hotel clock to make sure I wouldn't miss my dawn call on the set. At five, I gave up and dragged myself to the bathroom.

I was less than thrilled at the reflection gazing back at me from the antique mirror. My dark blue eyes—normally my most attractive feature—were now undercut with dark circles. I splashed my face with cold water, brushed my teeth, tied back my hair, and applied my usual minimal makeup, a bit of smudged eyeliner.

In the desk, I found a complimentary postcard featuring a sepia photo of the hotel and wrote a quick note to my mother: *First day on the set about to begin. Nervous and excited! I'm going to see Jake again!*

I opted for a scooped-neck, form-fitting T-shirt and jeans, pulled on my boots, grabbed my shooting jacket, with its half dozen pockets for lenses and film, slung my camera bags over my shoulders, left my postcard at the front desk to be mailed, and set out into the cool, gray morning mist.

When I reached that day's location the crew was already bustling about, unloading the trucks and setting up chairs for the cast. I found a safe corner of the camera truck for my equipment and loaded my Nikons. Then I navigated through a forest of light stands, apple boxes, and camera crates and finally found the food service table. Grateful for hot coffee, I hoped the caffeine would clear my head.

"Maddy!"

A squeal of delight accompanied Darlene's rush to embrace me, knocking my camera straps off my shoulders and splashing the hot liquid over my hand.

"I only just heard you would be on this shoot. I'm so glad you're here, girl! You have no idea. God… and I've just given you third degree burns…!"

Laughing as I shook coffee off my scorched hand, I hugged her back, my cameras swinging awkwardly from my elbows while she chattered on.

"Come on over to the makeup trailer, and I'll clean you up."

She dragged me along, babbling a mile a minute. "Billy told me he was going to gather the old crew for this one. He's been trying to get *Desperado* off the ground for years, and it's finally all come together. We're all going to get to play cowboy! Danny's mixing sound, Terry's operating camera… God, it's like being back in film school. This is just too great for words!"

I had to laugh. Except for her bobbed hair and the smile lines at the corners of her eyes, Darlene hadn't changed a bit. She hauled me up the steps and into the trailer, and I wiped the remaining coffee off my hand and sat down.

"Do I get an introduction, or am I just part of the furniture around here?" a slightly theatrical voice complained to Darlene from the far end of the trailer.

The graying fellow with an elaborate mustache gestured toward me. "I assume this is the famous Maddy. This should make things more interesting. Okay, Dar, where are we going to keep track of the broken hearts for this show? Should I keep a running notebook, or shall we just carve notches in the doorframe? We must be systematic here. I don't want to lose track of anything."

"You can rely on Franklin for the inside dope on anything going on around here." Darlene feigned a conspiratorial tone. "Franklin hears all, knows all, and, what's even better, tells all."

Franklin countered, "And I will always be Frank with you." He extended his hand to me. "Very pleased to meet you, hon. Don't worry, I can be discreet… if absolutely necessary." He gave me a wink before returning to grooming a blond wig anchored on a counter stand.

"The cast is going to be a handful, but manageable." Darlene plopped down in a makeup chair next to me. "Brett's a sweetheart, as long as you stroke his ego enough."

"That's not the only thing he likes to have stroked," Franklin interrupted, raising an eyebrow.

"But Amanda's a bit of a bitch," she went on. "Threw an outright tantrum when I took out the wrong lipstick during the wardrobe tests. Thought she was going to bite my head off. Tread lightly with that one."

"Actually, if you're planning to tread on her," Franklin

interjected, "I recommend wearing hobnailed boots. With spurs."

A knock on the door brought them to their feet as a perfect, shaggy, sandy-blond head peeked around the door frame, swiftly followed by an equally perfect six-foot-two-inch body in buckskins.

Brett flashed a dazzling smile at me. "Who is your lovely friend, Darlene, and where have you been hiding her?" He stepped past them both and came right up to me.

I extended my arm. "Hi. I'm Madeleine, the still photographer for this movie. I'm very pleased to meet you."

He lifted my hand to his lips and kissed it. "The pleasure is mine."

He flashed his famous smile at me again as Darlene and Franklin rolled their eyes behind his back, and I carefully retrieved my hand and added, "I hope you won't mind if I occasionally grab you after a scene to shoot some setups if the light is good."

"Honey, feel free to grab me any time." He raised an insinuating eyebrow, then turned to flash a grin at Darlene. "Touch me up, babe. They're ready for me out there."

I rushed out to the site of the opening sequence. I spotted Amanda Price consulting with the script supervisor and saw Terry riding the camera dolly, rehearsing the shot with a stand-in.

As the camera glided to a smooth halt at the end of the track, the dolly grip noticed me taking light readings. He grinned, looking me up and down, and said, "Hey, baby. Nice tits."

Terry leaned down and swatted him with the script. "Mind your manners, asshole. That's Maddy Garfield, and she's a very talented lady."

"She definitely looks talented to me." He wagged his eyebrows, leering.

Terry slammed him over the head with the script again, and the electricians behind him burst into laughter.

A tall figure stood in the shadow of the camera truck, watching the exchange from beneath a cowboy hat pulled down over his brow. An immediate thrill rushed through me.

It was Jake.

George, the first assistant director, brought our attention back to the work at hand.

"Last run-through!"

Everyone returned to their positions, and Brett joined Amanda under the lights. I found a perfect spot on Terry's left and focused on Brett. The light accentuated his famous features as he gave me a quick wink before assuming his character's steely expression. Pleased, I popped off a few frames.

Brett addressed Jake, who was hidden from me on the other side of the massive camera. "I'm ready, JT. Why don't we just shoot it?"

I took a deep breath and concentrated on focusing my lens.

George checked for a signal from the director, then shouted, "Let's roll!"

"Speed!" Danny replied as the tape in his Nagra sound recorder achieved synchronicity with the camera's pace.

The second camera assistant rushed in to slate the scene,

and a deep, familiar voice said, "Ready... and action!"

The camera slowly glided forward and ended in a tight close-up of Brett hardening his jaw and whispering his line. A perfect take... but they shot one more for safety, as was often the case.

"Cut and print," Jake called out. "Let's move on."

I turned and walked around the camera to get a good look at the notorious JT Morganstern. His back was to me as he consulted with Terry and Gordon Hayes, his distinguished director of photography, about the next setup. Then he turned, the early morning light behind him casting his face in shadow.

"Hello, Garfield."

He took off his hat and ran his hand through his hair.

I stepped closer, into his shadow, and looked up into his deeply tanned face. Laugh lines were now etched around those beautiful green eyes, and his dark, unruly locks were lightly sprinkled with premature gray at the temples, the backlighting of the sun glinting around the edges. He had matured, broadened across the chest, solidified, his height more imposing—a more overpowering presence than I had remembered.

I tried to suppress any evidence of my post-adolescent adrenaline rush.

"Hi, Jake."

"It's good to see you, Garfield. It looks like we're going to have ten weeks together."

The world around me went soft focus as Jake's eyes connected with mine. I opened my mouth, but the power of speech deserted me. I wanted to rush into his arms, rub my face against that broad chest, and feel those strong, warm arms around me again. He had visited me in my fantasies and dreams for so many years, and now, for this moment, it was just the two of us.

A beautifully modulated female voice with a slight British accent broke the spell. "JT, darling, I do need to talk to you about the dialogue in this scene."

Amanda Price stepped between us as if I weren't there and led Jake away. He glanced apologetically over his shoulder as the star dragged him toward her Winnebago.

Darlene stepped up behind me and whispered in my ear, "Does Jake look great, or what?"

I realized that I had been holding my breath and audibly exhaled, returning to the world, my ability to speak partially restored.

"I had no idea he was… I didn't… He's so… God! Listen to me. I sound like a babbling idiot." I took a deep breath and tried to regain my composure. "Yeah. He looks great.

"Whoa, Maddy. For God's sake, don't get hung up on Jake again. From what I hear, he's got more notches on his bedpost than Brett 'The Walking Erection' Shaw. In the last few months alone he's been out with at least a half dozen women. Like that actress from *Beachfront*… you know, the one who looks like an inflatable pool toy… and Marissa Harding, the ingénue from his last film…"

"Yeah. I've seen the tabloids."

"…and, brace yourself, there's even been talk about Jake and Amanda Price, the Queen Bitch herself. And of course he's been involved off and on for years with Christine Blake, last year's big-deal cover-girl. This is dangerous territory, hon. Honestly. Don't get sucked in over your head."

My heart sank into my boots, but I made a show of shrugging it off and smiled reassuringly at Darlene. "Don't worry about me, Dar. I'm not that easily taken in by charmers. I've been shooting 'em and dodging 'em for years." I turned and walked away, fighting down the ache that welled up in my chest and constricted my throat.

The next setup was the reverse of the previous one, but this time the emphasis was on Amanda. Gordon, the brilliant cinematographer, had softened all the lights with diffusion filters and placed them strategically to bring out her dramatic bone structure and luminous skin.

I found the only spot that would give me a perfect portrait during the scene and chose my 105 mm lens to flatter Amanda even more. Everyone took their places for a last rehearsal, and I focused on Amanda's eyes, pleased with the superb light and the sharp definition of her eyelashes. I popped off a few frames, eagerly anticipating the dramatic photos to follow when Jake would whisper, "Action."

Amanda turned off her mark, hands on her hips. "JT, get that damned woman out of my eye-line. I can't act with a still photographer right in front of me. Get her *out!*" She strode out of the lights and crossed her arms, waiting for compliance.

I carefully navigated my way past the light stands, sandbags, and assorted crew members to a spot well out of Amanda's view. From the far edge of the set I found a spot where, with a long enough lens to blur the background full of lights and flags and lounging crew, I could at least shoot Amanda's legendary profile. It was not the ideal publicity portrait I'd hoped for, and an image of Dunworth canning me loomed large, increasing the knot in my throat.

Amanda flubbed her first line, and they went on to a second and third take. Finally, Jake called her aside to discuss another approach to the dialogue.

He led Amanda into the best ambient light on the set, angled her toward my lens, and subtly cheated his own stance, so I had a perfect view of *"The Director Working with the Star."* He used his hands a lot, and it gave me one beautiful shot after another. His intensity kept Amanda too preoccupied to notice me.

I finished the roll of film just as he led Amanda back to the set to complete the scene. He glanced in my direction for a split-second, a hint of a smile on his lips, and I nodded to him, gratefully.

The majority of scenes over the next several days were exteriors in the spectacular Colorado Rockies, with plenty of room to work. I occasionally caught Jake watching me, which always gave me a little butterfly flutter in my stomach. I constantly found myself tongue-tied in his presence, but I managed to focus on the job at hand. I even found a free moment to browse in one of the town's quaint gift shops on the way back to the hotel after an early wrap one afternoon and bought myself a small, black, antique feather fan.

The unit publicist, Allen Singer, arrived from L.A. with

a small contingent of press, carrying my first batch of proof sheets. I was relieved to find that they looked beautiful, crisp, clean, and perfectly exposed. Allen couldn't have been more effusive.

"The shots are absolutely great. I brought a set of proofs for you and a set for JT. I can't understand why Dunworth has such a stick up his ass about you. Just keep getting the kind of stuff you're getting, and he's bound to ease off."

I photographed all the press interviews, making sure I got good shots of each interviewer with Brett and Amanda. A little diplomacy with the press went a long way, and Allen repeatedly acknowledged my initiative with a nod.

I was sitting on the steps of the camera truck, absorbed in studying my latest proof sheets, when I suddenly realized that Jake was standing in front of me, thumbs hooked in his jeans pockets, and looking down at me. I felt my cheeks flush and mentally kicked myself for reacting like a teenager with a crush.

"The shots are very good," he said, nodding toward the proof sheets. "I spent some time checking them out today. You have a remarkable eye. I hope the movie ends up looking half as good as your stills."

"I'm just documenting what you and Gordon have created. You're making a beautiful film, and that's to your credit, not mine."

"You need to learn how to accept a compliment." Jake grinned and tried again. "You are an exceptionally talented photographer."

I bit my lip and took a deep breath. "Thank you."

"Much better. I think I'll have to compliment you more often so you can practice."

I grinned back at him. "Sounds good to me."

* * *

The next day's scenes took place inside the existing Gold Rush–era saloon in town. It had been so lovingly preserved that very little was needed to prep it. The initial setup was a wide master shot of Brett and several of the supporting players, as a poker game turned violent. It was a visual feast, with hazy golden light flooding in through the saloon doors, and just enough smoke to create a dusty period look.

The next setup was more intimate, and I couldn't find a spot that would give me a usable angle. I could get a wide shot that included the crew at work, light stands, and the camera setup, but not the isolated key shot.

My frustration grew. I needed the same angle as the movie camera to capture the scene's impact, and I realized there was no way to get it. As everyone settled in for the first take, I leaned back against the wall and bit my lip, trying to swallow my disappointment and erase the image in my mind of Dunworth's gloating expression.

"Quiet on the set!"

The slate was in place for take one, and everybody settled in. George glanced at Jake and asked, "Ready, JT?"

"Hang on a sec." Jake turned in my direction. "Come stand here, Maddy." Jake waved me to a spot directly in front of him, right next to the camera. I crossed through the set and took the perfect location Jake offered… traditionally the director's spot. Jake nodded to George.

"Okay. Let's roll."

The scene was complex for the actors, the emotionally charged dialogue leading into a very precisely choreographed fight. It took the rest of the afternoon to nail down the master shot, and I was excited with the images I was capturing. Though my concentration was centered in my eyes as usual, I found myself distracted periodically by Jake's proximity.

When we wrapped for the night, I gathered my equipment and packed it up, labeling my film cans for the production assistants to mail to the lab back in L.A. When I finished, I turned to leave the now-deserted saloon but saw Jake leaning against the bar in the dusty, fading light. I left my cameras next to a barstool for the moment and approached him.

"I want to thank you. I wouldn't have gotten much today without your help. You really gave me what I needed."

"I'm always happy to give you what you need, Maddy," he said with such unexpected intensity that my heart began to pound. I broke from his gaze, staring awkwardly at the floor, unable to cope with the flood of foolish impulses welling up inside, the power of speech gone again.

"What an amazing woman you've become." He lifted my chin with his hand. "Balls of steel, and you still blush like a schoolgirl." He leaned down and softly brushed my lips with his. It sent a jolt of desire through me, and I had to catch my breath before it deserted me entirely. He slipped his arm around me under my shooting jacket and drew me closer, kissing me again, this time lingering, lightly stroking until my lips parted, then deeper, the warmth and softness melting my resistance. I met the tip of his tongue with my own as he lightly teased the inner edges of my parted lips, sending more shock waves through my system.

Darlene's warnings nagged at the edge of my mind, but I was too enthralled to care. He held me tightly now, and I could feel his hardness pressing against me through his jeans.

My whole body turned to liquid. I moaned softly as his lips teased mine, losing myself in the sensations flooding through me. I thought my heart would burst from the intensity of my joy.

"God, Maddy." Jake's voice was husky, whispering between kisses. "You have no idea of the effect you have on me." He backed me gently against the bar, one hand tangled in the hair on the back of my head, the other at the small of my back, pressing me harder against his body. I was overwhelmed, flooded with desire.

"I think I'm getting the idea," I joked, breathing heavily.

The sound of voices just outside restored my senses, and I lurched away from the bar and reached down to gather my cameras, trying desperately to regain control of myself.

A stunning blonde swept through the saloon doors. It was Christine Blake, much to my dismay, looking like a page out of *Vogue* in a fringed white suede jacket, a white cowboy hat with blue feather trim, skin-tight jeans, and embroidered white cowboy boots.

"Damn." Jake muttered under his breath as she strolled toward him. "When did you get here, Christine? What do you want?" She reached for the collar of his work shirt, but he crossed his arms to create a barrier between them.

"We have a little unfinished business, darling. We have to talk." She toyed with her elaborate turquoise necklace. "You'd better come back to the hotel with me. I've ordered some champagne and dinner," she purred.

I did not wait to hear Jake's reply. I hoisted my cameras to my shoulders, trying to ignore the drama unfolding at the end of the bar, and rushed out of the saloon.

As I ran down the dusty, dark road toward the crew hotel, I could hear the sound of female laughter in the distance behind me, and I cursed myself for my naiveté.

CHAPTER TWENTY

Starlight and Margaritas

Durango

Christine Blake hovered around Jake on the set for the next three days, watching him like a hawk from the high canvas director's chair that the crew had rushed to provide. She linked her arm with his every time he left the set. She leaned on his shoulder when he studied his shooting script. She monopolized his every free moment.

I tried not to notice, but my eyes constantly betrayed me, searching him out, my heart sinking at the endless intimacies Christine flaunted before the crew.

As if Christine's possessiveness was not enough, Jake's lead actress, Amanda, constantly demanded his attention regarding her problems with everything from script to wardrobe. By the time Christine left three days later, he looked noticeably haggard.

Feeling humiliated and foolish, I spent the next few days trying to avoid him. I concentrated on the work at hand and spent my time between scenes hanging out with Darlene and Franklin at the makeup trailer, a place Jake rarely visited. Their gossip kept me entertained and distracted. They had a wealth of unflattering stories about both Christine and Amanda that had me rolling with laughter and feeling a little less outclassed.

"Honey," Franklin reassured me, "next to those pretentious broads, you're a veritable queen. And I mean that in the very best sense of the word."

* * *

"Hey, Maddy?" Darlene joined me at the long folding tables and plopped her lunch tray down next to mine. "Did you happen to see Brett's stunt double, Tony Hansen? Oh my God, what a doll!" She took a quick bite of her salad before babbling on. "He's doing a shirtless fall from the saloon balcony this afternoon. Franklin made a blond wig so he will look as much like Brett as possible, and I get to cover all of his scars with concealer. I actually think he's better looking than Brett—more masculine and weathered—and his eyes crinkle up when he smiles at me… and so sweet and shy…"

I'd heard Tony was the best at horse "gags," falls, and realistic fight choreography. "You wouldn't think a guy who puts his life at risk as a profession would be shy."

"Honestly, he is truly sweet—not grabby like all the grips and wranglers. He actually blushed when I touched up the makeup on his chest… and it is a gorgeous chest. It's so refreshing to meet a cute jock who doesn't assume he's God's gift to women. I really like him." She lowered her voice so only I could hear. "If I pull down the curtain on the makeup trailer window, try to keep everyone away." She grinned, took one more bite, and rushed back to work.

Apparently the feeling was mutual. The chintz curtain had been closed for over an hour that afternoon when the AD finally knocked on the makeup van to say that everything was ready for Tony on set. He emerged, breathless but ready for his stunt, and headed for the saloon. Darlene followed, rosy-cheeked, slightly disheveled, and grinning, and gave me a thumbs-up.

* * *

By the beginning of our third week, Darlene knew the location of every scar on Tony's lean, muscular body. The curtain was pulled down so often that the trailer was no longer a reliable retreat for me, but I decided to stop hiding.

I had no illusions about attempting to compete for Jake's exclusive attention with several of the world's most beautiful, talented, and desirable women. I convinced myself that I had too much self-esteem to allow myself to become another notch on his bedpost.

After all, I'm an adult and a professional, not some simpering teenybopper. I have a job to do, and I can handle this.

We were just finishing a relatively easy day of shooting in the saloon again. I had plenty of room to work, and I enjoyed the easy bantering and complete cooperation of the grizzled old character actors who populated the scenes with Brett.

Brett himself had been charming and accommodating all day. Later I dragged him out to the raised wooden walkway outside the saloon to pose in character with the old geezers, delighting in the contrast between his beauty and their rough-hewn, deeply lined faces.

The late afternoon light was perfect, soft and golden. The men joked with me as they assumed every pose I suggested, giving me a wealth of usable stills in both color and black and white. I lined them up on the porch with their prop rifles and shot a series of Matthew Brady–style portraits, making a mental note to have them printed in sepia tones. Then I released the old-timers and kept Brett for a few more solo portraits while the light was still good.

When Brett's concentration began to drift, I peeked at him from around the edge of the camera. This was a trick I had found worked great with both babies and actors, to show them there was still a person behind the camera to relate to and interact with.

"Look right through the lens at me, Brett," I coaxed. "You're angry at me." He immediately adopted one of his famous steely-eyed looks. "Good. Now you're grudgingly forgiving." His eyes softened, the corner of his lip lifting slightly. "Great. Now flirt with me."

He turned on his famous charm and directed it straight through the lens at me, his eyes reflecting glints of light.

I finished the roll and straightened up, rewinding. "Perfect! Just what I needed. Thank you, Brett. You're a doll."

"I know, darlin'. That's why they pay me the big bucks." He gave me a wink and sauntered off toward his Winnebago.

I put down my cameras to stretch my stiff back and neck. Warm hands began to rub my aching shoulders. I could tell instantly whose they were but said nothing, grateful for the physical therapy. It was a major effort to remain calm while my excitement was threatening to blow my composure, but the tension in my neck was gradually easing, and an enveloping warmth was spreading through my body.

"You're not a bad director, either," Jake murmured in my ear.

I turned to face him, attempting to present a detached conversational air. "Thanks. I'm flattered."

He paused. "About the… uh… incident in the saloon…"

"Don't think twice about it. It didn't mean a thing." I tried to make a graceful exit, but he was quick to keep pace with me.

"Oh. Well. That's good." His voice did not carry a great deal of conviction. "Maybe we could just start from scratch."

I steeled myself and looked back at him. "You're a very charismatic man, and I can't deny that I'm attracted to you. But that doesn't mean I have to do anything about it."

He raised an eyebrow, both amusement and surprise in his expression.

His closeness was distracting me terribly, but I tried to be rational. "It seems to me you have your hands full as it is, and I doubt that you need one more complication."

I quickened my pace toward the hotel. He kept up with me easily, his long legs striding as I practically ran.

"Whoa. Easy there, girl." He grabbed my arm to slow me down. "I wasn't propositioning you. I just wanted to invite you to join us all at the cantina for drinks tonight. We have Sunday hiatus tomorrow, so we thought we'd celebrate a little."

"Oh." I gave myself a mental kick for my unnecessary confession of attraction, and I gave Jake a small, contrite smile.

"Sounds great. It would be fun to do a little carousing with the Wild Bunch."

"Okay. See you there. Margaritas on me."

I gave him a mischievous glance. "I'll just bet she is."

Jake laughed as we entered the hotel lobby. "I'll see you later, then."

I nodded, smiling and glad I'd lightened the tone, and retreated up the staircase. I could feel Jake's eyes watching me go.

* * *

I decided not only to go but to knock his socks off. The only way I could completely restore my dignity was to be the belle of the ball and keep Jake at a cool distance.

Yeah, right, my inner voice mocked me. *Let's see you keep your cool around that man. God, you're such a pushover.*

That simply made me more determined than ever to remain detached and rational.

I washed up and brushed my hair, leaving most of it to hang softly around my face, but with a few strands tied back with a ribbon. I applied slightly more makeup to my eyes than usual and even added a touch of lipstick, but a glance in the mirror at the garish effect the color had on my too-full lips made me wipe it off again.

I chose the only semi-dressy outfit I had brought, an embroidered, off-the-shoulder peasant blouse and a long, three-tiered skirt with a bright flower print in shades of purple and blue. I pulled on my black suede, high-heeled boots, wrapped my fringed silk piano shawl around my shoulders, and headed for the door, pausing only to grab my new antique fan and loop it over my wrist.

I was as ready as I'd ever be.

* * *

Bright light filtered through the stained glass in the turn-of-the-century wood-framed building. I paused in the cool purple twilight outside the cantina, listening to the sounds of laughter and the distant music of the Eagles, then took a deep breath of clean mountain air, and entered.

Billy leaped up from his table and swooped down on me, whooping with unrestrained enthusiasm.

"Goddamn, Maddy girl. Look at you!" A stranger would never have guessed he had academic credentials and an advanced degree. "Let me buy you a margarita or two or six. Billy escorted me over to the booth and swept off his hat to usher me in. Jake was only a few feet away, sitting at the bar, but I avoided his eyes.

I curtsied to Billy. "Why, thank you, sir," I replied in my best Scarlett O'Hara drawl. "You are a gentleman and a bullshit artist of the highest caliber, and I would be most honored to drink your tequila."

Danny, who had zero tolerance for disco music, had made tapes of everything he felt worth listening to and had rigged the sound system in the cantina to run off his production recorder. The melodic sounds of Poco, Linda Ronstadt, Gram Parsons, the Flying Burrito Brothers, and the Eagles filled the air.

Darlene was already on the dance floor, wrapped around Tony Hanson and oblivious to the world. The men on the crew outnumbered the women about twenty to one, so the few girls from the local college who had dared to stop in had more dance partners than they could handle.

So did I. After only one frosty margarita I was pleasantly intoxicated and took turns dancing with Billy, Terry, Danny, and the incorrigible Brett, who insisted on holding me too close and whispering come-ons in my ear. I just laughed, tapped him on the shoulder with my fan, and threatened theatrically to swoon dead away if he didn't mind his manners. Even silver-haired Gordon took a turn around the floor with me before bidding us all goodnight.

Periodically I would catch a glimpse of Jake sitting at the bar, watching me, a slight smile lifting the corner of his mouth. Finally I begged for a break and, feeling bold, walked to the bar, looking at Jake as brazenly as he was looking at me.

"Hiya, cowboy. Buy a lady a drink?"

"Sure. You can help me drown my sorrows." He sounded almost cheery.

"What sorrows are we drowning, exactly?"

"Christine and I have had a disagreement about the future of our 'relationship.'" He downed the shot of Tequila in front of him in one swallow.

"And what is the future of your relationship?"

"Ah. That is the question. Christine seems to have led her family to believe that we are engaged."

"Congratulations, Jake. I hope you and Christine will be

very happy together." I tried to ignore the constriction in my chest and turned to the bartender. "Give this man another shot."

"Thanks. I think I could use one. I can't imagine a universe in which Christine and I would be happy together."

I climbed onto the bar stool next to him, leaned on my hand, and studied him. "You don't seem to be very enthusiastic."

"If you knew Christine, you'd understand. I don't respond well to ultimatums."

Jake gave me a hint of a smile and signaled the barkeep to give me another margarita. We drank in silence for a few moments. I felt slightly dizzy and very relaxed.

"May I have the next dance?" Jake extended his hand. I looked up at him warily.

"Only if you are on your very best behavior, sir…" My feigned drawl made him smile. "… and do not take advantage of my ever-so-slightly-inebriated state."

"On my honor, ma'am."

I accepted the challenge, and placed my hand in his. He gave me his best Rhett Butler predatory grin and escorted me to the dance floor. The opening notes of the Eagles' "Desperado" began as Jake swept me into his arms. "I do believe they're playing our song, Miss Garfield."

I had intended to allow a little distance between us, but he gently pulled me close, his strong arms holding me against his body. It was easy to follow his lead. He emanated such warmth that I wanted to melt into him. He nuzzled my hair while I nestled against his shoulder and closed my eyes. I knew Jake wasn't mine and probably never would be, but I savored the moment, pushing everything from my mind and abandoning myself to his embrace.

We danced to song after song, moving together naturally, easily, swaying slowly to Linda Ronstadt's "Love has no Pride" and "Long, Long Time" and Jackson Browne's "These Days." The whole world faded away, and nothing existed for me but the music, the warmth, and Jake.

The music stopped between tape reels, and Jake retrieved my shawl and led me toward the door.

"I want to show you something," he whispered.

We passed Darlene and Tony on the dance floor, and her eyebrows rose. She gave me a thumbs-up and mouthed, *"... but be careful."*

We stepped outside into the crisp Colorado night, the strains of "Peaceful Easy Feeling" fading behind us. Jake led me down an alley next to the cantina and over a rise on the edge of the little town.

"Close your eyes, Maddy."

He took my hand and guided me to the crest of the hill.

"Okay. You can look up now."

I opened my eyes and was instantly overwhelmed by the vision above me. There were more stars than sky, more than I had seen in my whole life. It was all so bright that it dazzled me and so huge and overpowering that I lost my balance and fell backward against him. My shawl slipped from my shoulders, and he wrapped his arms around me to keep me from dropping to the ground.

"Oh my God, Jake! Isn't it the most beautiful thing you've ever seen?"

"Almost," he whispered, and kissed my neck and the exposed curve of my shoulder. The touch of his warm lips made my skin tingle.

He led me to a flat outcropping of rock and sat down with me between his legs, wrapping me tightly in his arms to protect me from the chill. I leaned back against his shoulder, staring at the endless, glittering sky, mesmerized by the vastness of the universe and the security of his arms. He kissed my temple, and I closed my eyes and sighed, wishing the moment could last forever.

"You're shivering." He took off his denim jacket, with the peace button still attached, and draped it over my shoulders. "I'd better take you back before you freeze to death."

He helped me up, and we walked back over the rise to the hotel.

We walked together up the sweeping staircase which led to the second floor and my room.

At the door, I retrieved the key from my boot and turned back to say goodbye to Jake. He rested one hand against the door frame. I reached up, took his face in my hands and kissed him goodnight.

He murmured like a purring cat and drew me closer. "I've missed you, Garfield." He pressed his lips to my forehead. My temple. My cheekbone. His lips were hot on my cool skin. He lifted my chin and brushed his lips gently on mine.

Heat radiated through my whole body. Everything began to blur.

"May I come in?"

I had fleeting doubts—I told myself that he was taken, that he belonged to Christine, and that there was no glory in being one of an endless parade of conquests, another notch on his bedpost. But a nagging little voice inside kept torturing me.

You are finally in his arms, you fool. Life is too short to let dreams go. Seize the moment.

I wanted him. I'd always wanted him. And now he was here, wanting me. I opened the door and let him in.

CHAPTER TWENTY-ONE

Carpe Diem

Durango

I grabbed his shirt and pulled him into the room. He turned and locked the door behind us.

"I can't believe we're finally alone." He took me in his arms. "I promise there are no planes to catch. Nothing's tearing me away tonight."

I couldn't ignore that warning inner voice. *Only for tonight?*

"It's not fair to give a girl a mind-blowing first kiss and then disappear."

"Mind-blowing? It was that good, huh?"

I rolled my eyes and mock-punched his arm. "That's not the point. I don't want to get hurt again. You broke my heart."

"I never meant to hurt you, Garfield." He kissed me between sentences. "But you were just a kid, and if I'd stayed, it would have been hard to keep my distance."

"I thought you didn't want me."

"I wanted you, but I knew you weren't ready, so I did the honorable thing."

"I'm ready now."

He slipped the blouse from my shoulders and caressed the

curve of my neck with his lips. The tingling spread through me to my core, my breath quickened, and my legs buckled. I almost fell, but he held me, his arm around my waist, one hand behind my neck supporting me, his thumb stroking the edge of my jaw.

He scooped me up in his arms, carried me to the brass four-poster, and placed me gently on the red velvet coverlet. He undressed me skillfully, slipping my skirt down over my hips and sliding my silk undies off while kissing every inch of exposed skin.

I unbuckled his belt, struggled with the buttons on his jeans, and freed him. He caught my hands, kissed the palms and backed away, pulling off his shirt and stepping out of his jeans as I watched. He was beautiful—his dark loose locks disheveled around his face, his body lean and sun-bronzed, his cock hard and ready. His raw power sent shock waves through the pit of my stomach.

"Just do me a favor, Jake."

"Anything, Maddy,"

I grinned and pulled him down on the bed. "Take your time."

He threw back his head and laughed at the memory. "Where have I heard that before?"

He kissed me tenderly, then teasingly, coaxing my lips apart, his hand gently stroking my inner thigh, his fingertips exploring. All coherent thought deserted me and the world dissolved.

The flat of his large hand covered my whole soft mound, the fingers between my legs gently massaging side to side. I could feel myself swelling and opening to his touch. A single finger slipped between the folds, stroking, spreading the warm wetness, making me moan.

Jake was leaning on one elbow, head resting on his hand, as if studying my every reaction. He gently insinuated a single finger into my tight warmth.

"Oh, God, Jake…" I moaned, my hips lifting involuntarily.

He leaned forward and kissed me again, his hand still coaxing between my legs, his finger circling and slowly sliding in and out. I caught my breath as he added a second finger, stretching and filling me. My hips rocked to meet the gentle thrust. I ran my hand through his thick hair, holding his teasing mouth on mine. I gently caught his lower lip between my teeth so he couldn't pull away, and he laughed deep in his throat like a lion purring. He moved over me, his long legs between mine. His erection was like velvet on steel against my thigh.

I ached with wanting him. My suppressed emotions welled up inside, and a tear broke free from the corner of my eye and dripped on the pillow. He kissed its trail down my cheekbone and along my jaw to my mouth. He took my wrist and lifted my hand over my head, running his lips over the soft skin on the inner side of my upper arm then down to the outer curve of my breast. His warm mouth on my nipple sent another rush of sparks through my body.

"Are you sure, Maddy?"

I answered by reaching down between us, encircling his shaft with my hand and guiding him between my slippery folds, swollen with desire.

"I really wanted you to be my first."

"This is *our* first," he whispered between kisses. "That's more important. It's all led to this, to us."

He reached down and stroked me with the head of his cock, slowly up and down, nestling deeper.

"We'll take it slow. We can pretend it's the first time for both of us." He kissed my lips, my eyes, my throat. "Let it go… let it all go. Just let me love you."

He kept stroking and circling, watching me as my eyes drifted closed and my breath deepened.

The last remnant of any rationality slipped away. I was entirely liquid, floating downstream on the sensations flooding through me. He advanced an inch, then withdrew slightly. I moaned and tried to pull him deeper. He advanced again, slightly more, and pulled back again as I floated between desperation and ecstasy.

He began to move, each slow thrust going deeper until he was buried to the hilt, filling me to my limit, and then paused again.

I opened my eyes to meet his, tightened my muscles to squeeze him inside me, and felt him surge.

He growled deep in his throat and began to rock against me, kissing me deeply as the tempo increased. I rode the wave of glittering pleasure, losing contact with the planet, swept away by the electric sensations pulsing through my whole body. Each thrust lifted me higher until stars exploded behind my eyes. It was as if a dam had broken inside me, a tidal wave of ecstasy carrying me over a precipice. My body convulsed, each thrust an explosion of light. I opened my eyes to see his intense, beautiful face looming above me, and as his eyes met mine, it triggered his orgasm, and he groaned and came in a powerful surge. Our bodies pulsed and throbbed, releasing all tension like bubbles in champagne rising to the surface together and bursting.

We stayed joined, letting the exquisite sensations slowly ease. We floated slowly back to Earth as I savored the fluttering aftershocks rippling inside.

"God, Maddy."

His breathing gradually slowed and he kissed my lips, my nose, my forehead, before easing from my body. He turned onto his back and drew me into his arms. I nestled against his shoulder, his warm hand stroking my back and coming to rest on my bottom.

I savored every second.

What a difference being in love makes.

"I've been fantasizing about you for so long… Nobody else could even come close."

His eyes widened. " Jeez, Garfield. That's a lot to live up to. I hope I haven't ruined it." He shook his head.

"You're better than my imagination. I couldn't be happier." My hand wandered down his chest, following his sprinkling of dark fur lower until I brushed his cock… and it began to rise again. His forearm was across his face, but I could see his smile beneath it.

"If you keep going, we might have to do it again."

"Promise?"

He laughed and kissed me, and spent the night exploring my body, learning all of my most sensitive places and ways to touch me that made me delirious with arousal. Dawn was breaking by the time we had reached total exhaustion. We spooned, my back against his chest, his face nuzzling the nape of my neck. I felt at peace. It felt right.

Pure bliss.

I fell asleep in his arms, a smile on my lips.

* * *

It was close to noon before we began to stir. I awoke to kisses on the back of my neck, and I snuggled against him as we spooned, feeling him rise against the back of my thigh. His hand cupped my breast, his thumb lightly stroking my taut nipple, his lips sending tendrils of arousal down my spine and to my core.

I guided him between my thighs, and he reached down to stroke me with clever fingertips until I was on the verge, then entered me as I came in rippling waves around his cock and he groaned as he released.

"Jesus, Garfield." He dropped back on the bed, out of breath, eyes closed, smiling. "If we keep this up, it may kill me. Have mercy."

"I have no intention of killing you." I turned to face him. "But we don't have to do it four times within twelve hours on a regular basis."

"But you're not ruling that out…"

I laughed and curled up against him, and we dozed off again.

In the early afternoon I felt him ease from the bed. Feeling satiated and content, I stretched and turned to watch him dress. He sat on the edge to pull on his socks.

"Leaving… again?" I was teasing, but some part of me feared this was history repeating. I sat up and held the sheet to my chest. I tugged on his shirt and he turned to kiss me.

"Duty calls." He rested his forehead against mine. "I have to meet with the key crew in less than a half hour to prep for the coming week, and I shouldn't keep them waiting… even though I want you again."

"Really?" The word emerged like a sigh.

"You have that effect on me, Garfield. It's beyond my control." He groaned and pulled away. "I would love to spend the whole day in bed with you, but we should probably try to be discreet. John Taggart is arriving Monday, and he's going to require a lot of attention." He sat up and pulled on his boots. "You can sleep in, but pull yourself together for work on Monday. I will try to contain myself, God help me."

He rose and grinned at me from the doorway before retreating to his room.

CHAPTER TWENTY-TWO

Meeting John Taggart

Durango to Bayfield and Back

Sunday had gone by in a haze, and I couldn't stop smiling to myself until our unit publicist ran past me on the set Monday morning.

"John Taggart is arriving this afternoon!" Allen shouted. "Harris Dunworth is bringing him in personally with a small army of press and the studio's special photographer, Spencer Grant. Got to make sure everybody's briefed!"

John Taggart was a Hollywood legend. He had made his mark as a laconic hero in dozens of films in the forties and fifties but had disappeared from the screen for nearly twenty years. He was notoriously reclusive, and his decision to play the idealistic rancher-turned-lawman in *Desperado* had made headlines in all the trade papers.

I was looking forward to working with Taggart, but I was not so thrilled at the news that Dunworth was arriving... or that he was bringing his own photographer. A knot of tension formed in the pit of my stomach.

Every studio occasionally brought special photographers to the set to shoot glossy, posed, gallery-style images of the cast to be used for promotional posters, ads, and key art. Sometimes that was unnecessary, if the unit photographer got everything the studio needed. I would normally not think twice about the slick, contrived setups the "special" would shoot—it had never seemed like a threat to me before. But in this case, I felt a vague unease at Dunworth's lack of confidence in my ability. Having him look for excuses to get rid of me with his own man standing by definitely raised my anxiety.

I headed for the makeup trailer to get the gossip. Franklin peered at me over his glasses. "Dunworth and his 'special,' huh? A very special couple, indeed. You mean the Liz Taylor and Dick Burton of the publicity set? And I do mean 'dick.' Don't turn your back on those two, honey, or you'll come away with a dagger in it, for sure."

I did not find the news particularly reassuring.

Franklin continued preparing the wig for Amanda's stunt double, who was arriving later in the week, and glanced at me out of the corner of his eye. "So… How is JT?"

I blushed to my boots and stammered incoherently.

"Just as I thought." Franklin looked at me like a disapproving parent. "Did Darlene neglect to warn you about the pitfalls of getting involved with the King of Heartbreakers, himself, the notorious JT Morganstern? I must have a word with her about dereliction of duty."

"Really, Frank, it's not like that at all." I was completely flustered. "Please don't start any rumors. I'm going to have enough to contend with without having to deal with crew gossip. Especially with Dunworth coming." I flopped down in a makeup chair, apprehensive and glum.

"I can't blame you, hon. JT is some beautiful piece of work, all right. Unfortunately, the man is notoriously straight… more's the pity. I'd go after him if it wouldn't mean making a complete fool of myself. You going to be okay?"

"I'm fine. Honestly. Nothing's going on."

"Sure there isn't." Franklin's skepticism was obvious.

I gave him a pleading look.

"Don't worry about me, hon. I can keep my mouth shut. With difficulty, but I can. You're the one I'm worried about. Just try to be as discreet as possible. Not that it will be easy. News like this has a life of its own… and Christine is a viper. Better watch your step."

Franklin gave me a sympathetic look and returned to grooming the wig. I sighed and walked back to the set.

During the morning's setups I tried to concentrate on the work, but every time I glanced in Jake's direction and our eyes met, it was as if lightning flew between us. I prayed no one else would notice.

We shot a scene inside a stagecoach, where Brett's desperado character meets Amanda's prim Eastern gentlewoman for the first time. It was a crucial production still to capture, one that would be essential for the press kit, but there was no space to shoot into the coach window alongside the giant Panavision motion picture camera.

I approached Jake while the lights were being set. "Can you let me have this one when you're done with it?"

His eyes softened, but he caught himself and gave me a

professional reply. "Sure, Maddy. I'll hold them here for you as soon as this take's in the can."

"Thanks." I didn't want to tear my eyes away. There was a hint of a smile on my face.

"My pleasure." He couldn't stop smiling at me either.

George cleared his throat loudly before announcing, "We're ready, JT." He glanced from me to Jake as the spell broke, and we attempted to look detached and businesslike.

"I'm ready, too," Jake replied, striding purposefully back toward the assembled crew.

George followed him, glancing back at me as he left. "Yes, indeed. Sure looks ready to me." He gave me a mischievous grin as they disappeared around the stagecoach.

It was a difficult scene with a lot of snappy dialogue, meant to establish both the characters' attraction for each other and their basic conflict. Between master shot, close-up coverage on each of them, and innumerable takes and retakes of lines, it was late afternoon before they finished. Everyone breathed a sigh of relief, and the electricians started to turn out the lights.

"Hold everything in place for a minute." Jake leaned into the coach to address Brett and Amanda. "I need you to do it one more time, for stills."

"Really, JT..." Amanda began to complain, but Jake interrupted her.

"You know it's part of the job, darlin'. Vital key art. You look wonderful in this light, and we need the shots, so just sit back down, and let Maddy get it over with."

Amanda pouted but sat down again. Brett gave Jake a sly

smile from over her shoulder, and I stepped in as the movie camera pulled out. They reenacted the entire scene for my lens. Occasionally I would stop them and direct the placement of their bodies to improve the shot or would halt them just long enough to switch cameras, making sure the scene was covered in both color and black and white.

I finished the last roll and breathed my own sigh of relief. "Thank you, guys! That was wonderful. I really appreciate it."

Brett gave me a wink. Amanda just nodded and exited the coach as quickly as possible, swishing past me with a rustle of taffeta and crinoline.

* * *

I was sitting on the steps of the camera truck, unloading my cameras and labeling my film cans, when I spotted the small army of press marching over the rise from town. In the center of the troop was the tall, lean, charismatic John Taggart. To his left was the much-smaller Dunworth, unmistakable with his red hair and business suit, walking double-time to keep up with Taggart's long strides. I grabbed my Nikon, loaded it quickly, and took a light reading off my hand, then scooted back to the set, close to where Jake was standing.

Like a flock of sheep, Dunworth and his press corps followed the Hollywood legend as he circled the set until he found Jake. Taggart extended his large, weathered hand, and I started shooting the proceedings.

"Pleased to meet you, son," he intoned in his famous, gravelly voice. "Since you talked me into this, I made a point of reviewing your work. Admire it very much. Lookin' forward to workin' with you." He pulled Jake closer with the handshake and whispered in his ear. "Any way we can dump these paparazzi and find ourselves a nice, quiet place to hang out and talk?"

Jake smiled and assured him, "I'll see what I can do, John."

"There's the man I gotta meet!" Billy strode toward us across the grass, grabbed Taggart's arm and nearly shook it out of its socket. "I've been waitin' all my life to work with you, sir, and this is the goddamn happiest day of my goddamn life."

Taggart laughed out loud. "This must be Mr. Branigan." He looked to Jake, who nodded confirmation. "I much admire your script, Bill. I think we should all get together tonight, get to know each other better, if it's alright with you?"

Billy beamed.

I was thrilled to be shooting this historic first meeting, capturing the animated expressions and warmth on film. Finally I joined the group. Dunworth ignored me, but Jake grabbed my hand and dragged me forward.

"This is Maddy, John... our unit photographer. She's damn good, and I think you'll like working with her."

"I know I will." John smiled at me gallantly, shaking my hand.

I thought I detected a twitch in Dunworth's eye as I gave John a little curtsy and said, "I'm very honored to be working with you."

"Well, the feeling's mutual, little lady." He squeezed my hand before turning back to the gaggle of press. "Okay, boys.

Back to the hotel so you can pick my brain for a while." He turned back to address Jake and Billy "And I sincerely hope I'll be seeing you gentlemen later."

Taggart sauntered through the ocean of press, and they parted like the Red Sea in the Pinnacle tank and followed him back up the rise.

That left me, Billy, and Jake surrounded by crew members wrapping equipment for the day as dusk turned into evening.

"Thanks for the introduction to John."

Jake nodded and replied, "Always glad to help."

He was smiling, and his eyes were riveted on me. I knew I was disheveled after the long day's work, with wisps of hair falling in messy tendrils around my face, and I could feel the faint sunburn on my nose and cheeks. He kept his hands in his pockets, but I had the impression it was to restrain them from grabbing me and completely blowing our cover.

Billy looked back and forth between us, his eyes in a suspicious squint.

"I guess I'd better go rescue John from the press," Jake said ruefully. "From what I've heard about him, this macho bonding session may go on all night."

"Oh." I couldn't keep the disappointment out of my voice. "Well. It should be very interesting." I tried to sound cheerful. "Think about how it will read in your memoir, carousing all night with John Taggart. I wouldn't pass up an experience like that."

"Stop being so damn sweet and understanding," he whispered in an undertone so none of the passing grips would hear, "or I'll have to grab you right here and have you on the grass."

Billy raised a shaggy eyebrow.

I grinned back at the wicked gleam in Jake's eye and blushed. "There's always tomorrow," I whispered back.

He ambled back over the hill with Billy's arm draped across his shoulders.

* * *

The next afternoon the Chapman crane arrived at our location in time for the night shoot. The wonderful device was so perfectly balanced that a grip could use one hand to transport a three-person camera crew up into the air to shoot sweeping mob scenes or to emphasize the isolation of a solitary figure in an empty street.

"Hey, Maddy! Come take a ride!" Terry shouted from fifty feet in the air, as the crane swooped down to within a yard of me.

To keep from disrupting the delicate balance of the machine, Gordon waited until I had climbed on before he stepped off. There were three swivel seats: one for the camera operator, one on the left for his assistant to pull focus, and one on the right for the director. I sat in the director's seat and was thrilled at the rush of wind against my face as we swept up above the Western town. Using my widest lens, which could take in the entire panorama, I captured a sweeping view of the crowd of extras in the street, the bustle of crew members hauling equipment and canvas chairs, and the arm of the crane falling away below us.

As we descended, I noticed Jake watching me from the saloon porch. He grinned and disappeared behind the set. I waited for Gordon to replace me on the crane platform, then wandered casually in the direction of the saloon and rounded the corner.

Jake swept me into his arms. "God, I've missed you," he murmured, stopping my reply with kisses and holding me tight against his body. I hugged him back, rubbing against him. His response was immediate. He growled into my ear, "How am I going to make it through the night?"

I laughed and covered his face with soft kisses. "How about if I meet you here between each setup?"

"By the end of the night I'll have a reputation as One-Take Morganstern, the fastest director in the West."

He buried his face in my neck, inhaling deeply before pulling away and steeling himself to regain some semblance of composure before returning to the set. I waited until my ragged breathing had returned to normal and then followed.

When the master shot was finally in the can, the crew rushed to set up the next shots while Jake and I stole away to our rendezvous spot. We surged into each other's arms and necked like teenagers, hungry for each other's mouths and the feel of each other's bodies through the denim and leather. The heat of our encounters sustained us through the brisk Colorado night and kept us both in a constant state of arousal and anticipation of our next stolen moments between shots.

When John arrived on the set, Jake gave him his full attention. I shot them working together, discussing the scene. John seemed somewhat unsteady, and Jake constantly had to reassure him.

I marveled at Jake's gentleness and perceptiveness in dealing with the old man, whom he coaxed into a wonderful performance. John's deeply lined face in the mob torchlight etched classic images on my film, and I felt a thrill each time I released my silent shutter.

* * *

Back at the hotel I let Jake in as dawn was breaking, and he collapsed on the bed, totally exhausted. I pulled off his boots, unbuttoned and removed his shirt, and rubbed his neck until he rumbled with satisfaction like a tomcat. He drew me into his arms, sighed, and fell asleep. I snuggled into his encompassing warmth and rested my face on his shoulder, inhaling his comforting male scent. Smiling, I fell into a deep slumber.

I awoke mid-afternoon to the radiating pleasure of lips on the nape of my neck and hardness against the back of my thigh. I feigned sleep but snuggled back closer in his arms and felt his surge of arousal. He growled deep in his throat and pulled me tight against him, one arm around my hips and the other around my ribcage. His warm hand cupped my breast, fingers gently stroking my nipple.

The rush of liquid heat inside me made me moan and turn toward him to catch his mouth with mine. The tip of his tongue teasing the inner edges of my lips sent little ripples of pleasure through me, robbing me of my breath and any semblance of rational thought. I grabbed his lower lip between my teeth, and he laughed and rolled me on my back under him, the heat of his skin almost burning mine.

"Hey, Maddy?" It was Billy's voice from the hallway. "If you should see Jake, tell him it's three-fifteen in the afternoon, and he has a script conference with John at three-thirty." His footsteps receded down the hall.

"Shit." Jake rested his forehead on mine for a second before wrenching himself out of bed and into his jeans. I searched under the bed for his socks, and the provocative position made Jake growl again and drop to his knees behind me, showering my bottom with kisses. I gasped, laughing, and twisted to intercept him.

I squirmed out of his grasp and grabbed his face between my hands. "Jake. It's three twenty-five. You have to go."

"I know. I know." He closed his eyes and took a deep breath, the tension and hardness of his body warring with his self-control. "Yes. Gotta go." He kissed me again.

I'd have given anything to leap back into bed and abandon myself to our mutual desire, but rationality prevailed. I pulled back from the kiss, but he still held me in his arms.

"Jake…" I kissed him softly. "I'll see you later."

CHAPTER TWENTY-THREE

Night Shoots

Bayfield Location

While the crew set up their equipment for the evening shoot, I sought out John Taggart. He was sitting on the steps of his Winnebago and waved to me to join him. I sat down next to him.

"So, how are you doing, Mr. Taggart?"

"You can call me John. Feels real good, workin' again. Been a long time."

"Why were you away so long? Tired of making movies?"

"That's a complicated question." He looked me in the eye. "You really want to know?"

I nodded.

"I made a lot of movies. Worked constantly. And when I wasn't in front of the camera, I was…" he took a deep breath as if summoning some inner reserve, "…usually drunk. I hurt a lot of people."

I squeezed his arm. "You've also inspired a lot of people. You've been an important part of some of the greatest movies ever made. Millions of people love you."

"But not the ones who counted most. I had a good thing and let it slip away. My wife, Betty, was a good woman. She took it as long as she could before she left me. Took the baby and walked out of my life. And I was too self-absorbed to go after her and try to make things work. Too much booze, too many willing women. I was a goddamn fool. Finally couldn't work anymore. Couldn't remember the lines. Couldn't walk half the time. Sort of exiled myself… for a long time."

I couldn't help but admire his courage in admitting all that, when so many other celebrities in his position were well-known for laying blame on others. I was touched that he had shared it with me.

"What made you come back?"

John smiled. "A couple of things. My daughter contacted me. She's all grown up now… a fine young woman. Wanted to find out who I was. She's quite a girl. Smart. Kind. Like her mama was. Real pretty. I realized how much I had missed, not seeing her grow up. Decided it was time to start living again. And then I read Bill's script. It said so many things I wanted to say."

I nodded and smiled at him, and he went on.

"It's a great part, Maddy. He told my agent he had written it with me in mind, and when I read it, I knew I had to do it."

"Where's your daughter now?"

"She was living in New York, going to school, but she graduated awhile back. Been teaching English at a high school. Real bright girl. I've asked her to come out to location to see what I do. Didn't want the press getting wind of it. Private thing, you know."

I nodded. "I'd love to meet her, John."

"And so you shall… so you shall." He took another deep breath and sat up a little straighter. "So how're you doin', Maddy? You gettin' all the shots you need?

"I can always use more." I grinned. "Especially when the light's this good."

"I'm all yours, little lady," he replied gallantly and followed me to a nearby grove of trees.

I was in photo heaven. His deeply lined face set against the gnarled tree branches made the images seem primal and evocative, as if he were the Earth itself in human form. And he was such an expert subject—knew exactly how to catch the light in his eyes, how to communicate volumes in a glance.

I documented each precious moment. Here was a man who had worked with Hawks and Ford, an icon from the glory days of Hollywood. The images had the mythic quality of a legend captured, and he was giving it all to me freely.

I was so wrapped up in the shots, I barely breathed during the entire session. As I finished shooting the last of the four rolls of film from my pocket, I exhaled and smiled at him.

"I can't tell you what a pleasure it is to work with you, John. You're a gentleman and a pro, and I'm very honored to be shooting you."

He laughed. "If I were a few years younger, I wouldn't be such a gentleman, and you probably would have to shoot me." He gave me a wink and put his arm around my shoulder, and we walked back to the set together.

One of the Native American character actors approached us and John reacted with delight.

"Is that Charlie Walking Bear?"

"In the flesh, John. Good to see you again. It's been a while."

John turned to me. "Maddy, this is my old friend, Charlie. We made a dozen westerns together back in the forties."

Charlie extended his hand for me to shake, and then the three of us sauntered back to the set.

The crew was ready for the key shot of the evening, which would be the last shot of the movie when the editing was completed. It was the scene in which Brett's character returns to the valley where Amanda's character still waits for him.

It was nearing golden hour, that brief time in the day when the sun was sinking toward the horizon, infusing the countryside with warm light. The camera was set on a dolly, running on a track parallel with Amanda as she ran to the crest of the hill overlooking the ranch. Her body was caught in the brilliant orange-gold backlight of the sun, her hair a glowing halo framing her perfect features as she watched Brett approach in the distance.

I staked out a shooting position just beyond the camera track, which gave me a perfect frame at the end of the shot: Amanda full-length in the foreground, her hair and skirt blowing in the wind with the breathtaking Colorado valley stretching out before her. It was key art if ever I saw it, the kind of picture that ends up on posters and billboards.

They got the shot in a single take.

"Cut!" Jake turned to Terry behind the camera for confirmation.

Terry grinned and held up his thumb. "*Perfectamente*, JT.

It doesn't get any better than that."

Jake breathed a sigh of relief as the sun slid below the horizon. "Print that, and let's move on."

Most of the evening hours were spent doing the rest of the coverage of the nighttime mob confrontation with John as he protects a Native American leader from a lynching. The part was played by Charlie Walking Bear. Jake worked with them closely, making suggestions, giving praise, rehearsing John between camera setups. I photographed their interactions—Jake's intensity, John's concentration.

They finished the scene just before dawn. George trotted around the set, signing out the actors, and Jake caught my eye and tilted his head toward the barn as he finished briefing Gordon on the next week's schedule. I strolled as casually as I could around to the back of the barn and waited, trying to quiet my rioting pulse.

Finally, Jake rounded the corner and swept me into his embrace. I slipped my arms under his coat and tilted my head back to look at him.

"I thought you'd never come."

He gave me his adorable predatory smile. "We can deal with *that* later," he buried his face in my neck. "No shooting tomorrow." He kissed the edge of my jaw. "A whole day to ourselves." He kissed my cheekbone. "Just us." He kissed my eyes and nose and lips. "Tomorrow."

As his lips caressed me, I could feel him grinning.

"What's so funny?" I pulled back to look up at him. "Are you laughing at me?"

"I can't help it. You *are* funny." Jake pulled me closer. "You make me smile. So macho in everything else you do, but then you just dissolve in my arms like melting ice cream." He grinned and kissed me again.

"Is that a bad thing?"

"Not at all. I think it's cute as hell."

He took a deep breath, put his hands on my shoulders, and held me at arm's length. "We're both complete zombies. Go get a good sleep before I lose all control and take you right here and die of exhaustion before we finish this damn movie." He kissed my forehead, turned me around, and pushed me gently toward the town. "I'll come by to pick you up in the afternoon."

I staggered back to the hotel in the cold morning mist and fell into bed, asleep before my head hit the pillow.

CHAPTER TWENTY-FOUR

Picnic at Wolf Creek

Pagosa Springs, Colorado

Jake showed up at around three in the afternoon. I grabbed my camera and a few rolls of film, and he escorted me downstairs to a waiting pickup truck. The back was loaded with camping gear and shopping bags.

I glanced down at my long flowery skirt and gave Jake a wary look.

"I'm a city girl, y'know."

Jake laughed and held the door open for me. "We'll just have to do something about that."

After about an hour's drive toward Pagosa Springs, we crested a hill and descended into the most beautiful valley I had ever seen. A river curved through the valley basin, with hundreds of lush green trees along its far bank creating punctuation between rolling meadows. Dramatic, swelling clouds were penetrated by bright rays of sun, throwing shafts of light on the glittering water.

I took out my camera and attempted to preserve that breathtaking sight forever on film. And I insisted on photographing Jake with the valley stretched out behind him. I loved the way he looked: his strong, deeply tanned face, his hair windblown, the male power he radiated, his eyes looking right through my lens into my mind and soul. I loved focusing on his dark eyelashes and the way the light accentuated his bone structure and reflected off his eyes. I shot a few frames before he took my camera from my hands.

"Enough. Nothing in between us for a change." He enveloped me in a hug.

I looked up into his smiling face. "I can't seem to get enough of you."

"We can work on that." He gave me a wicked grin and a quick kiss. "I want to know everything you've been doing the last few years."

We gathered firewood and set up camp. We spread out a large ground cloth, zipped two sleeping bags together, cleared a fire circle, and surrounded it with rocks. While Jake started the campfire and unpacked the shopping bags, I picked an armful of bluebells and wove them into a wreath.

Jake grinned at the sight of my crown. "My flower child," he said.

"But not a child, fortunately."

He nodded and hugged me, then spread his arms to show me his handiwork. "Check out our Colorado feast."

There were buffalo steaks in an iron skillet, potatoes to bake in foil among the coals, a fresh green salad, cleaned and sealed in a plastic bag, and corn to roast. He spread out a blanket on the soft grass, propped up his backpack to lean on, and unpacked a baguette of French bread, some pâté, and a bottle of rich, deep-red Bordeaux with crystal wine glasses.

"So this is what the cowboys ate, huh?" I asked as he poured the wine.

"Only if they spent too much time on other people's expense accounts."

We clinked glasses.

"Here's looking at you, Garfield."

I laughed and shook my head. "I don't mind if you want to call me 'kid' now."

"You are definitely not a kid anymore, thank God." He broke off a chunk of crisp bread and handed it to me. "This feels like home to me. Everything seems more real, somehow."

"Real? Playing cowboy and making movies is pretty divorced from reality. We're so lucky to have jobs we love, working with friends. But it's nothing like the real world." I gazed at the verdant valley and then back to Jake's face. "This is so amazing. Like a fairy tale… me and you and this incredible place."

Tears welled in my eyes, despite my best efforts to hold them back, and my voice cracked. "And it breaks my heart, because I know it can't last."

Jake took the wine glass from my hand and set it aside. He dragged me into his arms, pulling me onto his lap, my head against his chest. I leaned into his shoulder, immersing myself in the comfort of his embrace.

He buried his face in my hair and murmured, "Don't cry, Maddy. We can make it last." He kissed my tears away. "I'm so happy when I'm with you. Please be happy with me."

He kissed me from somewhere deep in his soul, as if his

life depended on it. The intensity took my breath away, and I responded in kind, throwing my arms around his neck as his hands sought my body. I was swept along in the torrent, abandoning myself to the sensations raging through me, my passion matching his.

I unbuckled his belt to release him. He pulled my peasant blouse off my shoulders and gently bit the skin of my throat, his lips tracing a path to my breasts, teasing and sucking my nipples, sending shock waves through me. His hand stroked between my legs, massaging, sliding, probing until I was filled with liquid fire, moaning, out of control.

And then he took me, easing himself inside in one long, slow thrust to the hilt. I cried out his name, and he stopped my mouth with his own as he pressed into me again and again, the waves of pleasure cresting and breaking deep inside.

With a muffled groan deep in his throat, he thrust one last time, leaving us both spent and trembling in each other's arms.

I held him tight, stroking his hair, so full of emotions I couldn't speak. I heaved a ragged sigh, and a tear spilled from the corner of my eye, slid down my temple, and dripped on Jake's arm.

He sat up abruptly and gathered my body tightly against him. "Oh, God, Maddy, I'm sorry. Did I hurt you? Have I upset you?"

I took his face between my hands. "I'm fine. Really. I'm not upset, just in love." I smiled, embarrassed by my tears, and kissed him gently. "I just have to learn not to turn into an emotional basket case every time you touch me."

"In love? Not just a schoolgirl crush anymore?"

"I've been in love with you since I was fifteen. And it killed me every time you left and every time I'd see you in the press with some gorgeous woman on your arm. I knew I couldn't compete with them."

"This isn't a competition. You were the inspiration for the heroines in my movies —strong, intelligent, fearless women, fighting injustice. No one else ever affected me that way."

"So I'm not just one more notch on your bedpost?"

"Is that what you think of me? That I collect women, like trophies?"

"All I have to go on is what I read in the press. All those beautiful, talented women throwing themselves at you… It seems to be quite a long list."

"Come on, Garfield. I'm not playing a game. My life bears no resemblance to the one in the tabloids."

"So… none of it's true?"

He shook his head and raked his hand through his hair. "I admit there have been many women in my life. It's flattering to be pursued, and casual sex is great at first—but sex without emotion is… empty… and somehow my thoughts always came back to you. The truth is that I've wanted you since the summer we met, when you were just a teenager, when I gave you your first kissing lesson. I always thought I'd see you again, and every time I have, it's brought back those feelings."

"How was I supposed to know? You left without even saying goodbye."

"Leaving was the best thing for both of us."

"I really thought you didn't want me." I reached up to touch the old scar above his right eye. He kissed my fingers, surrounding my hand with his own.

"Oh, I wanted you, all right. But fifteen was just too young... and most people don't end up with their first, you know." He kissed my forehead. "I always hoped we'd find each other again, when the time was right."

"I've never really wanted anyone else. I've had a very rich fantasy life with you."

"I've fantasized about you, too. I can't guarantee that I can live up to your expectations, but you've exceeded mine. I've been watching you." His lips brushed mine. "You're kind and honest and brave... and very talented." Kisses punctuated his words. "You make me laugh. You make me want to protect you. You make me crazy, and I've never wanted anyone the way I want you..." His mouth was warm on mine. "...my sweet, smart, opinionated, stubborn girl... with those infamous balls of steel."

I returned his kisses with pure joy.

If only this moment could last forever.

Jake held me in his embrace as we watched the spectacular sunset over our valley. Then we made our feast.

The brisk mountain air and the intensity of our lovemaking gave us voracious appetites, and we devoured our steaks and wine and then talked all night in each other's arms. Jake even pulled out a cassette player with one of Danny's custom tapes, and we listened to the Eagles singing, "Peaceful Easy Feeling."

I nestled against him, my head on his shoulder as he poured

out years of unspoken thoughts about his time in London, the films he'd made, and the people he'd met. As his suppressed emotions overflowed, I was surprised by his self-doubts. Despite his attempts to express his deepest feelings about the direction of the world through his films, he believed that he was still only a bystander observing the sweep of history, while others put their lives on the line to effect change.

"I wouldn't even have a career if it weren't for Christine's father. He financed my first film. I dated other women in a very public way to convince myself that I hadn't been bought, but he still assumes that my future is with Christine."

There was a long pause as I gathered the courage to ask the most important question. "Do you have feelings for Christine? Can you imagine a life with her?"

"God, no… It's been… at best it's been a tempestuous relationship. Christine lives on the edge, on a fast track in the London fashion and drug scene. It's not my world. And I can't keep being the one responsible for her, which is what her father wants. I can't control her and I don't *want* to control her. I don't want her constant crises dominating my life. I can't tell you the number of times I've found her unconscious or in potentially dangerous situations where I acted as her protector. I respect her father, but he seems to think of me as his heir apparent, the one who will assume responsibility for running the production division of his corporation… and the one responsible for keeping Christine out of trouble."

"But do you *love* her?" I couldn't help holding my breath before he answered.

"No…"

I regained my ability to exhale as Jake continued.

"…and I've told her so, but she won't accept it." He shook his head and sighed. "She was the one who sent my first feature script to her father. I owe my entire career to her and her family."

"Come on, Jake. They helped launch you, but you don't owe your whole life to them."

"You have no idea how powerful and influential Harrison Blake is. He made it happen. I still don't know whether it was because he recognized value in my script or whether he just wanted a responsible babysitter for Christine."

"But you paid your debt to him. Your film was successful. It brought him a lot of attention and respect."

"The success of my film was just icing on the cake for him. Now I'm profitable as well as useful, but he still expects me to take care of Christine"

"You can't live your life based on other people's expectations."

Jake laughed without mirth. "Everyone has expectations of what my life should be."

I held his hand. "You can't keep stifling how you feel to meet the expectations of others. You can't take on any more of these imposed responsibilities."

Jake nodded. "I know. I've earned back every dollar Harrison Blake has invested in me. I've spent years bailing Christine out of self-destructive situations and stupid indulgences. It's got to stop."

"So what will you do about Christine?"

"I told her to go home. I told her to find someone else. But she only hears what she wants to hear. She believes she's entitled to have me. She won't let go."

I sat up and looked him in the eye. "You've paid your debt. You're a great director. That's *you*. Not Harrison or Christine Blake. You're a free man. Your life should be the result of your own choices, without coercion from anyone."

He pulled me back down into his arms and kissed the top of my head. "You see things so clearly. You always make me feel better."

I felt better, too.

We lay comfortably entwined and talked into the night, the moon and stars rising in the vast sky above us. I told him about my adventures in London, Pakistan, and Jamaica, the friends I'd met along the way, and the events that made me realize how fragile life can be. I told him about the causes that inspired me, to which I freely gave my time and efforts, and how I had learned to focus my concentration on my photography instead of my self-imposed solitary existence.

Under the magnificent, glittering Colorado sky, we finally slept in each other's arms in total serenity.

CHAPTER TWENTY-FIVE

Meeting Hannah

Pagosa Springs and Bayfield, Colorado

The next morning, I awoke to the smell of coffee brewing over the campfire and Jake's kisses.

"Come on. I have more to show you."

He bundled me into the truck and took me down the winding road and through a grove of trees to a clearing overlooking the river, where a large, rustic house was in mid-construction. Several men were lowering a massive beam across the walls of a huge room to create a ceiling.

"Hey, Jake!" one of the men balanced near the beam yelled down. "How do you like the progress? We're going to start framing the second story this week."

He swung down, dropped into the center of the room, and walked over to shake Jake's hand.

"Maddy, I'd like you to meet Michael Redwolf. I met him in New York when I was a student and he was building highrises. Now he's building me a house."

Michael's deeply tanned, weather-worn face crinkled into a smile as he pumped my hand. He signaled the other men to take a break.

Jake led me around the periphery, describing his plans and pointing out the views from various future rooms. I was enthralled and overflowing with questions and ideas. Michael walked with us and gave his input on the flood of suggestions.

"Are you going to have time to visit with me and Hannah this trip? I bet she'd love to meet Maddy."

"That's exactly what I had in mind," Jake replied. "Can you take a break now?"

"I guess I could take off an hour or two, if the boss doesn't mind."

Jake laughed and slapped him on the back as we all climbed into the truck. He and Michael regaled me with stories from the days when Jake and Billy, having left New York to go on the road, had spent a chaotic six weeks in Colorado amusing and totally baffling the local Native American inhabitants. The tales Michael told of the wild, Kerouac-influenced but sadly misinformed young men and their unique but ill-conceived version of "vision quests" among the native population had me in hysterics.

Michael and Hannah Redwolf lived a few miles away in a small cabin that Michael and his friends had built. I wandered around admiring the carved-wood fireplace mantel, the smooth, dark banisters and newel posts, and other custom-made architectural details before making myself comfortable on their overstuffed couch.

Jake and Michael went over the blueprints. Thirty minutes later, Hannah came flying through the door.

"Thought that baby would *never* get here," she said as she

flopped on the couch with us. "Nothing quite like a thirty-six-hour labor to wring the energy out of you. Ten pounds of gorgeous baby, and everybody's doing great."

Michael made the introductions. "Hannah's not only a teacher of Ute culture at the community house and our local herbalist, but she's also the midwife around here. Sometimes I don't see her for days at a time. You guys got lucky." He squeezed her hand and went off to the kitchen to brew some tea.

Hannah gave Jake a hug. "Thanks for casting my dad. He's having a ball acting again."

"Charlie Walking Bear is your father?" I asked.

"Yes, and old friends with John Taggart."

I was fascinated by Michael's beautiful wife, with her waist-length, black hair, lightly streaked with gray, and luminous brown eyes with laugh lines at the corners. We spent the next three hours engaged in animated conversation. Hannah was a natural-born storyteller, and I enjoyed hearing tales about her most outrageous birthing experiences, but I especially loved the story of Jake's and Billy's adventures when they were "On the Road" heading west in 1964.

"We called Jake 'Wolf Brother.' Wolves are very loyal to the pack, and"—she added in an undertone so only I could hear—"they mate for life, you know."

"And Billy?"

Hannah laughed. "He was dubbed 'Skunk Dancer' after a rather unfortunate encounter in the woods. He was pretty embarrassed, so I wouldn't mention it to him."

I felt as if I had known Hannah all my life and was disappointed when it was time to go.

"Wait a minute."

I grabbed my camera and hustled Hannah and Michael out on the porch. I drew them forward into the golden fading light and took portraits of them together with the setting sun reflecting in their eyes.

Hannah gave me a hug as we prepared to leave. "You and Jake would make beautiful babies," she whispered to me. "Come back here when the time comes, so I can be your midwife!"

I laughed and hugged her back. "It's a lovely thought."

"You make Jake bring you back soon!" Hannah called after us as we drove off.

"I'll try!" I yelled back, waving until they were out of sight.

I turned back to Jake. "I really like your friends."

Jake pulled me close so he could put his arm around me. "I had a feeling you would."

* * *

Back at work the next day, the love scene between Brett and Amanda was set up in a relatively small room at a local ranch. The essential crew was crammed into one half of the room; an antique brass bed took up the rest. In the scene, Amanda's character, Elizabeth, nurses the injured desperado, Cody, played by Brett. He has suffered a fall while attempting to head off a herd of buffalo, stampeding toward certain doom at the hands of the local ranchers.

Jake sat on the bed discussing the scene with the actors.

"There is a basic conflict between what you think you should be feeling and what you're actually feeling for each other. I want to see the underlying powerful physical attraction to each other, as well as the reticence and the grudging admiration. Each touch should be full of electricity. Ready to try it?"

Brett grinned. "I'm *always* ready, JT." He gave Amanda a salacious grin.

"Keep it in your pants, Brett," she shot back.

Amanda was not amused, but Franklin was. He stifled a smile and cast me a conspiratorial glance as he fixed a few stray strands of Amanda's hair. Darlene finished touching up the very convincing makeup bruises she'd created on Brett's face and body, and she and Franklin retreated outside.

Once again, Jake motioned me to come join him right next to the camera, which was mounted on a low tripod. He knelt behind me against the wall as I sat on the floor giving me a perfect frame of Brett lying on the bed in profile, with Amanda sitting on his far side, tending to his wounds. Soft backlight through the lace curtains behind her highlighted her hair, and the kerosene lantern on the table next to the bed provided soft, warm fill-light.

The cameras rolled.

Amanda tentatively reached out to feel Brett's forehead. She pulled away as he opened his eyes, but he grabbed her hand and drew it toward him. They began the dialog.

>   CODY
>   (whispering)
>   Stay with me, Lizzy.

He kisses the palm of her hand.

>   ELIZABETH
>   You need rest.

>   CODY
>   There'll be plenty of time to rest when I'm in my
>   grave.

He kisses her. She tries to pull away.

>   ELIZABETH
>   I don't want to hurt you.

>   CODY
>   It's not a hurt I mind, Lizzy. It just reminds me
>   I'm alive.

Cody rolls her toward the camera so Elizabeth ends up on her back, looking up at him, both backlit in profile. He kisses her again.

>   CODY (cont'd.)
>   And I intend to stay alive for a long, long time.

They embrace.

Jake watched the scene over my shoulder as I shot. I longed to lean back into him, to have him wrap his arms around me. Flashes of moments from the night before sent unexpected currents through me. I wanted to kiss him the way Brett and Amanda were kissing, and it took all my self-control to concentrate on documenting the scene instead of living it along with them.

Jake called out, "That's a cut."

He checked with Terry, who gave him a nod.

"Works for me." Jake said. "Let's print and move on."

He gave me a little kiss on the back of the neck before standing up and pulling me to my feet.

I noticed Harris Dunworth and his photographer, Spencer Grant, were watching from the door. Grant had his arms crossed, his head slightly tilted to one side. Dunworth's mouth was set in a tight line. His eyes narrowed, and he nodded to himself as they turned and walked away.

CHAPTER TWENTY-SIX

Stampede

Pine River Valley, Colorado

Jake, Gordon, and Tony Hanson had gone out at dawn to meet with the wranglers in the corral to coordinate the day's major action sequence. It was the scene that would precede the love scene, in which the desperado attempts to divert the moving herd of buffalo away from the murderous ranchers who plan to eliminate them.

Tony's stunt for this scene was quite dangerous: a fall from horseback in the middle of a buffalo stampede. Franklin and Darlene had made him look as much like Brett as possible.

The camera was mounted on a flatbed truck running parallel to the herd, equipment locked down, crew tethered with straps. Between the camera and sound crew and all their equipment, the script supervisor, and Jake, the truck was packed solid. Not a single square inch was left for me.

Jake was adamant. "I don't want you anywhere near this scene. It's far too dangerous."

I clenched my fists and held my ground. "It's part of my job is to get this shot. It's important."

"It's *not* important. It's just a movie. I don't want to have to worry about you."

"I didn't *ask* you to worry about me. I am perfectly capable of taking care of myself."

"Like hell you are. Stop arguing with me, and go back to the makeup trailer."

He turned and stalked back to the flatbed for another dry run without the herd.

I hiked to a slight rise in the plain where I'd be out of the way, just behind the path the camera truck would follow during the shot. With a long lens, I knew I would be able to get a great shot of Tony surrounded by a sea of buffalo. I loaded my cameras, mounted them on tripods so I could shoot both color and black and white at the same time, took my light readings, and waited for the signal for the shot to begin.

In the distance the camera truck began to roll—slowly at first, then faster as the herd thundered closer and began to engulf it. It looked like the wranglers had miscalculated the animals' path, thinking they would be able to contain them all on the left side of the truck; but as the herd began to overtake them it branched in two, with several of the giant beasts veering to the right of the truck and up the slight rise.

Despite the confusion, I refused to miss the shot I'd set up so carefully. With my eye to my main camera, I looked through my telephoto lens to isolate Tony among the teeming animals. I couldn't imagine I might be in any real danger. Then I glanced toward the speeding camera truck as it grew closer, and I saw Jake rip off his tether and launch himself toward me through the air. He caught me across the shoulders and turned under me to take the impact. After we hit the ground, he rolled on top of me to protect me from the pounding hooves thundering around us.

I lifted my head, trying to orient myself. The camera crew, absorbed completely in the shot at hand, apparently had no idea that Jake had thrown himself from the truck until they had finished the take. When they didn't hear his voice telling them to cut, the camera truck turned and sped back to the rise. The wranglers rushed in to herd the buffalo back to the corral and to retrieve Tony.

Jake and I were lying in a tangled heap in the dirt. Jake was bleeding profusely from what looked like a scalp laceration, and his body was heavy over mine.

"Jake?"

He didn't move. I rolled him on his back as I slid out from beneath him. Just semi-conscious, he groaned, clutching his side, his face covered in blood.

"Oh, God, Jake—please be okay!"

I cradled him in my arms. Visions rose in my mind of my bruised and bloody father lying lifeless as he was lifted into the ambulance, and I started to cry. The pain I had suppressed to be strong for my mother seemed to well up in my chest and burst free.

"Please don't die!" With his blood staining my jacket, I rocked back and forth as I held him and sobbed uncontrollably.

"Jesus, Maddy," he groaned through gritted teeth. "Why do you have to be so goddamn macho?"

"I'm sorry. I'm so sorry!" Tears poured down my cheeks. "God! I thought I'd killed you!"

"Good try, Garfield," he mumbled and then passed out.

The crew came running with the set doctor, who signaled for George to radio for an ambulance to take him to Mercy hospital back in Durango. Darlene rushed out with a blanket to cover him up, and I held him until the medics arrived to carry him away.

As I followed the stretcher toward the waiting vehicle, Harris Dunworth grabbed my arm. I tried to pull away.

"Leave me alone! I've got to go with Jake."

"Mr. Morganstern will be well cared for. We have a very large investment in him and this picture, and we intend to protect that investment." He jerked me around to look at him. "You, on the other hand, are expendable. You have jeopardized this entire production. Go pack your things. You're fired."

He released me and strode away as the ambulance drove off behind me with Jake inside.

I turned and, through my tears, saw it disappear over a rise, leaving nothing behind but the taste of dust in my mouth.

* * *

I said goodbye to Darlene and Franklin at the trailer. Darlene hugged me.

"Oh, Maddy, this is so unfair. It wasn't your fault the buffaloes ran the wrong way, for goodness sake! You were just doing your job."

Franklin was indignant. "Dunworth is such a prick. If he thinks his life is going to be easier without you on this shoot, he's got another thing coming. You've got *family* here, honey."

I hugged them both and returned to the camera truck to gather my remaing equipment. Gordon and Terry were there with the rest of the camera crew.

Gordon shook his head. "I understand the photographer's imperative, but this is a major setback. Let's just hope Jake will be okay. I'm really sorry the publicity department is reacting this way. I've seen the stuff you've been getting, and I know they'll never have a better still photographer on this picture than you."

"Thanks, Gordon. That means a lot to me, especially coming from you. I was only documenting what you and Jake have created."

I gathered my cameras and returned to the hotel to pack.

As I had been in Spain, I was horrified at the results of my determination to "get the shot." It had always been a basic part of my photographer's psyche to be so wrapped up in capturing the essential images that everything else dimmed in comparison. But I also knew that I had unwittingly put the entire production in jeopardy… and what was infinitely worse, Jake might be gravely injured.

Billy drove me to the Common Spirit Mercy Hospital, about twelve miles away, and we located Jake. He was sleeping, one arm draped across his face. His head was bandaged, and his chest was taped. I touched his hand, and he opened his eyes and smiled at me.

Relief overwhelmed me.

CHAPTER TWENTY-SEVEN

Exiled

Colorado to Los Angeles

"You missed a great ambulance ride." Jake tried to shift positions and winced.

"I'm so sorry." I held his hand in both of mine. "I'm really, really sorry."

Billy came up behind me and joked, "So, asshole, what's the verdict? Terminal heroism?"

Jake grinned ruefully. "Cracked rib." His words were slightly slurred. "Not so bad. At least they've got me thoroughly drugged, so it could be worse. I can be out of here in a day or two. We can still finish pretty close to on schedule. No more buffalo stunts, though. Give me a rewrite with rampaging rabbits."

"You got it, compadre. I'll even line up the rabbit wranglers for ya."

Jake smiled and closed his eyes, still holding tight to my hand. "You going to stay with me, Garfield?

"Only for a short while. I'm being exiled back to L.A. in the morning."

Jake snapped out of his drug-hazed stupor. "Who's exiling you?"

He tried to sit up but fell back, an agonized expression on his face.

"Please take it easy, Jake. Don't hurt yourself. Nothing can be done about it now. Dunworth's taken me off the picture. I've 'jeopardized the studio's assets,' and they're not about to let me stay. He's been looking for an excuse all along, and I guess I've given it to him."

I was truly contrite and must have looked forlorn, since Jake squeezed my hand, trying to comfort me.

"That little weasel will have to deal with me…" he shifted and groaned… "eventually. Billy, until I can do it myself, I want you to give this guy some grief. He doesn't know his assets from his ass."

Billy laughed and patted Jake's shoulder. "How about if I write a scene where a smarmy little asshole gets tarred and feathered? He'd be perfect casting."

"Don't worry about it, Jake." I leaned over the rail and kissed his forehead. "Just rest and get well. I'll stay with you as long as I can."

Billy patted him gently on the shoulder. "Rest easy, buddy." He turned to me. "I'll be back later to take you to the airport."

He left us alone.

"Put down the railing and lie next to me, Maddy," Jake whispered, holding tight to my hand.

I feigned shock. "I've already been accused of trying to kill you. I'm certainly not going to give Dunworth the satisfaction of actually doing it. Please take it easy. I don't want to hurt you again."

"'It's not a hurt I mind,' Maddy," Jake deadpanned, giving a perfect imitation of Brett's gruff delivery. "'It just reminds me I'm alive.'"

"And I suppose you 'intend to stay alive for a long, long time'?" I punctuated the line with kisses and laughed through my tears.

Jake nodded. "Unless you find some other way to kill me."

"Then you better behave yourself." I kissed his forehead "And I'll stay as long as I can."

I lowered the side of the bed and gently cuddled up beside him.

* * *

I flew back to L.A. relieved that Jake would recover but convinced that my career was over. I called my mother, weeping into the receiver.

"I almost killed Jake and got fired. I've ruined everything."

"And did you intend to kill Jake?"

She managed to make me laugh. "God, no! Are you kidding me?"

"Yes. And I'm glad to know he's okay."

"My life is such a mess. I thought this job would truly launch my career. And now it's over. And Jake—I love him so much, and now I don't know if I'll ever see him again."

"Oh, honey. The best advice I can give you is to have no expectations. We never know what will come next. Keep an open heart. All we know for sure is that *this, too, shall pass.*"

* * *

Darlene called me a few days later to tell me that my friends on the crew had initiated a silent conspiracy against Spencer Grant, Dunworth's handpicked photographer. According to her report, every time he lifted his camera to his eye, a crew member would walk prominently through the frame. If the actors were rehearsing, Darlene and Franklin would hover around them, fixing hair and makeup even if both were already perfect, in order to make any shot unusable. Darlene took particular delight in leaving white tissue paper sticking up around the actors' collars between shots, ostensibly to protect the costumes from makeup stains, of course.

John Taggart made a point of keeping his back to Spencer at all times. He even chased the frustrated photographer out of his sight-line during takes, a self-indulgence John himself usually only attributed to "prima donnas."

Each time Spencer did manage to find a usable angle, Gordon would readjust a lighting flag so that the lights would shine directly into his lens. He found it impossible to get a single usable still. When Tony directed him to "a great spot" for capturing his next stunt, Spencer ended up coated from head to toe in dust. It took him a full day to get the fine grit off his cameras and out of his hair.

Darlene overheard Dunworth, completely unaware of the subtle sabotage, begin criticizing the useless proof sheets.

"I can only assume," he had seethed at his "special" photographer, "that Miss Garfield got her job by sleeping with the director. But at least she produced usable art. What's your excuse for this?"

"I guess I just picked the wrong person to sleep with," Spencer retorted and stamped away in a cold fury.

Over the next two weeks, Darlene called with regular updates. Dunworth's vexation with the whole production was growing steadily and visibly. Darlene told me with glee that Jake had ceased to cooperate with any of the press visiting the set; he would retreat after each scene to his own production trailer "to rest, under doctor's orders." John Taggart had taken to hiding out there with Jake and, despite Allen Singer's pleas, refused to speak to anyone.

They all felt sorry for Allen, being caught in the middle of the war of attrition with Dunworth, but they would not relent. A few days later Allen let me know that he had finally summoned up enough courage to confront Dunworth.

"You might as well pack up the whole publicity campaign," Allen had told him. "Nobody is going to cooperate with us, Harris. Not as long as Maddy's gone."

Dunworth was nearly apoplectic. "*I* am the head of publicity, and I will not have anyone usurping my authority. *I'm* the one who hires photographers. I do not need *others* dictating what I should or should not do or whom I should or should not hire. She jeopardized this entire production, and I was well within my rights to fire her. Get away from me before I fire you, too."

As Allen had retreated, he'd overheard Dunworth speaking on the phone behind him and turned to look back.

"I'm sorry, Miss Blake," Dunworth was saying, "but it looks as though I will have to let her finish the shoot." He had cringed at the apparent outpouring of fury on the other end of the line but replied, "No. I understand, but the situation is untenable at the moment, and there isn't much I can do about it."

Moments after I heard this report from Allen, my phone rang again. Dunworth's voice was very tight; it was obviously an effort to force out the words.

"Madeleine, we would like to keep a consistent look to the art, so we are considering allowing you to finish shooting *Desperado*. We've decided to overlook your irresponsible behavior on the set, pending your reassurances that there will be no further such incidents to distract or endanger the director or delay the production. If you can agree to that, you'll be allowed to return to location to complete the job."

My relief at the prospect of returning to the production, my friends, and Jake was palpable. I struggled to be diplomatic.

"Thank you, Harris." I knew the familiar use of his first name would annoy him, but I couldn't resist. "I would like to finish the shoot."

I pointedly omitted any "assurances" about my behavior, my only concession to my suppressed resentment over my banishment.

I took a plane back to Colorado the next morning.

CHAPTER TWENTY-EIGHT

Colorado again, and Grace

Durango

The crew had a twofold cause for celebration that night: my return and Grace Taggart's arrival.

John's daughter was in her early thirties, tall and big-boned like her dad, with long, straight, light brown hair and a gentle face… and Billy was smitten at first sight. He rose to his feet and took off his black cowboy hat whenever she came near. He sat with her at lunch break. He regaled her with stories. She was visibly in awe of Brett and Amanda and was fascinated by the entire process of filmmaking, so Billy personally escorted her through the various sets, explaining everything, the customary expletives noticeably missing from his speech.

Grace and I had an immediate rapport. She soon confided in me that she saw in Billy the same roughhewn charm as in her father and was flattered by his attention and kindness. And she confessed that she couldn't stop wondering what it would be like to be caught up in a bear-like hug and whether his shaggy blond beard and mustache would tickle.

As confidants of Billy and Grace, Jake and I found ourselves playing matchmakers, and we didn't need to work at it. They were soon spending every possible moment together, and it became obvious that the glamour of shooting no longer held half the fascination for Grace that Billy held for her. She told me that she loved his earthy masculinity and his constant good humor. She loved his writing and his jokes and his large, calloused hands that held her like some fragile creature who might shatter with too rough a touch. Jake let me know that Billy had confessed that he loved Grace's openness, honesty, and lack of pretensions and the incisiveness of her mind when they discussed movies and literature.

It was a match made in heaven, and Jake and I made sure to give them every possible opportunity to be together.

* * *

When I entered the saloon after the day's wrap, Billy and Grace were dancing, and I'd never seen such a blissful expression on Billy's face. John sat at the bar with Jake, watching the couple, his expression unreadable.

Jake rose to hug me as I rushed into his arms. He winced.

"Oh, God, Jake. I forgot about the rib." I clapped my hand over my mouth, but he pulled me back into his arms.

"Just be gentle with me, woman," he whispered in my ear.

And I was.

I escorted him back to his room, carefully removed his clothing, and helped him into bed. Then I kissed him all over, my lips softly tracing paths down his neck, across his chest, and down his belly, luxuriating in his warmth and responsiveness.

"Don't move. Let me do everything." I licked him slowly, watching his face. He groaned and hardened, watching me with eyes half closed, a slight smile on his lips.

"You are an angel of mercy, Maddy, my love," he murmured, his breath catching.

I loved his warm, smooth skin and the hardness beneath it. Soon my explorations and experimentations had him groaning with pleasure. He ran his hands through my hair, and his breathing deepened and quickened.

"I just mean to have my way with you," I replied with glee, moving up to straddle his waist. I reached up and pulled the clip from my hair, letting it fall around my shoulders, and leaned forward to kiss his chest above the bandage, my hair following the path of my kisses.

I reached down to guide him between my thighs, and the sensations made me dizzy. He purred deep in his throat and reached to stroke between my legs. The rush of arousal almost made me lose my balance, but he grabbed my hip with his free hand to steady me and slowly pulled me down to surround him with my heat. I caught my breath as he eased into me. I found my rhythm and rocked slowly, as he stroked me and seemed to be studying me. His jaw tightened as he held back his orgasm.

Spurred on by his hardness and his hands, I was overwhelmed by sensation until, with a cry that triggered his own climax, fireworks exploded behind my eyes and throughout my body, and I fell forward, catching myself on my hands to keep from collapsing on Jake's wounded chest.

After a few minutes of savoring the pulsing aftershocks, I took his face in my hands and kissed him gently. "Pure altruism," I murmured. "Just like Florence Nightingale."

Jake laughed and pulled me down beside him to cuddle in his arms. "Your place in heaven is assured, sweet Florence."

We both fell asleep smiling.

* * *

Only a few production days remained, and the thought of everyone going their separate ways brought a lump to my throat. The end of a shoot generally marked the end of those special relationships and friendships. No matter how close people had become, everyone would disperse after the wrap party, only to see each other one last time several months down the road at the cast-and-crew screening. Everyone typically went on to new projects with other actors and crew members. Some, if they were very fortunate, might work together on something else in the future, but it was more common never to meet again, short of stumbling across someone socially at a random industry event.

I had studied the entire stack of proofs from the shoot, choosing the best frames to show Allen. He was visibly excited when he saw them.

"This will make a dynamite press kit," he said, genuinely impressed. He copied down the proof and frame numbers to order prints from the lab. "I can get all kinds of coverage with this stuff—*TIME, LIFE, People, Rolling Stone*. And I'll make sure they don't forget your credit." He gave me a wink and prepared to head back to Los Angeles.

The remaining schedule was hectic, the days running to sixteen and eighteen hours before wrapping. Jake and I could only manage to cast an occasional longing glance at each other. We would try to meet behind the sets when possible, but inevitably Jake would be needed to consult about something, and I was constantly being grabbed by various crew members to record special effects being rigged, or wardrobe needing to be documented, or simply to snap shots of the crew with the actors, which they could show to their families and treasure forever. Shots with Taggart were especially popular, and I kept an extra camera with me at all times just to get those "family photos."

CHAPTER TWENTY-NINE

The Wrap

Durango

On the final day of shooting, I made sure the call sheet listed that there would be a crew shot at the end of the day. I assembled all the director's chairs, ladders, planks, and every apple box the grips could find to make sure there would be a place in the shot for everyone.

As soon as the final scene was in the can, and Jake had announced, "That's a wrap!" the celebrating crew gathered in front of the saloon for the final still. I placed Jake, Billy, Amanda, Brett, John, and Gordon in the chairs, with Terry and the rest of the camera crew to their right, and Danny with the sound crew to their left. Hair, makeup, wardrobe, and stunt crew members stood behind them, and the grips, electricians, and wranglers balanced on the ladders and sat on planks braced between the rungs. George and the other assistant directors and production crew sat on the ground.

I had set up my camera on a tripod, and I made sure that every one of the eighty members of the cast and crew was clearly visible. Using a delayed flash, I ran in to grab the spot they had saved for me in the front row. The flash went off, and the crew cheered.

We held the wrap party on Saturday night in the huge barn set. The studio had sent in caterers, and tables were set up around the vast room, covered with everything from barbecued ribs to giant steamed prawns and crab claws with cocktail sauce. The central buffet held hand-carved turkeys and slabs of roast beef, massive tubs of homemade mashed potatoes, sliced glazed carrots and green beans with almonds. Other tables were laden with huge bowls of fresh fruit, various salads, and dozens of assorted desserts.

The crew downed oceans of margaritas and laughed and hooted and made outrageous comments as they watched a reel of the funniest outtakes from the shoot.

A live country-western band played until ten. When they took a break, Jake jumped onstage and whispered something in the lead singer's ear. He smiled, consulted with the other band members, and then nodded to Jake, who waved Billy, Danny, and Tony to come on stage. Jake grabbed the microphone.

"And now, for the first and only time, I'd like to present the Pinnacle Outlaws!"

With Billy on bass guitar, Danny on rhythm guitar, Tony on drums, and Jake on lead guitar and vocals, they launched into a ragged but enthusiastic rendition of Del Shannon's "Runaway," to the delighted whoops of the crowd.

Darlene and I played the roles of adoring fans, screaming and reaching for them. Jake flashed a roguish grin at me, his hair falling forward into his eyes as he sang, and I felt like an adrenalized teenager again. When the makeshift band launched into "Dream Lover," Darlene and I jumped onstage to sing background vocals.

They finished with the Stones' "Satisfaction," to a roar of approval from the dancing crowd, and finally relinquished the instruments to the real band, followed by wild cheering and applause.

"So, you're a rock star too, huh?" I teased as Jake swept me back into his arms to dance.

"Well, I wouldn't go that far. Billy and I and a few other guys messed around at NYU, playing local parties for a while—the world's shortest rock 'n' roll career."

"I should have guessed you were a musician."

"Why? What was the giveaway?

"'Cause you're so good with your hands, of course!"

Jake pulled me closer. "Watch what you say, woman, or I'll take you right here on the dance floor. I'll show you how good I can be with my hands."

I laughed, thrilled at his favorite "threat," and pressed back against him as we turned and swayed to the music.

Darlene and Tony, Billy and Grace, and Jake and I danced until near dawn, when we were all barely able to stand, and the exhausted hired band finally called it quits. We three couples said goodnight to each other and wandered away from the barn in pairs.

Jake took me aside. "The studio thinks we have a good shot at Academy nominations if I can get the film done quickly, so it can go into release and qualify before the end of the year. The schedule they're demanding is insane. I don't know how

I'll finish editing and scoring in time, so please be patient if you don't hear from me for a while."

I swallowed back my fears of losing him and said, "I understand."

"We'll be together back in L.A. before long," Jake said, trying to reassure me as we finally made it to the hotel in the misty early dawn. "Once the movie is ready to screen, we'll have more time."

"I'm going to miss you."

I slid my arms under his jacket and around his waist, my head thrown back to gaze into his face. He smiled and kissed me softly.

"I'll miss you, too. I'll be living in the editing room for several weeks after we finish getting everything wrapped around here, but I'll definitely be seeing you again, Garfield. I promise you that."

He kissed me again, very gently, and I had a terrible premonition that he was saying goodbye.

CHAPTER THIRTY

The Sound of Silence

Los Angeles, California

I was totally exhausted when I arrived home at midday on Sunday. I dropped my bags and equipment in the living room and collapsed on the bed, too tired to unpack or even undress.

I slept for fourteen hours.

When I awoke, I felt dizzy and ill. I staggered to the bathroom to wash my face and was shocked to see how pale and haggard I looked.

I changed into some sweatpants and an oversized T-shirt and made myself a can of soup, but the smell of it made me gag. I finally climbed back into bed and curled up around a pillow and fell asleep again, drifting off while remembering the sensations of being enfolded in Jake's arms.

Tuesday, I forced myself out of bed to go meet Allen for lunch to discuss the press kit. As I climbed into my car, I was hit with another wave of nausea. I sat behind the wheel, breathing deeply and waiting for it to pass.

After a few minutes I started the engine and drove to Lucy's El Adobe Cafe, across from the studio, to meet Allen. He was waiting for me inside the iconic Mexican restaurant, where the dark brick walls were covered with hundreds of signed movie star headshots. He greeted me with a hug.

"Jeez, Maddy…" He escorted me to a booth before adding, "…you look like hell."

"Gee, thanks, Allen. Nice to see you, too." I gave him a wan smile. "Too many night shoots. I think I must be coming down with the flu."

The smell of the refried beans forced me excuse myself and rush to the bathroom. I dry heaved with nothing in my stomach to lose, then washed my face, took a deep breath, and returned to the table.

"I'm really sorry, Allen. I hope I'm not contagious."

I carefully sipped some vegetable soup and soon felt decidedly better.

Allen told me of his plans for the publicity campaign for the film and asked me to pick the photos I felt would make the best magazine cover shots and large blowups.

His enthusiasm was boundless. "The industry buzz on *Desperado* is amazing. The studio is already planning a campaign to get John Taggart nominated for an Oscar. Word is that this could be a huge commercial success. This could be JT's breakthrough from an art house audience to a mainstream one. It could be very big."

I tried to keep my voice light and conversational. "Have you heard from Jake?"

"Hell, no. He's been locked in an editing room round the clock, last I heard. The studio moved up the release date to get it into Oscar contention, so he's working under an impossible deadline."

I sighed. "He must be under a lot of pressure."

I forced down the last of my soup, hoping the nausea was gone for good.

On the way home, I stopped at the lab to pick up the prints of my portraits of Hannah and Michael Redwolf and mailed the photos off to Colorado. By the time I got home I was completely exhausted. The phone was ringing as I came through the door, and I rushed to grab it, hoping it was Jake.

It was Darlene. "Put on the teapot, girl. I'm on my way over."

I dragged myself to the kitchen and put on the kettle and rummaged through the cupboard to find some crackers. Darlene came breezing through the door just as the tea had finished brewing.

"Check out the rock!" Darlene flashed her hand in front of my glazed eyes. "Tony wants to marry me!" she sang, dancing around the room for a second before coming up short in front of me. "My God, girl. Are you sick?" She put her hand on my forehead. "Hmm. You don't feel like you have a fever. But you look awful."

"I don't know what's the matter with me. I've been feeling sick ever since I got back. I figured it was not enough sleep and too much good old L.A. smog to welcome me home. But it doesn't seem to be getting any better. I can't seem to hold anything down."

Darlene gave me a suspicious look. "Are you late?"

"Huh?" It took a second for the question to sink in. "Oh. God. I don't know. I didn't keep track during the shoot and… oh, God." I sank down on the couch.

"Wow." Darlene sat down next to me. "Did you and Jake take any precautions?"

"I was so swept away, I didn't care." I chewed on my lower lip, staring out the window at nothing.

"Jesus, Maddy. Are you serious? I thought you'd at least protect yourself, even if he wouldn't. You'd better find out for sure if you're knocked up." She fell silent momentarily and then asked, "What will you do if you are?"

I crossed my arms over my midsection. "It would be a beautiful baby," l whispered, more to myself than to Darlene. "Jake's baby."

"Hey. Hey, you with the faraway look. Back to planet Earth, girl. Are you talking about trying to go through with it? On your own? Shouldn't you maybe talk to Jake before any decisions are made? How the hell could you support yourself and a baby? You barely support yourself as it is. He should take some responsibility here, don't you think?"

"He has a lot of responsibilities right now."

Responsibility. I remembered our conversation in the valley… his resistance and reluctance to be coerced into being responsible for someone else. Having to live up to the expectations of others. A victim of circumstance. That's not the way I wanted this to happen.

I closed my eyes and groaned, sinking deeper into the couch.

I changed the subject to chat about Darlene's upcoming nuptials, and then we gossiped awhile over our tea until she patted me on the knee and rose to leave.

"You better find out for sure about your condition. And call Jake."

I nodded. "I don't want to pressure him. But don't worry. I won't be stupid about it. No rash decisions. Please keep this between us for now."

I knew she was right, but I also realized the tremendous pressure he was already dealing with.

"Well, keep me posted."

Darlene closed the door behind her, and l closed my eyes. I imagined Jake's arms around me and my arms around our baby.

* * *

It was three weeks since I had officially discovered that I was strong, healthy, and pregnant, and the late-August heat wave felt unbearable. I'd phoned my mother, who'd asked if I wanted to come home to Berkeley, but I reassured her that I was fine and could handle it myself.

Jake had not called since my return to L.A.

I was torn between wanting to shout my joy about the baby and give in to despair over Jake's absence. I kept telling myself that he really loved me and was just under tremendous pressure to get the film finished. But another voice kept reminding me of his reputation and the fact that I hadn't heard from him at all. Worse still, I worried that he might consider the pregnancy another burden, another imposed responsibility.

I sat by the phone for an hour, trying to summon enough courage to dial the Blake mansion, where he always stayed in L.A., and I almost hung up during the long interval while the phone rang on his end of the line.

Finally a voice answered… a refined female voice. In the background I could hear sounds of a raucous party in progress.

"May I speak to Jake Morganstern, please?"

"Who is this?" The voice at the other end was decidedly hostile, and I could guess who it must belong to.

I tried desperately to keep my own voice strong and steady, but I was shaking all over.

"Would you tell him Maddy Garfield is on the line?"

"Oh. Madeleine, isn't it? That photographer from the shoot? Jake is far too busy to speak with you. If you have questions about the film's promotional campaign, please contact the studio publicity people." She overemphasized the words as if I were hard of hearing.

"Christine?" I found myself rapidly losing all semblance of calm, panic rising rapidly to constrict my throat. "I… I thought you and Jake had separated."

There was a pause before she replied evenly, "I can't imagine why you'd think so. That's not the way these things go. Why throw away a perfectly good relationship of many years' duration over a location fling? He's decided to be a good boy, and I've decided not to leave him."

I was in shock. I tried to keep my voice from rising. "I don't believe you."

"It doesn't really matter what you believe, dear. You may delude yourself in any way you choose, but it isn't really our concern. Don't bother to call again."

The line clicked and went dead.

I was incredulous. My hand trembled as I hung up the receiver and fought the anger and despair rising in my chest.

A "location fling"? Is that all it was?

I wanted to trust my instincts. I had to believe that what we had was real.

I refused to cry myself to sleep. As always, my last thoughts before drifting off were of Jake's arms around me, his warm lips on mine.

* * *

Darlene was furious. "That bastard!" she raged. "How can he play around with people's emotions like that?" She flopped down on the couch. "Really, Maddy. I can't believe you're going through with it."

I stared out the window, stroking my still-flat belly through my T-shirt. "It doesn't matter. I want this baby. I don't know if it was love for him, but it was for me." My eyes began to blur with tears. "This part of him is mine. I can do this on my own if I need to. If he wants me, he knows where to find me."

"You have to let him know!" Darlene fumed, then hugged me. "Okay, I might think you've lost your mind, but you do know that I'm here for you, Maddy. You just let me know what you need, hon, and I'll do whatever I can."

* * *

Without the option to call again, I wrote a letter to Jake at the Blake mansion, telling him I needed to see him, but got no reply. Finally, I called Billy to find out where Jake was editing the film.

"He's at Pinnacle, but he's losing it from the pressure. He's not taking any calls, and he's told the studio staff not to admit visitors. I know. I've tried."

Knowing that Dunworth would never call in a drive-on pass for me—I was still persona non grata with him—I tried to drive onto the lot without one but was turned away. In a stealth maneuver, I parked across the street near Lucy's Café, went back to the studio entrance on foot, and entered at the walk-in gate by blending in with of a group of executives who were returning from lunch.

I stopped at the commissary to ask for directions to the editing rooms and then headed there. As I approached the editors' building, I saw Christine leaving, and my heart sank. I waited while she got into her convertible and drove off without noticing me.

I climbed the steps and wandered around the building until I heard the sound of John Taggart's recorded voice coming from the end of the hallway, speaking the dialog from the lynch-mob scene. I peered through the door and saw an editor at the Moviola, surrounded by dozens of strips of film hanging on racks. A rumpled sleeping bag lay on the floor amid a pile of empty pizza boxes, bottles, and cans.

Then I spotted Jake at the back of the room, looking disheveled and gaunt. He was arguing with the editor about the sequence of shots, pausing only to lean over a table and snort a line of white powder, which I figured was cocaine. He glanced up and saw me.

"Maddy?"

I turned and ran back down the hallway with Jake in pursuit.

He reached out and grabbed my arm. "What are you doing here?"

I couldn't hide my anger and disappointment. "Coke? Really, Jake?"

"Give me a break, Garfield. Don't be so fucking judgmental. I've been awake for days and just have to get through this. Somehow."

At the other end of the hall, the editor stuck his head out the door. "Come on, JT. No time to socialize."

I jerked my arm out of his grasp. "I get it. Finish your movie. We can 'socialize' another time."

I fled down the steps, across the lot, and out the gate, tears blurring the surroundings as I ran. I wept all the way home. I didn't know what the future would hold for me, but I knew I could have no expectations and that I needed to be strong enough to handle this on my own.

My answering service's operator reported the calls I'd received: my mother worrying about me, Darlene worrying about me, a few possible job referrals, and a call from Jake Morgenstern. The message they related to me was short: "Tell her I'm sorry."

* * *

As late summer turned to fall, I tried to push thoughts of Jake from my mind. He had a job to do, and so did I. I concentrated on finding work and preparing for the baby.

I landed a job on a TV series at Universal called *Scary Tales*, an anthology of supernatural stories that needed a photographer two or three days a week. At least for those hours, it kept me active, out of the house, and away from the telephone.

Work was enough to cover the rent and basic bills and to keep my mind occupied most of the time. But my swelling midsection was an inescapable reminder of my situation and of Jake. Though my emotions were a roller coaster of joy and despair, the show provided me with a community of people who enjoyed my company and an outlet for my skills. It kept my sanity intact.

When I felt the baby's first butterfly movements inside me, I wanted to shout and laugh and share it with someone. The crew of *Scary Tales* treated my belly as if it were community property, constantly patting it and rubbing it. This phenomenon never ceased to amaze me. I couldn't imagine anyone walking up to a woman they barely knew and rubbing her stomach under other circumstances, but it happened almost daily as my mid-section expanded.

My mom flew down and joined me and Darlene to march in an antinuclear rally, which I shot for an extensive article in *Rolling Stone* The recent opening of several nuclear power plants near populated areas like Three Mile Island, had awakened a lot of former peace advocates to a new threat to the future. The small life growing inside me made me even more committed to stopping the spread of such facilities and to protecting the environment for future generations.

My mother hugged me. "Gotta make the world safe for my grandchild!"

Between work assignments and other pursuits, I was active and felt useful and was rarely at home with time to brood.

Rolling Stone contacted me about shooting a new British band that had specifically requested me. When I heard the band's name, I knew why: *Percy Verance* had a new hit single written by Colin Jones.

Colin, resplendent in rocker velvet and leather, was visibly surprised at the sight of my prominent belly.

"Maddy! My God. You're going to be a mum?"

"Apparently so."

"I don't see a ring on your fingah. Did the bloke who did this desert you?"

"It's not that simple, but I can handle this on my own."

He got down on one leather-clad knee. "Marry me, Maddy-girl. I'll make an honest woman of ya."

He winked, and I laughed, pulled him to his feet, and hugged him.

"A very kind offer. How would you like to be the baby's godfather?"

He looked both relieved and pleased. "I would be honored."

I spent the entire day with the band members as they posed in alleys, in trees, on fire escapes. The session was playful and filled with laughter, everyone contributing ideas. On the Venice Beach boardwalk, the band was accosted by screaming girls, so I documented the frenzied pleas for autographs and recruited the fans to be background "extras" in another round of shots.

"Is stardom everything you hoped for?" I asked Colin as I rewound my last roll of film on the drive back to the record company offices.

He shrugged. "It's better than being a roadie. Lots o' lovely birds makin' a fuss. Can't deny that."

When we said goodbye, Colin hugged me and whispered, "If you need anyfing, luv, you let me know. I will always be there for you, my girl."

* * *

In late November I received an invitation to the press, cast, and crew screening of *Desperado*. I was torn between wishing to avoid the humiliation of being perceived as Jake's discarded plaything and my desire to reunite with all my friends, to see the finished film, and—as hard as it was to admit—to see Jake again. I resolved to go and to do so with pride.

CHAPTER THIRTY-ONE

The Screening

Beverly Hills

On a hurried shopping excursion, I had found a burgundy velvet-and-lace dress with tiny gold buttons down the front and an empire waist, which accommodated my round-but-compact belly. The neckline of the dress exposed the new fullness of my breasts, so I put on an antique gold-and-garnet necklace, which drew additional attention to my neck and swelling cleavage, and added matching Edwardian earrings.

I tied part of my hair back with lace and ribbons, leaving the rest to fall in curling tendrils around my face, and was just finishing applying eye makeup when Darlene and Tony arrived to take me to the screening.

When I made my entrance into the living room, Tony's jaw dropped.

Darlene practically squealed. "You look absolutely gorgeous! You're going to make him eat his heart out," she crowed, breaking into giggles as they whisked me out the door.

I didn't hear a word of the conversation in the car. I looked out the window, rehearsing my meeting with Jake in my mind and planning how calm and composed I'd be.

"Yeah, right," my cynical inner voice replied. *"You? Calm around Jake? That'll be the day."*

We pulled up to the Academy Theater on Wilshire, and Darlene and I got out and walked to the check-in table, while Tony drove around the corner to park in the garage. Press members and the film's crew were gathering at the entrance. The crowd spilled out to the sidewalk, where barricades held back some avid movie fans, including many who haunted the facility regularly, hoping to catch sight of arriving stars.

After we checked in, Darlene went back to the door to wait for Tony while I entered the lobby. I glanced up, then stopped short and caught my breath.

The vast space was filled with huge blowups of my photographs, displayed gallery-style on every wall and on broad, square pillars around the room. The prints ranged from sixteen-by-twenty-inch to poster size, and they documented all my favorite moments.

There was John Taggart's craggy face, both among the ancient tree branches and in the glow of the mob torches. There was the saloon fight, the dust-filtered light giving the impression of a classic Western painting. There were the sepia portraits of the old-timers with their guns and the steely-eyed portrait of Brett. There was the massive panorama of the entire set from high up on the crane, the backlit love scene with Brett and Amanda, and the final shot of Amanda on the hill at sunset with Brett returning across the valley.

There was the crew shot, with every single one of us clearly visible. And there was the photo of Jake, standing at the crest of our valley, his hair windblown and his eyes soft, looking back at me from the photo as if he could see me in real time.

I was overwhelmed. A lump rose in my throat, and I fought back the tears that began to well up as I remembered that perfect moment.

"Garfield?"

The familiar deep voice penetrated my reverie, and the baby kicked in response. I turned to face Jake, my hand resting protectively on my belly. My heart was in my throat, and I could barely breathe.

He had aged in the previous four months. He was only thirty-two, but there was more premature gray at his temples. Though he still looked gaunt and tired, his eyes held all the warmth and amusement of the face in the photo of him behind me.

"How do you like what they've done with your photos?"

"It's wonderful, Jake. I'm a little overwhelmed. I didn't expect…"

His eyes traveled from my face to my belly and back again.

"Maddy, are you… are you…?"

I had never seen him at a loss for words before.

"I'm fine, Jake."

I suddenly realized I was unconsciously stroking my belly and lowered my hand. "How are you?" I lifted my chin and straightened my back. "And how is Christine?"

As the overhead lights flickered to signal that the film was about to start, the crowd in the lobby began surging toward the huge staircase that led to the enormous theater upstairs.

"Christine? I don't know what you're thinking." He took my hand. "But we'll talk about all this afterward. You're not getting away from me tonight."

He wrapped my arm around his, held my hand in place so I couldn't pull away, and escorted me to the east side of the lobby, where we took a small elevator up to the theater level.

Embarrassed by the spontaneous rush of joy I felt at his touch, I struggled to maintain an air of detached dignity as we went inside to get seats and listened to the producer's greeting and introduction. I saw Darlene and Tony at the entrance to the theater behind me, and I waved, but they couldn't see me in the dim light as they found vacant seats farther back.

After the screening began, I was intensely aware of Jake's presence next to me and could sense his eyes on me in the darkness. He held my hand, stroking it with his fingers and wreaking havoc with my resolve to remain calm and analytical. I forced myself to concentrate on the film.

Desperado flowed with the natural pace of a river, each scene contributing more depth and breadth to the whole, with action, humor, and drama perfectly blended. The performances were spellbinding, and John's in particular was a revelation of subtlety and heartfelt emotion.

When the lights finally came up to a burst of sustained, enthusiastic applause, I realized I had been holding my breath during the credits. I turned to congratulate Jake, but he leaned over and gently touched his lips to mine before I could utter a word. The current that shot through me made the baby kick and turn, and I jerked and put my free hand over the traveling small lump beneath the velvet. Jake noticed my reaction and glanced down, a sweet mixture of amusement and concern on his face.

He stood and leaned down, still holding my hand, and whispered, "Don't even think of leaving. Just stay with me until this is over. We must talk." I nodded and accompanied him back to the lobby, where a lavish reception was already in progress. Massive tables overflowed with food, wines, and elegant desserts.

Billy came flying across the room with Grace in tow, laughing and breathless, and lifted me off the ground.

"Hot damn!" he bellowed. "Do we have one helluva movie or what?" He grunted and set me back on my feet. "Jeez, Maddy, have you gotten heavier since last time I picked you up, or am I just getting old?"

He glanced down and suddenly realized my condition, and words momentarily deserted him. He narrowed his eyes at Jake. "This your doin', old buddy?"

Grace gave Billy a not-so-subtle elbow in the ribs and said, "The movie was wonderful, Jake." She hugged him briefly and turned to me. "And your photos of my dad are the best I've ever seen. We should all get together for dinner, very soon."

She hugged me and dragged Billy off before he could ask any more questions.

"Looks like Billy's being taught the fine art of diplomacy," Jake whispered to me as we were surrounded by well-wishers.

Across the lobby I spotted Brett shaking hands and accepting congratulations. When his willowy companion turned in my direction, I realized with a shock that it was Christine Blake, who briefly locked eyes with me, nostrils flaring, and then returned to fawning over Brett. I felt a moment of sympathy for the actor but was relieved that she had found another date for the occasion.

Jake and I fielded compliments for his film and my photos for an hour. Finally, he led me past a wide-eyed Darlene and Tony and out a side exit into the crisp November evening, pausing only to wrap me in his coat before practically dragging me to his car.

He sped up Crescent Heights Boulevard to Laurel Canyon, tearing along the narrow, winding roads up into the hills. He pulled through double gates into a long drive leading to a rustic cabin surrounded by pine and eucalyptus, where he parked and ushered me into the house.

Everything was made of redwood and oak, and it was much larger and more spacious than it appeared from the outside. Jake piled some logs in the massive stone fireplace and lit a fire before joining me on the dark leather couch.

He took my hand. "Talk to me, Maddy. Why didn't you tell me? I should have known about this…"

He tried to pull me into his arms, but I resisted, my back stiff, my chin set.

"I tried to tell you. I tried to call you and wrote to you, too. I even went to the editing room intending to tell you, but I didn't realize you were still with Christine. She told me you never wanted to hear from me again."

The hurt came bubbling up, and my self-possession

threatened to dissolve in angry tears.

"Christine told you... God, Maddy! I never even knew you had called or written. That woman is a witch! I wouldn't live with her if my life depended on it."

He sat back and ran his hand through his hair, seeming to gather his thoughts.

"We broke up months ago. She only decided to invade my life again when she returned to L.A. and just hung on because she heard that *Desperado* might be a commercial success. She didn't want to miss out on 'her' share of the glory if I was going to make anything from this. She brought the coke to the editing room, too. What a mistake that was. I was crazed, just living in there, trying to get this movie done... but the drugs only made things worse."

"So you're done with that? And with Christine?"

"Completely. She stayed at her father's house, and I moved here. I got this place so I would have a retreat, so I would never have to see her again." He turned and took my hands. "I tried to call to apologize for my crazed state and not being able to spend time with you, but you were never home, so I finally just left a message. I figured you were okay and busy and that I'd finish the film, and then we'd be fine... but I lost track of time, working round the clock, and I was so exhausted. I just kept thinking you'd be there when it was all over. I wanted to surprise you tonight with the display of your photos. I had no idea what you were going through. I didn't realize..."

He took me into his arms. "I'll never take you for granted again. Oh, God, Maddy, I'm so sorry. How could you have gone through this alone?" He pulled back suddenly, his brow furrowed. "You haven't found someone else?"

"I didn't want anyone else. I just wanted you. And since I couldn't have you," I stroked my belly, "at least I had part of you."

Jake took my hand and kissed the palm. Then he leaned down and kissed my belly.

"You have all of me, sweetheart."

The logs in the fireplace crackled and sent up sparks as I ran my hand through his hair and pulled his face to my lips. He swept me into his arms, his gentle mouth locked on mine, tender, searching, hungry for me. My veins flowed with warm honey, melting my resistance as his hands unhooked the tiny gold buttons of my gown.

"I want to see you, Maddy."

He kissed each inch of soft skin he revealed as he opened my dress and exposed my breasts and belly. "You're more beautiful than ever."

His warm lips and hot breath caressed my skin as his large hands supported my full breasts. His mouth was gentle on my nipples, his tongue circling and pulling.

I moaned and dissolved into the riot of sensations flooding me. He moved lower, his arm around my hips, his hand gently stroking the taut skin, his lips warm on my belly.

Our baby moved.

Jake looked up into my face with wonderment and delight in his eyes. "Wow. I think I just got kicked."

"You deserve it," I replied with a mock frown.

"I know." Jake looked contrite. "And you deserve so much better."

My dress was completely undone, the burgundy velvet now simply a background for my bared body.

With a mischievous gleam in his eye, he moved lower. "You can have faith in me. I promised to always try to give you what you need." He slid my panties off, slipped his hand under my bottom, and lifted my leg over his shoulder. "And I meant it."

He ran his lips up the inside of my thigh as his free hand stroked me. I felt myself swelling and blossoming, opening to his touch. I gasped as his warm tongue gently stroked between the soft folds, exploring, circling, the rush of pleasure sweeping me away, the world once again dissolving into bright shimmering light.

Nothing existed except Jake's mouth joined to my body and the torrents of liquid fire flooding me. His fingers and tongue urged me on, my excitement mounting beyond any semblance of control until, with an explosion of color behind my eyes and deep in my womb, all tension released, pulsing deep inside, tendrils of fire flying off into space as I floated back to Earth.

When I opened my eyes at last, there was Jake's face above me, observing me. I could see many things in his eyes. I saw a certain cocky pride for having caused such obvious bliss… but also an affection so gentle and true that it left me without defenses.

He looked so pleased that I began to laugh and covered my face. "Oh, God, I've done it again. I can't resist you. It's terrible."

Jake laughed and gathered me into his arms, smoothing down my disheveled hair, stroking my belly, and kissing me lightly on the lips.

"No, Maddy. It's wonderful. I can't resist you, either. We're perfect for each other. I know it will take time to sort everything out, but please bear with me. Stay here with me. You can have your own room to retreat to whenever you can't stand to spend another second with me. There's plenty of room for a nursery. Stay with me, Maddy. Let's do this together."

He kissed my belly again, and I grabbed his face and kissed him fervently.

"Oh, yes, Jake. I want that, too. God, I'm so happy."

He swept me into his arms and hugged me and, taking my hand, led me upstairs. I surrendered again… this time, to sleep.

CHAPTER THIRTY-TWO

Creating Family

Hollywood

We were awakened just after dawn the next morning by the sound of a ringing phone. Jake tried to ignore it, but it wouldn't stop, so he finally relented in case it was urgent.

It was Billy on the other end. "Jake! Wake up, man! You gotta come quick. It's John. They think he's had a heart attack."

We jumped in the car and headed downhill to the newly opened Cedars-Sinai Medical Center, a mile south of Jake's canyon house. In the hospital waiting room, Billy was giving Grace emotional support as best he could, and I hugged them as we anxiously awaited an update on John's condition.

Eventually Jake couldn't sit still anymore and walked away to stretch his legs. After awhile I saw him leaning against the gray-green wall of the nearby corridor, deep in thought. I stood up to join him when the studio's infamous head of publicity suddenly approached him.

"Any news? Will he be able to do press?"

Jake shook his head in disbelief and, eyes narrowing, lifted his gaze from the floor to Dunworth's face. "That's not exactly the highest priority at the moment," he replied through clenched teeth.

"No. Of course not. We're all very concerned for John's well-being, of course."

I could see that Jake's temper was rising. "I'm sure the rest of us would be more than willing to fill in for John to help promote the film."

"But the studio does need to know if he's going to be able to complete his contractual obligations. Not the best timing for this, was it?"

Jake had been trying to keep his anger in check but failed. He grabbed Dunworth by the lapels of his expensive Italian suit and slammed him against the wall, with his toes barely touching the ground. "Have a little respect. This may be inconvenient for you, but it's a matter of life and death for John, you fucking weasel."

"You're upset," Dunworth sputtered. "Understandably upset. Perhaps this is just not the moment or the right place to be discussing the promotion of the film. Perhaps we should all calm down and discuss this at another time."

"Perhaps we should."

Jake released him, and Dunworth dropped to his heels. He straightened his tie and his hair and turned to leave, scowling as he caught sight of me standing quietly several feet away, wearing my burgundy dress from the night before. He glanced from me back to Jake, raised an eyebrow, then left quickly through the double doors. I walked over to Jake and put my arms around him.

"Isn't my former boss charming?" I cocked my head, trying to keep a straight face. "I suspect that I'll never work at Pinnacle again."

A nurse stuck her head out of the intensive care unit door. "Mr. Morganstern? Mr. Taggart is asking for you."

Jake gave me a quick kiss and followed the nurse.

I watched from just inside the doorway as Jake entered the intensive care unit, obviously disheartened by the tubes and wires and blinking lights surrounding John. From where we each stood, Taggart's face was in profile, as if chiseled out of some great, craggy mountain. Intermittent blips sounded from the machine behind his head.

Jake approached the bed, with Grace seated on the other side.

"How are you feeling, John?"

Taggart opened his eyes and gave Jake a grim smile. "I can recall having felt better," he joked in a hoarse whisper. "Come close, boy. I want to talk to you."

Jake leaned in to catch every word.

"You've done me a great service, Jake, letting me play the part of Harlan James. You gave me back something I thought I'd lost a long time ago. You gave me back the joy of creating something again. And getting to know this daughter of mine better. What a gift she's been! I've done a lot of stupid things in my life. But the worst was having love and then letting it slip away from me. I missed so much… so much. Lived too solitary a life, wasted so much precious time. You're a good man, Jake. You're smart…" He paused, struggling for breath.

"Maybe you should rest now." Jake started to straighten up, then added, "John, your whole career is a legacy to the world. There isn't a person alive who doesn't appreciate what you've given them."

John shook his head. "Smoke and mirrors, boy. Play acting. It's a wonderful game, and we're lucky to get to play it, but it's not life. Listen to me, Jake. Don't end up alone. You need to make a life with a good woman… make a real home, have a family…" His voice trailed off, his breathing labored.

The nurse hurried over. "You'd better go, Mr. Morganstern."

John gave him a last glance. "That Maddy's a fine girl," he whispered.

Jake smiled and nodded, and we left the ICU hand in hand.

* * *

Desperado premiered just before Christmas, qualifying it for Oscar consideration, and was Pinnacle's biggest opening of the year. Jake was jubilant. The film established him in the big leagues, beyond the limitations of an art house director. We were relieved to learn that John survived by-pass surgery, was recovering from his heart attack, and was thrilled that the studio had launched a campaign to nominate him for an Academy Award.

As the new year began, I turned my energies inward. I prepared a nursery for the baby at Jake's home in Laurel Canyon and read every book about birth I could get my hands on. I kept thinking about how wonderful it would be to have Hannah as my midwife. Jake did his best to attend birthing classes with me, but Dunworth and the studio had him on a brutal schedule of promotional appearances on talk shows around the country that kept us apart too much to maintain any real continuity.

* * *

A few weeks later I was curled up reading in a giant, overstuffed armchair when the phone rang. It was Jake, calling from out-of-town.

"God, Maddy, I miss you! Listen… the promo tour will be ending in Denver in ten days. Why don't you meet me at the Colorado cabin? It's all finished and ready for us. We could even invite your mom, if you want. I can arrange plane tickets for both of you."

I was thrilled at the prospect. I immediately phoned my mother to tell her a ticket was coming, so she could make arrangements to cover the club during her absence. Then I called Hannah to let her know I was on my way there.

CHAPTER THIRTY-THREE

A Storm

Pagosa Springs, Colorado

Since our flights arrived just an hour apart, we connected in the terminal, where my mother hugged me and remarked on how "compact" I looked, even though I felt enormous. We chatted while waiting for our connecting flight to Durango, where Hannah would be meeting us for the drive to the cabin.

When we stepped outside the smaller airport building in Durango, we were greeted by a blast of icy air that stung our faces. We loaded our bags into Hannah's truck and headed out into the starkly beautiful countryside on the way to our valley. Hannah and my mom got along like long-lost sisters from the moment they met, which made my heart sing with joy.

Michael greeted us at the cabin with hugs, everyone's breath making little clouds in the frigid air. They bundled us into the house, where he had built a fire in the massive stone fireplace and stacked piles of wood on the hearth and porch to keep it well supplied.

"The pictures you sent us are the best we've ever had," Michael told me as he carried our luggage in from the car. "It's the first time I've ever seen a photo that really shows how beautiful Hannah is."

She chimed in. "I didn't realize what a handsome guy I was married to 'til I saw those photos. I guess I did all right." She shot a teasing grin at Michael. "The whole community was impressed."

Mom went to put her things away, while Hannah unpacked warm quilts for the bed and food for the kitchen as she checked me out with her expert eye. "When are you due?"

I groaned. "Not for another month yet, but I already feel like a beached whale."

Hannah hugged me. "I know exactly how you feel, but you look good. I'd guess only few weeks away at most. Nice big baby."

I shuddered. "Oh, please don't say that! Say 'Nice *little* baby,' please."

She laughed. "Babies are designed to be born, whatever size they are. They mold themselves to fit their mamas. So don't panic. It's going to be just fine. You're still carrying high; you've got some time. I'm glad your mom's here to keep you company. And I'm not far away if you need me." She hugged me again. "I'll be coming by to check on you."

"We're planning to be back in L.A. at least two weeks before I'm due, but I'm glad my mom is here and you're nearby. Takes some of the worry out of it for me. God knows Jake wouldn't have a clue if he tried to deliver this baby."

We shared a laugh just imagining that scene.

* * *

The storm had already lasted more than a week by the time Jake was due to arrive. The wind was wailing outside, and drifts had piled up against the house, but Mom and I had hauled in enough firewood to last an entire winter, and her vegetable soup was simmering in a huge pot on the stove.

By afternoon, Jake still hadn't shown up or called. I figured his plane had to have come in several hours earlier, but I hadn't heard a word. I finally lifted the receiver to my ear to try calling the airport, but there was no dial tone.

"Damn." I bit my lip and contemplated being completely without contact with the outside world.

"No phone service?" My mother's eyes widened. "What if you go into labor?"

A thump from outside sent me rushing to the front door, only to be greeted with a blast of icy air and wetness. A tree branch had broken off and landed on the porch… but no sign of Jake.

I struggled to close the door against the force of the wind, and my stomach tightened. I'd been having "Braxton Hicks" contractions all day, off and on, accepting them as my body's warm-up practice for labor, but this one seemed more intense and lasted longer.

"Stop it," I said to my belly. "You're *not* getting born yet, so just cut it out."

I curled up on the couch with my birthing book and tried to keep my mind off Jake and the storm. My belly tightened again, even more intensely, and I checked my watch. It lasted about forty-five seconds—much longer than any trial contractions.

"If this is the real thing," I said to my tightening midsection, "your timing is even worse than your father's."

My mother shook her head. "You know they knocked me out cold when I had you, and I never thought I might have to play midwife in the middle of a storm. I can do a lot of things, but delivering a baby... that would be a first."

I debated my choices. We could attempt to drive three miles to Hannah's and Michael's house in the worst snowstorm in recent Colorado history and risk being lost or stranded, or we could stay put, stay warm, and trust Nature to pull me through... and pray that Jake would make it.

The sound of the wind was enough to convince us to stay put.

To my mother's surprise, I suddenly had a burst of energy and decided to clean and organize the entire cabin.

* * *

Six hours into my organizational mission, I had no doubts that I was in labor.

I could no longer continue with my activities around the house. Each contraction forced me to stop whatever I was doing and breathe deeply, centering my energies on the life within me, the intensity absorbing my entire concentration. It crossed my mind again to attempt to get to Hannah's cabin, but the force of the contractions doubled me over, rendering me incapable of walking, and I realized I wasn't going anywhere. I gave up trying to do anything and just curled into fetal position on the couch in front of the fireplace. My mother held my hand, brought me water to drink, and brushed my damp hair off my face, all while trying to study my birthing books, but I knew she felt helpless.

* * *

By midnight the contractions were so intense, I felt as though I were being hurled out of myself into space, into some flaming vortex of pain. I was in a complete state of panic.

Should it hurt this much?

None of the books had said anything about blinding pain, only about breathing and focusing. Maybe something was wrong. Maybe I was dying, me and my baby, in the middle of the woods. Each time a contraction ended, I wept with relief and waited in dread for the next one to hit.

Another contraction ripped through me like a blazing thunderbolt wrapped around my belly, pain radiating white-hot as I tried desperately to breathe.

The door flew open with a crash, and Jake blew into the room in an icy gust, with Hannah behind him. He spotted me curled in a heap on the floor before the fading fire, with my mother beside me, holding my hand. He threw off his ice-covered coat as he rushed to scoop me up in his arms.

"Oh, God, Maddy!" He wiped sweaty strands of hair from my face as he cradled me. "Are you alright?"

I tried to reply, but another contraction tore through me, and I could only grip Jake's shirt, struggling to breathe over the blinding pain.

Hannah closed the door, tore off her coat and hat, and rushed into the kitchen to wash her hands. She hurried to join us on the floor.

My mother must have been holding her breath, because she released it all at once. "Thank God you've come!"

"What's the big idea of starting without us, huh?" Hannah joked as I emerged from the vortex of pain into the world again. "Let me check how you're doing, okay?"

I nodded and buried my face in Jake's shoulder as Hannah gently examined me to check my dilation.

"Hey, mama. You're almost there!" Hannah gave me a big smile and took out her stethoscope to listen to my straining belly. "And this kid has a super-strong heartbeat. You're doing great! Guess you didn't really need us at all."

She began massaging my trembling legs.

"I'm so glad you're here. I was so afraid. I thought—"

Another contraction stole the power of speech as Hannah softly talked me through it.

"Let it come, Maddy. Just look in Jake's eyes and let it wash over you. Let everything go, and breathe pure white light to the baby."

I looked into Jake's beautiful eyes, so filled with love and concern, and let myself melt into the warmth and security of his arms. He was my only anchor to the planet. Without him, the pain would have thrown me to a place so far away that I'd never make it back. But he held me and whispered to me, and slowly I returned to him.

"It's so much easier in your arms," I whispered when I could speak again.

Jake kissed my forehead.

"Time to get up, girl." Hannah stood and reached out her hands to me.

I looked at her as if she'd gone insane. "I couldn't possibly move."

Hannah was adamant. "You will feel so much better when you're upright, you'll see. You'll be glad you did it."

She directed Jake to sit on the couch, and piled pillows on the floor at his feet so I could kneel on the floor and rest my arms and head on his lap. Jake stroked my hair and held me in his arms, while Hannah massaged my back and legs between contractions. During each contraction I tuned deeply inward, concentrating on imagining breathing white light to surround the baby, listening to the soft murmur of Jake's voice, and letting the sensations carry me away. I swayed to accommodate the movement of the baby inside me. I was amazed at how much easier it was to cope with the unbelievable intensity while on my knees with my arms around Jake and his around me. I focused my mind on helpful images — flowers bursting into bloom, lenses opening from a tight $f22$ to a wide $f1.5$.

Hannah added more wood to the fire, noting that the baby was finally settling deep into my pelvis. Gravity was helping us, along with my natural movements.

Hannah nodded, watching me sway in the light from the fireplace. "You do a fine baby-dance. You know it's okay to make sounds, too. Sing a baby-song... let come out whatever needs to come out."

On the next contraction, I let out an open-throated moan, a soft sound, vibrating, emanating from deep inside.

"Yes. That's good!" Hannah's eyes caught a gleam from the firelight. "Yes, Maddy. Let it all come. You've got it now."

When the contraction ended, I lifted my head from Jake's lap and gazed up into his eyes, my face perfectly relaxed. "I feel so much better," I whispered.

Jake looked astounded at the sense of peace radiating from me. "You're amazing."

Hannah whispered, "This is the calm before the storm, Jake, my friend."

She smiled as I closed my eyes and was pulled into another contraction, but this time there was a catch in the middle of my soft moan, which made her nod. "Pushing urge?" she asked.

"Wow! Yes." My eyes were wide with surprise at the new sensation. "What a feeling!"

"Hard to mistake it for anything else, huh?" Hannah grinned. "Just relax and do whatever feels right. When you feel like pushing, push."

Hannah warmed some olive oil on the stove and returned to sit behind me on the floor. I alternated between pushing and being kissed and petted by Jake. My mother fetched a wet washcloth to cool my brow as Hannah gently rubbed the olive oil in circles between my legs, stretching and lubricating me.

The baby moved downward. I felt so full I thought I would burst… until Hannah announced that the top of the baby head had touched her hand.

"Ring of fire?" Hannah asked.

I gasped. "Yes! Ow, ow! Exactly like a ring of fire."

"Don't push at all. Just let the baby ease out."

Hannah gently supported the tender tissue, stretched nearly to the tearing point, as the baby's head slowly emerged.

There was a long pause when I just breathed deeply. Then another contraction pushed the rest of the baby out in one swift rush, and my sigh of relief almost sounded like laughter.

I looked up at my mother, who clasped her hands together and wept with a huge smile on her face.

As I turned, Hannah passed the baby face-down between my legs and into my hands and then showed me how to rub the natural, protective, white cream into the baby's back. The baby made little coughing sounds as he spit out the mucous in his mouth, and I turned him over.

"What a beautiful boy!" Hannah winked at Jake. "Is his daddy that well hung?"

Jake and I burst into laughter as our son regarded us with wide, serious eyes.

Jake reached out to touch the baby's cheek, and the infant turned toward his finger. "I thought babies are supposed to cry when they're born," he said to Hannah.

"I think he found this a very interesting experience. But if you don't feed him soon, he just might start to cry."

Hannah showed me how to position the baby to nurse, and he latched on, pulling strongly at my breast, his large, dark eyes locked on mine.

"He's got eyes just like yours, Jake. Look at those eyelashes. He looks at me just like you do."

"He can't help it. He has the most beautiful mother in the world."

Jake sat back in the deep couch with me sitting between his legs, leaning back against him as I nursed. He kissed my temple as he studied his son.

"How are you feeling, Maddy?" Hannah asked as she cut the cord, tied it off and tended to the afterbirth.

"Like tap dancing on the ceiling!" I laughed. "I've never been this high before in my life."

Hannah nodded. "It's a pretty amazing experience, for sure. You have no idea what you're missing by not being able to give birth, Jake."

"That's okay with me," he replied, grinning. "I'd just as soon leave the birthing to you. I know I couldn't deal with it half as well. That was as close to giving birth, myself, as I ever want to be. It was such an amazing experience… I'm still in shock."

"I am, too," my mother said as she headed toward the kitchen. "I may be a mother, but this is the first birth I've ever actually witnessed. My daughter never ceases to amaze me."

She returned with soup and crusty brown bread for us all. While Jake and I ate, Hannah weighed and measured the baby, sprinkled a little goldenseal powder over his umbilical cord to dry it out, and wrapped him securely in a receiving blanket. His little face regarded her solemnly.

"You have another heartbreaker on your hands," Hannah said, laughing as she handed him back to me. "A seven-and-a-half-pound heartbreaker. Thought of any names yet?"

Jake laughed. "There aren't any names in my family that I'd

willingly torture this child with. I'm not going to name him Seymour or Stanley or Manny."

"My father's name was Gabriel. I've always liked it." I looked up at Jake hopefully.

My mother's jaw began to tremble, and her eyes misted. "What a lovely thought. You father would have been thrilled."

"Around here we often give a temporary name to a baby, based on the circumstances of his birth." Hannah listened to the howling of the wind outside. "How about 'Storm'?"

Jake smiled and kissed me. "Gabriel Storm Morgenstern, huh? A bit of a mouthful for a kid to say, but I like it." He stroked the baby's cheek, and Gabe furrowed his brow and turned toward the touch. "If he decides to go into rock 'n' roll, he can always shorten it to Gabriel Storm."

Hannah came up behind the couch, put her arms around both of us, and gave me a kiss on the top of my head. "You did a good job, Lenswoman."

Jake lifted an eyebrow. "'Lenswoman?'"

"That's what my dad and the tribe started calling her after he saw all those beautiful photos. She earned her name. She's a very talented lady."

As I cuddled Gabriel to my breast, Jake added, "In more ways than I can count."

EPILOGUE

A Triple Wedding

Spring, Wolf Creek, Colorado

Come spring, there were three weddings: Darlene and Tony, Grace and Billy, and Jake and me. We celebrated on the hillside overlooking our valley, surrounded by our closest friends. Much to my surprise, Jake invited Colin and his band, and they played the song Colin had written about me.

"You better take good care of our Maddy…," Colin said as he shook Jake's hand, "…or I will steal her away."

Jake laughed. "So noted. But I won't give you that opportunity."

My mother recited her version of the traditional "seven blessings" and then took Gabe from Hannah's arms so Hannah could give a traditional Ute blessing:

"Now you will feel no rain, for each of you will be shelter to the other.

Now you will feel no cold, for each of you will be the warmth to each other.

Now there is no loneliness for you.

Now you are two bodies, but there is one life before you.

Go now to your dwelling place to enter into the days of your togetherness,

and may your days be good and long upon the Earth."

Jake leaned down and whispered in my ear, "And let's make lots more movies… and babies."

And so we did.

Seven Blessings

I originally wrote the Seven Blessings to read at my goddaughter's wedding, but it might also be considered as Maddy's mother's version of the traditional seven blessings in a Jewish marriage ceremony. I offer it freely to couples who might like to incorporate any of it into their own wedding ceremonies.

1. *May there always be laughter in your life. If you keep your sense of humor and find ways to make each other smile every day, it will be much easier to navigate the inevitable bumps in the road.*

2. *May your bed always be comfortable… and may you always find comfort in each other's arms.*

3. *May you always appreciate the beauty of life and this planet and, most important, each other… and remember to express that appreciation often.*

4. *May you always feed each other well. This means: May your food always be delicious, delighting the taste buds and filling your stomachs… but also, may you feed each other's brains—stimulate each other's creativity and intellectual curiosity. In other words, may your gardens of both earth and mind always bloom abundantly.*

5. *May all your children have healthy bodies, brilliant minds, a great sense of humor, and kind hearts. (We already know they will be beautiful!)*

6. *May you always inspire the best in each other, cheer each other on to achieve your greatest potential, and make the world a better place by your actions.*

7. *May this journey together be an amazing adventure story you can tell to your grandchildren and great-grandchildren.*

   Praised is love! Blessed be this marriage!

ADDITIONAL NOTES ON THE TEXT

Music plays an important role in *Lenswoman in Love,* and many readers have asked about the songs that comprise the soundtrack to Maddy's and Jake's romance. Here is a partial list of artists and a few songs mentioned in the book, along with my recommendations to introduce you to them. Go buy some—you won't be disappointed.

NOTE: Please do not pirate them. Musicians deserve to have income from their creations. The only good-guy pirates are in romance novels.

Del Shannon – "Runaway"

Martha and the Vandellas – "Dancing in the Street"

The Kinks – "You Really Got Me"

Bobby Darin – "Dream Lover"

Bob Dylan – "My Back Pages"; "Like a Rolling Stone"

Buddy Holly – "True Love Ways"

The Everly Brothers – "All I Have to Do is Dream"

The Drifters – "Save the Last Dance for Me"

Patsy Cline – "Crazy"; "I Fall to Pieces"

Sam Cooke – "Wonderful World"; "You Send Me"

The Shirelles – "Baby, It's You"; "Will You Still Love Me Tomorrow" (Carole King)

Eagles – "Desperado"; "Peaceful Easy Feeling"; "Take It Easy"

Linda Ronstadt – "Love Has No Pride" (also sung by Bonnie Raitt); "Long, Long Time"

Jackson Browne – "These Days"

Gram Parsons & Emmylou Harris – "Love Hurts"

The Beatles – Everything!

The Rolling Stones – "(I Can't Get No) Satisfaction"

The Animals – "We Gotta Get Out of this Place"; "Don't Let Me Be Misunderstood"

The Zombies – "She's Not There"; "Tell Her No"; "Time of the Season"

The Doors – "Light My Fire"

Grateful Dead – "Uncle John's Band"

Janis Joplin – "Take Another Little Piece of my Heart"

Tom Lehrer – google him – you'll love all his satirical songs!

And for those curious about folk music:

Pete Seeger – "Where Have All the Flowers Gone"

THANK YOU...

To the community of writers who so generously advised and helped me;

including my Women's National Book Association critique group: Joan, Ellen, Kathrin, Margaret, Alexia, Christina;

to my editor, the meticulous Deanna Brady, (getwords@gmail.com / dbwords.com);

my patient and talented designer, Charlotte Mouncey, https://www.bookstyle.co.uk/;

my agent, Eric Lincoln Miller;

the wonderful women of the Women's Fiction Writers' Association's HISTFIC group;

my friends at the Greater Los Angeles Writers Society;

my dialect consultant (Jamaica) – Niambe MacIntosh and her nieces;

and my always supportive and brilliant husband, Jeff.

ABOUT THE AUTHOR

Kim Gottlieb-Walker's career as a photographer spanned over 50 years, from rock & roll and popular culture heroes of the '60s and '70s to motion pictures and television unit photography. She was an elected representative for still photographers in the International Cinematographers Guild, IATSE Local 600, for over three decades. Her coffee table photo books "Bob Marley and the Golden Age of Reggae" and "On Set with John Carpenter " (covering *Halloween*, *The Fog*, *Christine*, *Halloween II*, and *Escape from NY*) have had multiple printings and also have editions in Japan, Russia and France. She also worked at Paramount as the unit photographer on *Cheers* for nine years and *Family Ties* for five, as well as the pilots for *Star Trek: Deep Space Nine* and *The Next Generation*, and the last Bob Newhart show *Bob*.

She lives in beautiful Laurel Canyon in Los Angeles with her husband of over fifty years, Jeff Walker, one of the smartest men in Hollywood.

www.ingramcontent.com/pod-product-compliance
Lightning Source LLC
Chambersburg PA
CBHW030330230225
22393CB00011B/445